Congratulations

Congratulations

Darrin Lowery

Urban Books, LLC
78 East Industry Court
Deer Park, NY 11729

ISBN 13: 978-1-61664-178-8

Printed in the United States of America

Distributed by Kensington Publishing Corp.

Acknowledgments

I would like to thank the following people for their support: God, Carl Weber, Natalie, Maxine and everyone at Urban books. I would like to thank Brenda Hampton, my friend, fellow author and agent. Brandi Higa, Leslie Swanson, Melanie Palmer, Nicole Logan, Travis Hunter, Eric Jerome Dickey, E. Lynn Harris (RIP), Michael Baisden, Sistah Souljah, Kw'an, Nichelle Walker, Verl and Leesa from Da Book Joint, Naleighna Kai, JL Woodson, Devonshe Person, Mary Morrison, Kiberly Lawson Roby, Wahida Clark, Glenn Murray and 220 Communications, Nikki Woods, Common, Twista, Da Brat, Do or Die, Marc Gerald, 50 Cent, JM Benjamin, Rawsistaz.com, OOSA Online Book Club, Power 92, WGCI, V103, The Divine Sisters Book Club, Reading Renzdevous Book Club, Sugar and Spice Book Club, Readers Paradise Book Club, The Windy City Book Club:Phalon Carpenter, Spanneshia Bouldin, Latoya Hazelwood, Antoinette Powell Sonja Evans, Marla Seals, Darrien McKinney, Mr. Phillip, Mr. Rada, Mr. Lopez, Elbert Muhammad, Solanna Bullette, Venture Berry, Ms. Rose, Kristy Yanney, Kristie and the ladies of Dolce Vita, Carmen Buick, Yolanda Hooks Buick, My MySpace friends, my TAGGED friends, Tiffany Higa, Denise Torres, Boomer {yeah you get a shout out}, Ms. Toni, Trista Russell, Jo Oliver, Nicole Logan, Leslie Allen, Joy Johnson, Erica Bramlett, Susan Cullen, David Allen, Charles and Jonathan Gandy, Lisa Thomas, Yolanda Epps, Tina Davis (Big Tina), Mr. Kelly Williams, Ametra Self, Denise Bolds,

Earl Sewell, Farrah and Timel Ellison, Ireta Gasner, James Beasley, Jamie Rose, Robert Smith (POPS) Sandra Smith, Lynette Smith, The Lowery Family, Katrina Robertson, Kelly Granberry, Kimm Farrell, Myrtle Rycraw, Neil Jackson and the "I get's down jack crew," Tracey Lynn Deis, Adrienne, my bartender, Wanda Saunders, Deon Cole, and to all my regular readers. Without you I am nothing.

Chapter One—Tiffany

TIFFANY WITHOUT A CLUE

"You need to get the hell up out of my house!"

As Thomas walked out the door I slammed it behind him. I slammed it so hard that every neighbor on my floor in my apartment complex had to hear it. I couldn't believe the things he just said to me. I couldn't believe we had yet another senseless argument. You don't talk to someone you love the way he had just talked to me. You certainly don't put someone down who is working hard in her position to be the best she can be professionally.

I couldn't believe that I went all out for him this evening. I could have gone out. I could have worked on projects around my house or even taken in a quiet evening at home. Instead, I called him and left cute but nasty messages on his phone, I rested up for this evening and I put on my sexual best. I did all that I could to get ready for my man and to tease and please him in every way, and this was how he repaid me?

Tonight was different from every other Wednesday night that we shared. Usually, Thomas came over with chardonnay or some other type of wine and fresh flowers. I prepared one of his many favorite meals and we usually ate, talked about our mutual coworkers at Third National Bank, as well as where we thought the future of the bank was going. These days, most banks were in trouble with mergers, high gas prices, and a failing economy. Thomas, who was a senior V.P., had assured me that our jobs were fine, at least for right now.

Still, we'd been arguing a lot lately and I couldn't help but notice that the arguments seemed to be intentional. Each time we argued it seemed to be about something petty. I was either taking too serious of a position on a social matter, or we argued about something on TV, or he would say something ridiculous like he thought I might be cheating on him. These days we would argue and he would tell me that I was being immature or childish. There were a lot of senseless arguments about nothing. Arguments, where I was always the one who was wrong. We could never seem to agree to disagree.

I often joked with Thomas about both of our names beginning with the letter T, and to me, "T and T was an explosive combination." Thomas never found that barb amusing, and joking with him these days wasn't in my best interest. He'd accuse me of being corny, or say something mean and sarcastic. What really threw me off were the petty excuses Thomas would use to stop talking to me. One day he would be fine, but the next day, he'd give me the cold shoulder or the silent treatment. The good times between us will always be unforgettable, but the bad times were starting to outweigh the good.

I viewed this as me being the one with the problem. The first thing that comes to mind is my weight. I'm not a size four—hell, not even a size six. But being five feet, five inches tall, light pecan in color, and a curvy 180 pounds, some changes needed to be made. I'm far from being "fat" by black standards, but rather "thick" in the hips. My round face and high cheekbones resemble the child star Raven-Symoné, and I consider both of us to be good-looking women. For most of my life, though, I've struggled with my weight. At twenty-eight I'd been on every crash diet and purchased several exercise machines seen in infomercials. I try hiding the "extra fluff" by wearing my hair down, sporting darker colors that are said to be slimming, and starving myself on occasion. None of this brought true satisfaction or results to me, and by this point in my life, I'd heard enough men complain about my weight. Sometimes, they'd bluntly ask me to try dieting, and some have offered to work out with me. It seems as if every man who walks in my life wants to change me, and their dissatisfaction attacks my self-esteem.

It's like men want to mold me, as if God had made some major mistake or wasn't paying attention when he created me. What hurts worse than anything is how often people tell me how pretty I am in one breath, but in the next, tell me I would look so much better if I simply lost some weight. That's why it's hard for me to swallow that a woman of my size landed an office heartthrob like Thomas.

Perhaps that's my self-esteem talking. Perhaps that is my own personal issue. I've never thought I was good enough to get the better-looking men. I never thought I deserved better than the men I had dated thus far in my life. I always settled when it came to men. I always let them get away with things no other woman would let them get away with. I always loved them first, rather than loved myself. I was never the leading lady in any man's life. I was always that "in-between woman." You know, that woman you date between relationships. I thought it was different with Thomas. I thought this was the real thing. I was still hoping and praying it's the real thing. I couldn't understand why we were fighting so much these days.

While still in bed, I pulled aside my nightgown and revealed my thick thighs. I sighed and shook my head in disgust. *It is my weight*, I thought. *It has to be.* I'd become self-conscious about everything I ate, and started to doubt that I was capable of holding on to a man. My self-esteem had taken a major blow because of the recent arguments with Thomas, and this was the last straw. It was almost as if Thomas had been looking for reasons to sabotage our relationship. I didn't want to lose him; after all, what woman in her right mind would want to lose a man like Thomas? I planned to make some changes to my appearance, but my previous efforts had caused him to distance himself. *Why?* I thought. I knew it was because of my weight, and slapped my thick thighs good-bye. I was losing him, and it was time to get myself together. When I did, I knew Thomas would be singing a new tune and it would help remove this strain from our relationship. *I'll show my man how much he's loved and let him know that I'm willing to do anything in the world to keep him. By all means, I do mean anything!*

Thomas and I kept our relationship a secret at the office. Relationships were frowned upon in the workplace and Thomas used to always go on about how cliché they were as well. He thought it would also be a good idea to hide things from our friends and family. At least until we saw where the relationship was going. His rationale was that we were always friends first. For the first few months we were in a phase where we were trying to see where our relationship was going. The months that followed had us madly in love. And now these past few weeks, we couldn't seem to go more than twenty-four hours without arguing.

I worked as an administrative assistant for another V.P. in the bank. Thomas, known to everyone as Mr. Thomas Young or T. Young, was the financial wizard on the floor. Fraternizing at work was sometimes frowned upon, so I usually sent Thomas e-mails from my Yahoo! account to his, under an alias. The code of conduct for the bank is very specific about office romances and the damage they can do to work performance. Through e-mail, we confirmed either dinner plans or secret getaways. Thomas was known as the "Dark Knight" online, and I was "Ms. Nicety." Thomas had enough clout to get us special "dummy sign-ons" that were used by the trainees in other departments.

Basically, our e-mails could be considered nasty-grams

that were sent all day, every day, and this was primarily how we communicated during the hours of nine to five. After hours, we spent time on our cell phones, and our text messages to each other were quite graphic. For those late nights that we couldn't see each other, we often graduated to phone sex.

I sat at my desk and smiled at the thought of seeing Thomas tomorrow night. Planning to have his bath drawn, dinner on the table, Kem playing on the stereo, and scented candles throughout the apartment, I e-mailed Thomas and inquired about his arrival time at my apartment in Hinsdale, Illinois. I had just purchased a sexy pair of lace boy shorts with a matching bra and silk robe, and wanted to rock his world. Ending my cycle always made me horny as hell and I was anxious for him.

Pleased with my seductive e-mail message, I clicked "send" and the message was gone. I wanted to show him my alter ego, Ms. Nasty. I wanted to do something *different* tomorrow, and the warmth between my legs became more pronounced as I thought about our weekly lovemaking session. I wasn't able to see Thomas more than once a week these days, because the bank was always sending him to seminars, training, or meetings with new clients. I took pride in the fact that I got to see him most days at work, and we saw each other, no matter what, on Wednesday nights after work.

From where I sat on the floor, I could see into Thomas's office, which was in the east wing of the downtown bank office. My desk was by the window, and across the way I could see the inside of his office through the opened blinds. He was on his computer, and I knew it would be just a matter of seconds before he responded.

Fifteen minutes had passed, and my eyes traveled from his office to my inbox. I even rebooted my computer, just in case something was wrong, but there was no reply from Thomas. Curious as to why he hadn't responded, I tapped my manicured nails on my desk and my eyes stayed glued to his office. He talked on the phone, typed on his computer, removed his suit jacket for comfort, and took a few minutes to eat a sandwich.

What if he didn't get my message? I thought. I sent him a second e-mail at 2:00 P.M., another at 3:00 P.M. and yet another at 4:00. Still . . . nothing.

By then, I figured he was probably too busy to respond. I assumed that I could talk to him after work, but that didn't discourage my thoughts about going to his office to ask him why he hadn't replied. I didn't want to raise any suspicion, but I pondered my decision. Since we worked in two different departments, I had no reason to visit his office, unless it was personal. I knew it would be viewed that way, so I brushed off this incident as nothing. I had to admit that during our eleven-month relationship, he had never totally ignored me like this. If he was busy, I'd at least get a message that said so. A text message wouldn't hurt either, but today he was different and I couldn't seem to put my finger on why.

At 5:00 P.M., I took once last glance at Thomas's office and hoped to get some insight in his apparent lack of communication. He knew I'd be leaving for the day, but a man I had never seen before stepped into his office. They hugged and gave each other dap, as some black men often do. Afterward, he reached for his briefcase, turned off his lights, and they departed. Not once did Thomas look in my direction—not once!

I swallowed the huge lump in my throat and gathered my things to go. As soon as I got in my car, I rushed to call Thomas, but got his voicemail. I tried his number again when I got home, and left a simple message for him to return my call. I didn't want to seem clingy, possessive, or desperate, but he had some explaining to do. I didn't think that an eleven-month relationship gave me license to question his whereabouts or behavior, and I was sure that my questioning him would disturb him. I had never dated a man as fine as Thomas, so I second-guessed myself about how to approach him with my concerns. Losing him was something I didn't want to do, so I had to be very cautious. I reached for the phone again and took a deep breath. "Hey, it's me." I paused and swallowed. "I . . . I was just calling to confirm whether or not we were still meeting tomorrow. Give me a call when you get a minute."

That minute never came. I cleaned the kitchen, took a bath, and read a book. The book didn't keep me from being distracted, or from checking my cell and house phones to see if Thomas had called. I was wasting my time. I placed the book on my nightstand and chalked it up to his being busy, or simply needing some personal time. Guys need personal time, right?

The next day, I got to work extra early. I checked my twenty e-mail messages, but none of them were from Thomas. The e-mails were from my book club friends, my brother, my girlfriends at work who had no idea that I was seeing Thomas, and the usual spam. Dark Knight hadn't made any attempts to contact me.

I shifted my eyes to Thomas's office, but he hadn't made it in yet. He was usually the first person in the office and sometimes the last to leave. This particular Wednesday, he didn't get in until almost 11:00 A.M. I watched him take a few sips from his coffee mug, then boot up his computer and type. Minutes later, the cold and automated voice on my computer responded, "You've got mail!"

I opened the e-mail, which read, "See you tonight." A huge smile covered my face, but when I glanced in his direction, he never looked my way.

I was somewhat relieved that we were back on track, back in our routine, and things seemed to be back to normal. I figured I would inquire about how distant he was at a later time, but only if the opportunity presented itself.

I sent Thomas a few messages about our plans for the evening and his desires for the night. Not once did he respond, but again, I assumed he was busy with work. Sometimes, I would try to entice him by asking what color he wanted to see me in that evening. He loved boy shorts, and there were other times we decided to role-play. I'd dress in leather, teddies, or simply one of his dress shirts, with a thong and heels. Whatever turned on Thomas, whatever fantasy he had, I wanted to fulfill. He never replied to my e-mails, so I was left with making the decision of the night's events on my own.

Yesterday evening I scurried around my bedroom to get ready for my man. Normally, Thomas left work at 5:30 P.M., and he got to my place by eight. He worked late sometimes, too, and after the cleaning crew left, I'd sometimes return to work to keep him company. We'd make love on his leather couch or recliners that sat in front of his smoked-glass desk. If his office wasn't an option, then his Cadillac truck was.

I placed new satin sheets on the bed, showered, and moisturized my body from head to toe in scented lotion from Bath and Body Works. I sprayed a dash of Vera Wang on my neck and calves, and between my 34D breasts. Many people referred to me as "thick," but I had some dynamite legs that rivaled those of a professional athlete. Not only were they strong, but Thomas said they were smooth like silk.

I prepared the fettuccine Alfredo, garlic bread, and garden salad, and chilled the chardonnay. An apple pie I had purchased earlier from Bakers Square went into the warm oven and I returned to my room to get dressed. The black lace boy shorts worked my curvy hips and the matching bra gave my breasts a boost. I covered myself with a robe and stepped into my black high heels. I made sure that everything was ready by 8:00 P.M., and just at the last minute, I lit some floating candles in a dish, put on some soft music, and dimmed the lights. Then I sat back on the couch with a glass of wine in my hands.

Thomas was never late, but eight o'clock came and

went. So did nine, ten and eleven, and by then, I had called him four times. He didn't answer, nor did he return my calls. Not one! He had never stood me up before. I was beginning to get worried. It was one thing to stand me up; it's another to stand me up and not call. This was not like Thomas at all.

I gulped down the rest of my wine, and slammed the glass in the sink. It broke into pieces, and I used my fingertips to massage my temples. Frustration was written all over my face, and it hurt like hell that Thomas hadn't called. I didn't know what was happening to us and the thought of him ending our relationship drove me crazy. I tried to make sense of his behavior, but there was no excuse for how he'd played me.

By 11:30 P.M., I had blown out the candles and eaten dinner by myself. The leftovers went into the fridge, and before I knew it, I was slumped on the couch, feeling sorry for myself. My eyelids felt heavy and I cursed Thomas's name before going to sleep.

There was a knock at the door and I jumped from my sleep. The clock showed 12:35 A.M., and it took a few seconds to get my bearings and figure out what the knocking noise was. I looked at the door, then back at the clock, and couldn't believe the time or his audacity.

No, he didn't! I thought, rising from the couch. I opened the door, and standing in the doorway was Thomas, all smiles.

"Hey, baby." He smirked.

"Hey, baby, my ass!" I yelled, and attached my hand to my hip. "Where have you been? Why haven't you called? I called you four times this evening . . ."

"So, I take it you aren't happy to see me?"

"Should I be?"

"What if I said that I was sorry?"

"Sorry doesn't explain where you were this evening, and as a matter of fact, yesterday night also. Thomas, what's going on?"

He gazed at me with his puppy-dog eyes and reached for my waist. "Tiffany, baby, come here."

I felt myself getting weak and my voice softened. "What, Thomas? Why are things changing between us?"

"Trust me, nothing has changed or will change between us. I've been a bit busy lately, but nothing is going to stop me from coming to see you."

He lifted my lowered chin and closed the door with the bottom of his size-fourteen shoe. When his tongue entered my mouth, I closed my eyes. I couldn't resist his pleasure.

THE BEDROOM

Round one wrapped up quickly, but because we hadn't discussed his recent actions, I felt dissatisfied. Thomas was a fine-ass man, which is the only reason why he got away with the BS he was pulling. This was the first time he had ever ignored, or stood me up. I didn't want him to make this a habit, so I pushed back his chest as he leaned in to peck my neck.

"You know I'm still mad at you." I spoke with certainty. "I know you said you've been busy, but that still doesn't explain where you've been."

Thomas stared sternly into my eyes and let out a huff. He held himself up with his muscular arms and my eyes dropped to his chiseled midsection. His chest was like a bodybuilder's and his addictive dick had to be lined with cocaine. I felt like an addict and he was definitely my drug.

"I said I've been working, Tiffany. What more do you want me to say?"

I guessed his busy excuse was enough, and as he gently sucked my earlobe, I touched his wavy black hair that reminded me of Blair Underwood. I tried to resist this Hershey's chocolate, six-foot-two man as best I could, but his looks were so rugged and his touch was simply electric. No doubt, I was concerned about some things with him, but his 8.5 was poking me in the right place and had me rethinking my level of madness.

I opened my legs. Whenever Thomas made love to my body, it seemed like not only was I in heaven, but the earth moved, the bed shook, and my body reverberated with waves and waves of orgasms. I responded to his touch, his sweet whispers and the almighty thrusts that he brought to the bedroom. Thomas was a tender and patient lover when he needed to be. He could also give a sista some of that thugged-out love when I needed that as well. No matter what, Thomas seemed to have the answer my body was seeking on Wednesday nights, and tonight was no different.

I've had some good lovers in my time, but none of them had taken me to the level Thomas had. He stretched my vaginal walls, and I could still feel him inside me long after he was gone. He aimed at making me feel good, loved, wanted, and dirty all at once. My body was worked like a high-end sports car on miles of open road. Sex between us was always powerful, yet dynamic and smooth. It went on for hours, and Thomas made it a habit to compliment me, kiss me, lick me . . . devour me with abandon, and make love to me for hours on end.

More than anything, I loved the way he looked into my eyes as we made love. I loved the way he ran his hands up and down the length of my body. I longed for his touch, his caress, and his deep and methodic slow strokes inside of me. The way he touched and licked my breasts drove me crazy. He cupped them and pinched my nipples when he was inside of me. Yes, I was still bitter this late-Wednesday, early-Thursday morning, but I needed him to stay inside me. I needed a hit of my drug, and for now, it was doing its job.

Thomas rolled over in bed and let out a deep sigh. Satisfaction was written all over his face, and when he held me in his arms, I knew my performance was the best I could have given. He kissed my forehead and pulled back the covers to get out of bed.

"Are you leaving so soon?" I asked.

"Yes, I have to get up early."

I watched as Thomas reached for his clothes and headed for the bathroom. I didn't want him to go, and I needed him to stay and finish the all-nighter I had planned for us to have. I re-lit the candles on my nightstand, and when he came back into the bedroom, he was fully dressed with his car keys in his hands. His eyes examined the flames.

"What's this?" he asked.

"I was hoping that you'd stay a little while longer. A few more hours might bring great rewards. Besides, I promise to make you the best breakfast you've ever had."

My eyes traced up and down the front of his body and watched him attentively. I smiled as he unzipped his pants and pulled out my dark chocolate treat. When his boxer briefs hit the floor, I rushed in front of him. He stroked my back and rubbed my apple bottom. That, along with him rubbing between my legs, brought a combination of warmth and moisture.

I stood on the balls of my feet to kiss him and our tongues danced together. "Moments in Love" was playing on the stereo, setting the mood. Up and down my neck he nuzzled me. My nipples hardened and my heart began to race. Thomas kissed down my midsection and wasted no time tasting my special place. I held on to his head and helped him feast upon me. He was starving for me and me for him. I fed him all of me and treasured his tantric lovemaking. Each time that I thought I was close to reaching a climax, he would stop, kiss me passionately on the mouth, and begin his foreplay all over again.

As the night went on, my spring became a river of juices, and my thighs glistened with the statement of my passion. Thomas turned me over and entered me from behind. My vaginal walls accepted his entry freely. We both let out gentle moans as he took long and deliberate strokes while experiencing my warmth. He sighed a sound of relief as he went deeper and deeper inside me. I felt satisfied and full all at once. He began to pick up his pace and stab me with his sword like a villain in a Shakespearean play. Over and over, and over again, I welcomed his assault. The deeper he stroked inside of me, the more I moaned. The more I moaned, the closer he came to "his special place." His muscles flexed throughout his body, and because he was almost there, he slowed down. I loved that he had such a hard time holding back his orgasm with me. I loved that my sex was so wet and so good that it took him to that special place. I loved the screw face that he had, and only because of what I had to offer, he was ready to come. My kitten was able to command his manhood. He was the one taking the strokes, he was the one seeking to prove a point, but I was the one with the power. I was now his drug and I knew that he slowed down to experience every second of the intoxicating high that we shared.

"I have to slow down," he confessed.

I smiled a smile that he couldn't see. He held on firmly to my hips to hold himself in place. He tried desperately not to move, afraid that he might explode either inside me or all over my backside. His breathing was now erratic and I knew he was very close because of the way his member throbbed inside of me. I felt his pulse and could feel his heart race. I didn't press for more, and just let him get his composure together.

We both collapsed, knocked out by a mightier opponent. I lay on top of him, breathing heavily. He kissed me again on the mouth and cupped my ass. My body felt tired and I was ready to sleep. He was still inside of me and I loved every second of it, until finally, I drifted off. Thomas jokingly called it the sleep of the dead.

       Thomas got up from my bed of sin to do his usual ritual of relieving himself and then washing up to go home. When I looked at the clock in the bedroom, it was 5:30 A.M. In just two hours we both had to get up, and the breakfast that I promised him wasn't going to happen. I could hear the jingle of his belt as he dressed in the bathroom. I watched the ghost-like shadows of his silhouette as he searched for his clothing, which was strewn about my bedroom. It didn't take him longer than ten minutes to get dressed. Before he left, I thought he was going to hit me with a good-bye kiss, but instead, I was hit with an unpleasant surprise.

       "I'm going to be out of town for a few days."

       "Oh? Where is the job sending you now?"

       "Minnesota."

       "Are we buying banks in Minnesota?"

       "Uh, yeah. Otherwise, I wouldn't be going," he said sarcastically.

       "How long will you be gone?"

       "A few days, maybe a week."

       "Which is it, a few days or a week?"

       "I don't know. It depends on how things go."

       "So which bank are we considering buying now?"

       "Why?"

       "I'm just asking."

       "Well, why are you asking?"

       "What do you mean why am I asking? I always ask you about these sorts of things."

       "Yeah, you do, and it's always gotten on my nerves."

       "I . . . I'm sorry."

       "I don't mean to sound harsh, but when you come at me like that, you sound like my mother or something."

       "What?" I was taken aback by his comment, and folded my arms in front of me. "Your mother?"

       "Yes."

"I don't understand. I'm acting like your mother because I'm asking about the well-being of our company?"

"My company, not our company."

In recent weeks he had been a bit sarcastic, but never this condescending; never this mean.

"What do you mean, not our company?"

"I mean, let's face it, I'm a V.P. and you're just a receptionist."

Just a receptionist? I thought. *Who the hell does he think he's talking to?* "Excuse me? First of all, I'm an administrative assistant. Secondly, don't minimize what I do."

Thomas chuckled. "Yeah . . . right. Uh, what's the difference between a receptionist and an AA?"

"One answers phones, the other keeps departments afloat."

"You have got to be kidding me, right? No matter how you look at it, Tiffany, you're a damn secretary. Oh, I'm sorry, I mean administrative assistant. And haven't I seen you relieving the receptionist on the floor from time to time? That doesn't look like keeping a department afloat, it looks like temp work."

What the hell has gotten into him? How could he say something like that? His words are hitting me hard, like bricks on pavement. He's never been like this before, never. What's going on? I mean what's really going on? Moments ago we were in a passionate embrace. Once again, for whatever reason, we seem to be going down this path again. Is it me? Did I do something wrong? What gives?

I had just about had enough of his insults and I stood face-to-face to correct him. "What the hell is that supposed to mean?"

"It means that AAs are a dime a dozen. Any temp or high school student could do your job. It's not like the company would be in jeopardy if you resigned or something. I think you're making your job seem a lot more important than it is. You do the mindless work, work that doesn't require a lot of thought and reasoning. I mean, admit it, the shit you do is basically routine, right? All of you secretaries, receptionists, AAs, or whatever you want to be called, depends on people like me to even have jobs."

I poked my finger at Thomas's chest. "Excuse me, but the name of the bank is Third National, not the Bank of Thomas Young! And as far as being a V.P. is concerned, they too are a dime a dozen and any kid with a B.A. could do your job. Hell, even a C.P.A. could probably do your job. Don't you dare come in my goddamn apartment insulting me and telling me what you think I'm worth! You need to show me some respect."

He backed away from my poking finger and threw back his hands. "Yeah, whatever."

"Whatever? Thomas, what the hell has gotten into you? Why would you insult me like that?"

"I was just thinking out loud, and you're the one who got defensive."

"It doesn't seem to me that you were *thinking at all*. By the way, and since we're on the subject, where were you Tuesday?"

"Excuse me? What does one thing have to do with the other? Besides, I already told you I was busy. Must we go there again?"

"Cut the act and answer my question."

"Hold up!" he said, taking his voice to a higher level. He frowned and his forehead wrinkled. "I'm a grown-ass man!"

"Okay, grown-ass man, where was your grown-ass on Tuesday? Why didn't you respond to my e-mails or my phone calls?"

"For the last time, I was busy."

I tooted my lips and placed my hand on my hip. "Busy doing what?"

"Working!"

"But you left the office."

"I don't have to be at the office to work."

"So where were you? What client were you with, and why didn't you at least text me?"

He shook his head and reached for the keys in his pocket. His eyes shot daggers at me. "Dammit, Tiffany, I was busy! Now, I'm leaving and thanks for already screwing up my damn day."

I continued to press as he made his way to the door. "Busy doing what?"

He quickly turned to confront me. "Look, I'm sick of this shit! One of us has to be at work and you're holding me up with a bunch of nonsense."

"Both of us have to be at work and my concerns are legitimate. What do you mean by one of us?"

"I mean, we both have to be there, but it is only important that one of us shows up."

His words stung again and delivered my self-esteem a major blow. I didn't know why he was tripping all of a sudden, but I did know one thing, he and his bullshit were about to get the hell out. I directed him to the door with serious hurt in my eyes. We had started with snide comments and sarcasm, but now he had graduated to belittling me. I loved him, but I couldn't . . . I let him continue to disrespect me like this. Not in my own home.

"Get out and don't come back until you get your lies together."

Thomas saw how hurt I was and he leaned in to give me a hug. I backed away from him.

"I'm sorry," he said. "Maybe I—"

At this point, I couldn't accept his apology. "You heard me, Thomas. Don't apologize now, nigga, just get the hell out!"

His eyes widened. "What did you call me?"

"You heard me and don't force me to say it again."

He curled up his lip and bit down on it. We had argued before but I had never cursed, let alone used the "N" word. His eyes and expression darkened and he looked at me like he was Ike and I was Tina. Just like Anna Mae, though, I refused to give in. I had no intention of eating cake or my words.

Instead of responding, he made his way to the door. I slammed it and I watched my picture on the wall crash to the floor.

What the hell was that all about? I thought.

I went to work mad as hell about my dispute with Thomas. I don't know what had gotten into him, but he had some explaining to do and was about to get an earful from me about his earlier comments. I could still feel him inside of me and his scent was still on me, too. I always felt satisfied with his lovemaking, but that didn't excuse him from being an asshole. I marched into work expecting to give him a piece of my mind. I went to his office, and to my surprise, he wasn't there.

Where the hell is he at now? I thought. I knew he said that he was going out of town, but I didn't think he meant today. Besides, didn't he say that one of us had to be at work? Wasn't he referring to himself?

I walked over to my computer and booted up the PC. I checked my e-mail account and there were no messages. Curious to find out why he wasn't there, I called his cell phone and was surprised by the message on the other end of the phone. "The number you have reached . . . 773-607-9248 is temporarily out of service."

Mr. V.P. hasn't paid his cell bill? I thought. *He has got a lot of damn nerve talking about me.*

I sat at my desk wondering what the hell was going on and why Thomas had been so petty lately. He was *different*, but I couldn't figure out why. Since I had so much work that needed to be done, I got busy, but was sidetracked with thoughts of him again. His words about me just being a secretary did indeed make me think. Was I wasting my time in my current position? Why hadn't I done more with my life? Was my job unimportant?

I did more of my day-to-day work, and then checked the human resources site to see if there was another position in the bank I might be qualified for. I had looked at the HR site at least once a month, but truth be told, I wasn't qualified to do much else. Everything these days required a degree or years of experience—I had neither.

Maybe we were having problems because Thomas desired a woman who wanted more out of life. Maybe he wanted more for me than I wanted for myself. Or maybe, he wanted me to bring more to the table. It was either that or my weight. In either case, I had to fix this before things got worse.

For the next two days, I didn't hear from Thomas at all. I was pissed that he was taking our latest argument this far. I hated the silent treatment, and it ate away at me more than any stupid argument. At this point, I didn't know where we stood, and I started to wonder, was this the beginning of the end?

Initially, I asked myself how he could walk away from all of this. Then it dawned on me that we didn't have much more than a good fuck on Wednesday nights. We used to have more than this. We used to mean something to one another. I didn't know why I hadn't seen things more clearly before now, but in recent weeks it seemed that all we really had were great sex and sexual messages during the week. It's like his messages were the tools he used to string me along and his sex was the thing that kept me hooked. He wasn't making love to me anymore. He was fucking me and fucking me well. I was beginning to wonder if I had mistaken great sex for misplaced love. I was beginning to wonder if I was using the way he made my body feel to mask what it was my heart wanted from him.

In the beginning were long walks, romantic dinners, and the occasional out-of-town trips. These days things were different, and I had to ask myself was he really giving up a lot, or was he simply moving on? Now it was obvious that I wasn't the type of woman Thomas would want to someday marry.

We had never discussed marriage, but when every woman is into a man, she writes his last name next to hers and sometimes wonders, *What if?* At twenty-eight years of age, I was guilty of that as well. I'd written his last name next to mine. I'd thumbed through the wedding magazines at the store. I'd also watched the wedding channel a night or two and although I had nothing planned on paper, I had planned my wedding to Thomas in my head.

Perhaps that was why Thomas had been arguing with me so much lately. He could tell I was under the impression that things were starting to get pretty serious between us, and maybe he was disappointed about my shortcomings as his potential wife.

Since he hadn't called, I was beginning to wonder if he had somehow been testing me and I failed. I did what a lot of women do when faced with relationship issues. Rather than evaluate the man, I wondered what I could have done differently. I had spent the last two days trying to answer that question, and when I came up with a long list of things I considered, I finally realized why Thomas had turned cold on me.

Chapter Two—Tiffany

When Saturday rolled around, I woke up mad at the world, but most of all, mad at myself. I wanted to hear from Thomas and I'd hoped that we could put our issues aside and reconcile our differences. I knew he'd been under a considerable amount of pressure lately at the job. I knew that he wanted more out of life than most men. I knew that being a black man in corporate America meant a ton of pressure. Perhaps this was where his scornful words stemmed from.

Being in a relationship couldn't be easy, and one with me wasn't a cakewalk either. I'm moody, opinionated, and I have no formal education. I only went to college for three semesters, and would have gone longer had tragedy not hit my family. Had things just been a little different, I could be the V.P. at the bank.

I was the oldest child in a family of four. When my parents were killed in a car crash when I was twenty, I had to take care of my younger brother, Kyle, who was seventeen at the time. I saw to it that he went to college two years after I withdrew. I made him go to school and I found a job.

The money left after burying my parents only amounted to about five thousand dollars. They had second and third mortgages on our home that had to be paid before we saw any money come to us. Even after the banks were paid, we still lost the house. That five grand was enough to get us moving in the right direction, but I needed to keep us afloat. We were all alone in the world and had no one to depend on but each other. That's when I got a job as a temp at the bank. I worked my behind off and eventually was brought on permanently.

Once I started working in the bank, I never again saw a need to go back to school and increase my own marketability. I never thought about having a huge house, fancy car, or luxurious lifestyle. I was just happy to have all my bills paid at the end of the month and a place to lay my head. In helping my younger brother succeed and get his degree, I felt I had done all I really needed to do in life. It wasn't easy, but I raised my younger brother, saw to it that he had all he needed to finish school, and helped to shape him into the man he is today.

There were plenty of days when he was in school that I didn't eat. There were days that my lights were cut off, and times I gave him spending money and I had none. But the good thing is we made it. From student loans and financial aid, as well as Kyle working part time; we made it. The only thing is I sacrificed a lot of my own goals and dreams so my brother could reach his.

Looking back, I don't regret the sacrifice I had to make. It brought us closer, and I know if there is one man in the world I can depend on, it's Kyle. I love him with all my heart and I think my parents would be proud of the job I did with him.

I guessed now that he was grown and successful, it was time for me to start living life for me. At twenty-five, he not only had his bachelor's degree, he's two semesters short of his master's degree; a degree he was getting from a full academic scholarship.

Perhaps making a sacrifice for my brother was now compromising my relationship with Thomas. I knew that he wanted more for me, and since our argument, I'd had nothing but time to think. How could I not see that I wasn't good enough? I hoped like hell that I hadn't let a good man like Thomas get away.

I got out of bed, and fixed a plate of scrambled eggs, turkey bacon, and toast. I then went to the gym, walked my two miles on the treadmill, and hit the light weights. Sweat rolled down my body, and I decided to stay for thirty more minutes to work the elliptical machine. When I got back home, I took a shower and headed for my room to watch the weekly programs I recorded on the DVR.

Once I was settled in bed with the remote control in one hand and a bag of chips on my lap, the phone rang. It was my best friend, Alicia. I hadn't seen my girl in about three months because I had been so busy with work and Thomas. I never got the chance to introduce them, but Alicia had to work on Wednesday nights. Thomas was always too busy on other days, so I gave up on the introduction.

"Hey, girl, what's up?" I said with excitement in my voice.

"Tiffany, where have you been? I started to put an APB out on your ass."

Alicia was a Chicago police officer. She had four years on the force.

"Girl, you know I've been busy with work."

"Work, my behind; you've been busy with that mystery man of yours. I forgot, what's his name?"

"Thomas."

"Yeah, Thomas. So how are things going with you two lovebirds?"

"Girl, I have major drama."

"Drama that I can't wait to hear. Are you seeing him today?"

"Nope, not today."

"Then I'm coming over. I have the day off so I can go to my snooty ass cousin's wedding. We can catch up for a few minutes before I have to leave."

"That sounds like a plan, come on over."

We hung up, and I got dressed in a pair of jeans, a sweatshirt, a baseball cap. My apartment wasn't that tidy, so I turned on a new album by Musiq and started cleaning. That didn't take long at all, and once I was finished, I booted up my PC. I surfed the Net for at least an hour, then heard the doorbell ring. I turned my TV to channel three to see who it was on the front door camera. I had to make sure that Alicia was alone because she sometimes had a habit of bringing people by my place when I looked a hot mess.

"Who is it?" I said jokingly while pressing the intercom.

"It's your lesbian lover!"

"Girl, don't even play like that. You know that I'm strictly dickly."

"Well, strictly, let me in."

I laughed and buzzed Alicia in. We hugged and I had to take a minute to check girlfriend out. She was dressed to the nines and looked like Kelly Rowland. Her complexion was dark copper, she had shoulder-length black hair and dark brown eyes. She was a size six, but was also thick. Her big behind, tiny waist, and perfect breasts attracted many men, and I always considered her to be the prettier of the two of us. She was the one person in my circle of friends who took very little shit. She used to be a mild and meek woman. Four years of fighting crime as a Chicago police officer in the roughest Chicago neighborhoods changed all that.

Alicia wore a black, form-fitting dress with spaghetti straps and her back was out. She looked like she was on her way to a party or walk on somebody's runway.

"Alicia, you look fantastic!"

"Thank you, honey. You're looking rather good yourself."

"Thanks. Did you lose some more weight?"

"I lost another ten pounds. I weigh about 125 now."

"I don't know how you do it."

"I gave up red meat, go to step class at least twice a week, and gave up drinking anything other than water."

"Shit, I wish I could be that disciplined."

"You can. You just have to get there mentally before you try making the actual physical change."

"Yeah, well, mentally my mind is somewhere all together different."

"Really, what's going on?"

Alicia and I took a seat on my sofa, and I recounted my story of Thomas and me, including the comments he made about me just being an administrative assistant.

Alicia frowned. "Girl, fuck that! Don't let any man ever try to tell you what you are worth! A woman's value goes well beyond what she does between the hours of nine to five. If that nigga can say some insensitive shit like that, then, baby, you don't need him!"

"It may seem insensitive on one hand, but on the other he may be right."

"Why, because you don't have a degree? There are plenty of educated fools out here who don't know anything outside of their damn school books. There are too many people out here with a ton of book sense and not a nickel's worth of common sense."

"I know that's right!"

We laughed, and for the next half hour, Alicia and I did what we did best—bash men. Don't get me wrong, we love men and agree that the world wouldn't be the same without them. But from time to time, black women need to vent about the unbelievable drama that black men sometimes put us through. After we were done signifying, I saw a light go on in Alicia's head. She was planning something. She smiled at me and spoke.

"Look, I have an idea. Why don't you come with me to my cousin's wedding? There will be plenty of eligible and *sensitive* men there. If nothing else, we get to party a bit, eat some good food, and catch up."

"I don't know. I'm not feeling a wedding right now."

"Come on, Tiff, we can go and at least make an appearance at the wedding. From there, we can go shopping or something. Besides, when was the last time we got to really hang out? I miss you, girl."

I threw up my hands. "You know what? You're right. I guess I could hang out for a while. Besides, I could use the distraction. It's just that I don't have anything to wear."

"I'm sure you can find something in your closet to wear."

"What time is the wedding?"

"Four o'clock."

"Today?"

"Today."

"Shit, I only have a few hours to get ready!"

I jumped off the couch and raided my closet for something sexy to wear.

Chapter Three—Tiffany

Since the wedding was taking place after 4:00 P.M., that narrowed my choices down to something black. Every woman should always have a little black something in her closet, and being unhappy with my current weight, all I seemed to wear these days was black. Black is slimming, and the first thing I thought of was the black knee-length dress I wore to my godparents' twenty-fifth wedding anniversary party. It was silk, with cap sleeves. I accentuated the V-neck with a Y necklace.

"Hey, Alicia, what do you think about this?" I asked, pulling the dress from the closet.

"That's really cute and sexy. Can I borrow it?" Alicia joked.

"Girl, this dress will swallow you."

"What shoes are you going wear?"

I knelt to the floor. "I'll wear the shoes I bought to go with it, if I can find them."

Getting irritated, I searched through my shoes, and finally pulled out the two-inch, sling back, and open-toed black shoes from the back. I put the dress up to me and held one shoe up.

"Okay, how does this look?"

"That's good, with or without stockings?" Alicia asked.

"Stockings."

"No, grandma, no stockings."

"Then why did you ask?"

"To see what you would say."

"Okay, no stockings."

"Good. The wedding starts in two hours so can you put a rush on it?"

I showered in ten minutes tops, moisturized my body, and sprayed myself with perfume that Thomas bought for me. Although I was angry with him, wearing this perfume was my little way of carrying him with me. I hadn't heard from him and that still had me concerned. My thoughts put a sharp twitch in my stomach, and whenever I felt that twitch, I knew something wasn't right. Perhaps there was another woman. It quickly dawned on me how busy he'd been with work and seeing me. There was no way another woman was in the picture, unless he had a woman out of town on one of these business trips he was frequently taking.

I put those thoughts out of my head and focused on enjoying my day. It had been a while since I spent time with my girl and I didn't want to be poor company.

My long, auburn hair was pulled to the back in a simple, thick braid. That allowed me to show off the tear-drop earrings that went with the necklace. I slipped on my panty girdle to control the jiggle from my hips and ass, and knew my granny would have a fit if she knew I was going into the house of the Lord barelegged. Once I slipped into my dress, I stood in the full-length mirror, looking left to right at my ass. *I swear if it gets any bigger, I'll need a wheelbarrow to carry it around.* Just then, Alicia came into the room and a wide smile covered her face.

"Tiff, you look gorgeous. Thomas don't know what he's missing."

I chuckled and continued to look at my behind in the mirror. "Look at how big it is. I'll never be able to work off all of this."

"Baby, that's just your ethnicity, now hop to it! Knowing my cousin, she probably has Saint Peter himself doing the valet parking at the church."

Before rushing out, I grabbed my favorite black shawl from behind my bedroom door and we left.

Alicia was in her Ford Expedition with the windows down and the sunroof open, blasting T.I.'s "You don't know me." I laughed out loud as I hit the alarm on my Hyundai Sonata, unlocking it. Alicia turned down her music.

"No, ma'am, you're riding with me!" she shouted.

"What?"

"I know you, Tiffany. You'll try to leave early. Not tonight, Cinderella, you won't be home until well after midnight."

I didn't argue with Alicia because it had been awhile since we'd last hung out. I threw my beaded drawstring purse in the backseat with my shawl and climbed into her mammoth vehicle. I put on my seat belt and braced myself for the ride.

Although I loved my girl, I hated the way she drove. Once I almost peed on myself as she weaved in and out of traffic, topping speeds of fifty miles per hour on side streets, and almost seventy five miles per hour on the expressway. No sooner than she heard my seat belt click, she took off.

Within minutes, we were in front of one the most beautiful churches I'd ever seen. It was built with grey stones and had medieval-type doors that were solid oak wood with metal hinges. As Alicia parked, I couldn't take my eyes off of it. I walked up to it, and a feeling of peace and serenity came over me. The wrought iron banisters were decorated with white and lavender bows. When we went inside and signed the guestbook, I could smell a hint of lavender in the air. The sanctuary was a few steps away from the foyer, and before taking a seat, Alicia spoke to and hugged people she knew. Three pews from the front, I saw Alicia's mother waving at us to come sit next to her. As I walked down the center aisle, I imagined what it would feel like if it were my wedding day. I mentally critiqued everything and made note of the things I would change. I really liked the pew decorations of white calla lilies with the stems wrapped with lavender ribbons. The colors went well together, but what would my colors possibly be? We got closer to Alicia's mother, and she scooted over for us to sit near the aisle.

"I know my mother is going to cry, so you sit next to her," Alicia instructed.

I sat down and exchanged pleasantries with her mom while Alicia chatted with another woman in the pew in front of us. The wedding was soon about to start, and although it was not my day, I was anxious for it to begin. Weddings had sentimental value for me. I guess they have sentimental value for all women. I was happy for the bride whom I didn't know. I felt it was a great day for any woman getting married in a time where people change partners every few years, just as they do with their cars.

I felt that any woman getting married in the new millennium belonged to a secret sorority. A sorority of women who wanted more out of life and still believed in family, and raising children. I was definitely a member of this sorority, although my membership had yet to be validated by my walking down the aisle. I often imagined Thomas and myself standing in front of a minister, with our family and friends. I imagined Thomas and me confessing our undying love for one another to God and the world.

Of course, I visualized what we'd be wearing. He'd be in a black Pierre Cardin tuxedo, with a red silk tie and vest. I imagined myself in a custom-made gown with a long train by none other than Vera Wang and a cathedral-length veil. Like most women, I imagined the weather being perfect on my wedding day and me being the most beautiful woman in the history of brides. I imagined that my man, my husband, was such a good catch that I was the envy of every woman who met me. This was my recurring daydream and the dream that consistently invaded my thoughts since I was fifteen.

When the music began, I snapped out of my trance. Alicia's mom leaned forward and put her finger on her lips, signaling Alicia to stop talking. I wasn't really interested in seeing anyone come down the aisle but the bride, because I was anxious to see what she was wearing. I took a second look at the program that was given to us when we came in. I was really impressed with how beautifully the lavender ink bounced off the white card stock paper. I imagined how it would look with red on white for my day. As I studied the program, I felt someone walk by me toward the front of the church. I didn't see who it was; peripherally I saw it was two individuals.

I assumed it was the groom and his best man because they were wearing pants, one in black and one in white. I knew it wasn't the bride so I continued to read the program and look at the design to see if there was a style I might mimic on my special day.

"Hey, Alicia," I heard a voice whisper from behind us.

Instinctively, Alicia and I looked back to see who it was. It was another of her female cousins I had never met. As I turned to face forward, I was horrified to see Thomas standing at the altar speaking with the pastor. My eyes widened to see if it was actually him, and as I focused hard, I gasped and put my hand over my mouth. Luckily for me, no one noticed. Alicia was still whispering to the woman behind us and her mother was whispering to Alicia's father, who had strolled in late and taken a seat on the opposite side of her.

Oh my God, what the hell is going on here? I thought.

I looked at the program again to check the names. It read *Anthony and Meagan,* just as I had read the first time. What was Thomas doing here, though? *My eyes must be deceiving me. He has to be standing in the wrong spot. He must be the best man and the other guy is the groom.* My blood pressure was on the rise, and I took a deep breath to calm myself. To be sure, I leaned over to Alicia. I was hot, light-headed, confused, and almost intoxicated all at once.

"Hey, who's the guy in the white tux?"

"That's the groom, silly," she responded sarcastically.

"That's Anthony."

"Are . . . are you sure?"

"I'm positive; I've only seen him a dozen times."

"Shhh," her mother remarked to us both.

My stomach turned in knots and I could've died right there. As the music began for the processional, my heart began to race and my breath became erratic. Couple by couple, the bridesmaids and groomsmen marched in, taking their places on opposite sides of the altar. I was getting very warm and pulled a tissue from my purse to wipe my neck and face. This was not happening. There is no way in hell this was happening. I must have been asleep and this was just a nightmare or something. I must have eaten something spicy before going to bed, and this was my penance for my late-night snack.

Minutes passed and I soon realized this was not a dream but my worst nightmare turned real. At first, I wanted to cry, but then I wanted to stand up and shout his name at the top of my lungs. I felt betrayed, deceived, and angry all at once. More than anything, I was wounded. It was a wound that words could not describe.

While Thomas stood at the front of the church preparing to pledge his life to another, I was dying a slow death from heartache. I felt so much pain it was as if someone were sitting on my lap, pushing hard on my chest. I wondered if I was experiencing a heart attack or a panic attack. Whatever this new pain was, it was not going away. I felt faint and high all at once.

No one else knew my plight, but I felt so used and so utterly embarrassed. How could he be getting married? What happened to his being out of town? How could I have been so stupid, so naïve, so . . . *wrong?* I decided it was time for me to go. I couldn't just sit here and watch the man I'd imagined marrying, marry someone else. *Someone else!* I screamed inside. *Then that means he's been cheating on me all this time. Even worse, I'm the other woman!*

I felt like the man in the car commercial when he puts his hand on the vehicle and he starts seeing quick images of himself driving the car. Except my images were of all the times I spent with Thomas; times that I kissed him and made love to him. All the while, all this time . . . he was engaged to another woman. I suddenly became ill and finally decided to get up. Just then, Alicia put her hand on my thigh.

"My cousin should be coming in now," she whispered. "She's cute, but she's a real bitch."

Everyone stood up as the organist began playing "Here comes the bride." This was a perfect time to excuse myself since everyone had their eyes on her. All I had to do was walk carefully to the opposite side of the church and leave through one of the rear doors. Then it dawned on me that getting up would bring unnecessary attention to myself, as well as the bride. How rude would it be to walk out as the bride was coming in? No, I was stuck. I started to get up, but I forced myself to sit back down. Besides, I had an urge to see her. I needed to size up the competition. Although it was obvious that I was not the woman Thomas wanted to marry, so there really was no competition. Still, I had to see her. I wanted to see the type of woman that was capable of capturing Thomas's heart. Why wasn't I good enough? And how did I find myself on the outside looking in?

I asked Alicia to switch places with me so that I could get a good look at the bride. She moved aside, and as I held back tears, I waited patiently for the double wooden doors to open. I quickly shifted my eyes to Thomas, who was staring solely at the doors where his bride would soon enter. When the doors opened, revealing her, everyone gasped and so did I. Everyone seem stunned by her beauty, and I was horrified because she was the *total opposite of me*.

Meagan, the bride-to-be, was gorgeous—if I must say so myself. She was so tiny that she couldn't weigh more than one hundred pounds, soaking wet. The white, strapless dress showed off her toned shoulders and arms, and she had curves for such a petite woman. The beading around the waist drew attention to her flat stomach, and the dress was certainly something I would've chosen if I were her size.

No doubt, she looked like a model from *Bride Magazine*, and appeared as every woman's fantasy on her wedding day. She was the *perfect* bride, and a single tear escaped from my eye as I realized there was no comparison between us. Now, I knew why Thomas had chosen her. I watched attentively as she made her way down the aisle to the man who I thought, just forty-eight hours earlier, was my boyfriend, my man, *my potentially future husband.*

The closer she got to me, I could see through her bicep, length veil. She had the complexion of Lisa Raye and she looked very much like her, just smaller. As she passed, I was practically blinded by the diamonds on her choker. I got a whiff of her perfume, and if I didn't know any better, I would say it was the same scent that I was wearing.

I continued to take mental notes of her. I watched the way her jet-black hair was rolled into a love knot at the nape of her neck. I was jealous at how small her back was and how firm her butt appeared. I bet she wasn't wearing a fucking panty girdle either. I was too jealous to compliment how luxurious her fish-tail train followed her. I looked at Thomas again and I wanted to kill him for staring at her like he was. Just as the thought crossed my mind, his eyes connected with mine for the first time. For a dark-skinned black man, he turned a whiter shade of pale. He looked at me with wonderment, panic, and confusion as he tried to figure out what, if anything, I would do. He had to be wondering the same thing I was: *Why am I here?* I watched him take in a deep breath and lick his lips with nervousness. He tried to avert his eyes, and then forced a fake smile at his bride. Again, he glanced in my direction, almost as if to confirm that it was really me.

His sudden look of panic confirmed my reality. This was indeed happening, and as much as I wanted it to be, it wasn't a dream. I figured his heart was racing just as fast as mine was. Our hearts were both racing just as fast as they had been two days ago while we made love in my bed, in my apartment. Thomas exhaled slowly and smiled at his bride again. He straightened his jacket and sighed, as if he were trying to regain his composure. It was good to see that he was in one hell of a situation, just as I was.

The bride took graceful steps as she walked in Thomas's direction. She smiled at him and he continued to display a forced, fake smile. His eyes connected with mine, and I could almost see through him; if looks could kill, my God . . . if looks could kill, I would unleash a death on Thomas that would shame the devil with my conviction. With each step the bride took in his direction, a memory of our relationship invaded my psyche.

I tried to shake the memories. I tried to keep my emotions in check. I tried oh so hard not to have a mental breakdown in the house of the Lord. Thomas made his choice. He was about to make that choice in front of his family, friends, and God almighty. Right or wrong, I had no right to ruin his day or hers. Then I thought, *Fuck that! If anything she has a right to know. Black women need to stick together. I would want to know if it were me. I should say something. I should do something.* Instead I was frozen with fear, uncertainty, and pain. Once again, just when I thought a man couldn't hurt me any more than other men in my past had, a new one came into my life and turned my heart inside out and stepped on it.

I watched Thomas and he tried his best not to look in my direction. But every few seconds or so, he did. With each step I found myself locked in a carnal memory. Most of the memories were from just a few days ago.

His bride was ten paces away from him, and although I looked in her direction, I didn't see her. With the next step she took, I saw Thomas in my mind's eye in all his naked glory. With the ninth step, I imagined him entering me from behind as I bent over my dining room table the other night. With the eighth step, I imagined him kneeling before me, tasting me. The seventh step had me kneeling before him, pleasing him orally.

Step six I was on top of him. Step five he was on top of me. Step four was Wednesday's 69 position. Step three, was his whispers in my ear. At step two, the bride looked in my direction and saw my single tear joined by many others. They were tears that I am sure she mistook for joy. I never saw her look in my direction. I was in a faraway place. Later on, I would wonder what made her look in my direction at that exact moment in time.

As she stood before Thomas, I imagined very clearly he and I climaxing simultaneously Wednesday night, early Thursday morning. I imagined that very last moment when everything in my life was normal. I then thought about the senseless fight that we had and all the senseless fights that preceded that one. I then wondered if his anger was genuine or by design. I looked in his direction again and he was almost rigid as he faced his bride. I knew that no matter what, he would not look in my direction again.

With his eyes full of water, the question was if he did let the tears fall, would they be tears of joy or sorrow for a betrayal that had boundless depth? As the congregation sat down, the preacher spoke.

"Who gives this woman to this man?"

"Her mother and her father," her parents replied.

Thomas cleared his throat and wiped the sweat from his brow before taking Meagan's hand. I knew enough about my lover to know that clearing his throat was his way of clearing his mind. He often did that at work, when we would argue or when something pressing was on his mind and he was searching for a solution to a problem.

He was probably now telling himself that everything was under control, which I'd often seen him do at work when problems arose. I was getting more upset because he was obviously choosing her over me. I knew the last thing he was going to do was announce his lover who was sitting three pews away.

I was now a mad black woman with the devil sitting on my shoulder. I watched as the ceremony moved forward, and listened to the brief scripture spoken by the pastor. All the various faces in the room turned and their eyes to the happy couple. Some were deep in thought, while others were deep in prayer. Many of the women had a look of either reflection or regret regarding their own nuptials.

My mind raced in a million different directions. My heart experienced an array of emotions. The chief of which were hurt and betrayal. So when the preacher asked if there were any objections, it took all I had not to stand up and scream our sin to the world. I wanted someone to hurt as much as I was hurting, and at this moment, if I would've objected, the hurt could've easily fallen on Meagan.

I didn't know her and didn't give a damn about *who* she was. Then it dawned on me the level of hurt she would experience if I were to let the cat out of the bag. I was torn. On one hand, I thought she had a right to know. On the other hand, I didn't feel it was my place to say anything; after all, I wasn't supposed to be here. I couldn't help but wonder if she was just as in the dark as I was. She had to be. I felt a need to say something, but I was in enemy territory and could be a casualty of this war. Although Alicia couldn't stand her cousin, Meagan was still family and I wasn't. There was no telling whose side she would take and I refused to put her in an uncomfortable situation.

When the preacher asked the congregation again if there were any valid objections, Thomas instinctively looked right at me. Without a blink, I stared deeply into his eyes and licked my top lip from one side to the other. I didn't say one word, but I was sure that my look put a bit of fear in him. For now, he thought he'd dodged a bullet and was in the clear. I was pissed that he looked at me with any semblance of confidence, as if he knew I wasn't going to say anything. I decided to shift in my seat, and when I cleared the tightness in my throat, his eyes got big as quarters. His look of confidence quickly changed to fear. It was obvious he no longer felt like he was in control. He had no idea what I was going to do, and the discomfort that showed on his face made me smile.

With no word from anyone, the preacher continued with the service. I sat there listening as the couple vowed to love, honor, and cherish one another. I witnessed the man I loved vow to forsake all others for someone other than me. If our relationship wasn't over, it was certainly over when he said, "I do." Then he kissed her, and as they kissed, I leaned my head to one side to watch him perjure himself in front of his friends, family, and God.

This relationship had to be a lie. It had to be. I thought of how he had committed adultery in his heart and in body not even two full days ago; if not adultery, then fornication. *What's happening here? What did I do to deserve this? How does he plan on facing me at work? Or does he even care? Did he ever feel anything for me? Was I not his woman all this time? Was I not the one who opened her house and her life and her heart to this man? How could he do this to me? Was I just some damned fling? Was I just his last go-round as a bachelor? What the hell!*

The preacher announced them as husband and wife and the congregation cheered. As the newlyweds walked down the aisle and passed by me, he snuck a peek at me. I felt like I'd been dismissed from my duties as what I thought was the role of his woman, but was actually the role of his lover.

After the wedding party and their parents exited the church, the other guests followed suit. Alicia quickly grabbed my hand and we rushed out to the foyer where the receiving line had been formed. Although there was a line, Alicia went right up to her cousin. They gave one another a very phony cheek-to-cheek kiss. As they greeted one another, Thomas seemed as if he were in a state of shock. His eyes looked glossy, and it was obvious that he couldn't believe what had just happened. Here we were now, just three feet away from one another, whereas two nights ago, there was no breathing room between our entwined bodies. I gazed at him, while holding back tears. He looked away from my hurt, and forced himself to smile and greet others with a handshake and head nod.

"Meagan, this is my friend Tiffany. I didn't include her on my response card but I'm sure you don't mind paying for her, right?"

"Um . . . sure. The more, the merrier," she responded and extended her hand to shake mine. "Tiffany, you're more than welcome to join us."

"Thank you and . . . and you look absolutely stunning."

"This is my fiancé, oops, I mean husband, Anthony."

He nodded and gave me a look that begged, "Please be quiet."

I extended my hand to shake his. He reciprocated and there was a momentary silence. His chest heaved in and out, and it was obvious to me that he was trying to control his reaction to my close presence.

"Excuse me," Meagan interrupted, "Do you two know one another?"

"Well, I thought he looked familiar to me as he stood at the altar; but now that we're face to face, it seems that I don't know him at all."

Thomas exhaled as I released his hand.

"Good, let's go," Alicia remarked as we stepped away to speak to other members of her family.

After the last guest kissed the couple and exited the church, it was time for the wedding party to go back into the sanctuary to take pictures.

"Okay, everyone, the faster we get these pictures taken, the faster we can get to the reception," the coordinator instructed. "I'm sure you're all hungry by now."

"Meagan, go on in and I'll be there in a minute," Thomas said.

"No, Thomas, we have to take pictures and I'm hungry." Meagan whined.

"Baby, I need to use the restroom," he told her politely, but his hand was yanked in her direction.

"Can't you hold it until we get to the reception?"

"Meagan!" he said firmly. "I'm going to the washroom."

He snatched away and Meagan was left standing with a wondering look on her face.

Chapter Four—Thomas

What the hell is Tiffany doing here? I thought as I looked at myself in the bathroom mirror. I splashed water on my face as my mind raced in a state of confusion, trying to figure out what Tiff was doing here. This was my wedding and my fucking girlfriend was at my wedding! *What the hell do I do now?* I asked the man in the mirror. My stomach was tied in a tight knot. I was so light-headed that I thought I might pass out. I wiped my face again with the water and tried to mask the beads of sweat that forced their way through my pores. My heart raced, my breathing was at a fast pace, and there wasn't much that I could do to keep myself from having an anxiety attack on the bathroom floor. I felt like crawling in the fetal position or hiding. I briefly thought about running out to my car and speeding off in any direction. It took me a few minutes to calm myself enough not to throw up or pass out.

"Shit!" I said in a voice just above a whisper. "Jesus, what have I done?"

I paced the bathroom floor and tried to figure out my next move. Minutes later, I heard Meagan's voice just outside the door.

"Sean, please ask him to hurry up. It's our wedding day."

My best friend and best man, Sean Jackson, walked in and smiled at my wife's impatience. When he saw the look of panic and confusion on my face, his smile quickly went to an expression of concern. We'd known each other for about ten years, and he knew me well enough to know that something was going on.

"Dawg, what's wrong?"

"I got mad drama, man. I don't know what to do."

"Well, it's too late for that now, player. You married Meagan and it's a done deal." He laughed.

"Meagan's not the problem."

"Then what is?"

"I don't know how to say this."

"Just say it, bruh."

I had a hard time confessing my sin to my boy. Sean would have my back no matter what, but he didn't advocate cheating, which was why he didn't know anything about Tiffany. Sean is one of those good brothers. You know the type? He pays his bills on time, doesn't cheat on his woman, and pays his child support religiously. He is going to make some woman happy should he ever decide to get married. Sean believes in God and believes in karma. He would have my back regarding the situation with Tiffany, but he would definitely lecture me and give me shit for it later. I debated telling him because I wasn't in the mood for a lecture. Not now—not today.

"I cheated on Meagan," I confessed.

"What? When?"

"I've been cheating on her for the past few months. Actually, for the past eleven months."

"Let me guess, that's why you've been missing our Wednesday night poker games, right?"

"Yeah."

I used to play spades, bid whist, and poker every Wednesday and Friday night at one of my boy's cribs. We used to each alternate hosting card parties. It was our way of staying in touch with one another. We were all Omegas, frat brothers until the end. We saw a lot of chapters hook up with each other back in school and over the years everyone always seemed to lose touch with one another. My frat brothers, Sean, Don, CC, and Chuck were my closest friends in life.

We all agreed that we would never stop hanging out, which is why since I graduated from undergrad years ago, we have all kept in touch. At twenty-eight years of age we were all successful black men; only some of us, it seemed, hadn't stopped acting like teenagers in spite of our success.

"Who's this woman you cheated on Meagan with, and why is it pressing on your mind now?"

"The sister out there in the black dress who Meagan and I were just talking to, that's her. Her name is Tiffany and I've been seeing her for a little over eleven months."

"She's here?"

"Yes, she's here."

"Ant, you have got to be kidding me."

"I wish I was."

"Well, it's been a long time since I was out there like that, but if she is the other woman, she will understand if I ask her to leave. I mean, I'm the best man. My duty is to make things run smooth for you, right? I'll just tell her that I know you guys' situation and she needs to bounce out of respect for your wife. It's not like she didn't know that you were getting married. I mean, who does she think she is just walking up in here?"

Sean saw the expression on my face, which gave everything away. He stopped speaking mid-sentence.

"Ant . . . you didn't."

I shrugged my shoulders before speaking. "She thinks she's the only one, or at least, she *thought* she was the only one until today. She considered me her boyfriend, I mean, up until today."

"And why would she think that?"

"Because we've gotten really tight this past year."

"Okay, fine. But what is she doing . . . *here?*"

"That's the thing, I don't know. I don't fucking know. She came with Alicia or something. I didn't even know she knew my wife's cousin. My wife? Shit, I have a wife now."

Sean paced back and forth as did I. Meagan was becoming impatient in the hallway and was beginning to trip. She called my name. I also heard her call my boy Don and ask him to check on me and Sean because she was becoming worried.

I was worried that she would think I was having second thoughts about our marriage, which wasn't even twenty minutes old yet. While she spoke to Don, Sean and I thought about my next move. Don walked in, joking as he usually does.

"Hey, what's goin' on? Should I tell your new bride that you two fools are in love and on the down low? What the hell is taking you guys so long? Your wife is waiting to take pictures."

Don was the ultimate player in our pack. He too took one look at us both and saw that something was seriously wrong.

"Okay, what have you two niggas done?" Don joked.

I quickly recounted the story to Don about me and Tiffany, and how she was now here at the wedding. I was hoping Don would take this matter seriously and offer a solution Sean or I hadn't thought of. Instead, Don was being Don, and soon after I told the story, he smiled and broke out laughing.

"That shit . . . is funny as hell!" he said.

He could see by the look on that neither of us was amused.

"Fool, stop laughing. Tell me, what the hell do I do?" I asked Don.

He tried hard to gather himself. "Has the other woman been tripping?" he asked.

"No, so far she has been cool."

"Then play that shit off."

"He can't just play it off, Don," Sean added. "If this other woman opens her mouth, that's it. There is no coming back from that shit! Meagan's friends, family, and everyone

we know is out there, including Ant's coworkers and VIPs
from his office. This shit blowing up in his face does not look
promising on a resume."

"Yeah, you're right," Don agreed.

Sean and I continued to pace the floor while Don sat
on the counter.

"Think of something, Mr. Player!" I said sarcastically.

"Shit, you got yourself in this shit, *player*, think of
something yourself."

I cut my eyes at Don and pounded my chest. "I thought
we were boys. Player or not, I need somebody to think of
something—quick."

"I'm just fucking with you and you know I got your
back," Don said. "We'll think of something."

"I hope so. The rest of my life lies in the balance here."

Don hopped off the counter and snapped his fingers,
as if he had an excellent suggestion. "Why don't I just simply
walk the bitch out of here?"

"Then we'll really have some drama, and that will
bring attention to the situation and arouse suspicion." Sean
said.

"Then, Ant could act sick," Don said.

"Meagan ain't going for that shit. I could have fucking
Ebola or Leprosy and she would tell me to hold on until the
end of the night," I responded.

"Damn. How did you get hooked up with this chick
in the first place? I mean, she's cute but she looks like she
needs to push the damn dinner plate away."

"Can we not get into that shit right now?" I asked.

"Thomas Anthony Young! Come out here, right now!"
we all heard Meagan yell.

We all looked at each other like three boys in trouble.
We had been thick as thieves growing up, but had never been
in a situation like this.

Just then, Chuck walked in the bathroom. Now, almost half of the wedding party was in the bathroom.

"Man, what the hell are y'all doing in here?" Chuck asked.

"Where is CC?" Don asked.

"Trying to holler at one of the bridesmaids," Chuck said.

"Which one?" Don asked.

"Don!" I yelled.

"Oh, right. We got drama, my bad."

Don told Chuck the whole story and his mouth was wide open. "You mean, he's sexin' the cute heavy-set girl with the nice smile?"

We all nodded.

He threw his hand back. "Aw, man, y'all straight. She already left."

The news had me ready to tap dance. "For real? You straight up saw her leave?"

"Yes, she's gone. And before your wife kill us, can we get out of this bathroom and go take some pictures?"

We all let out sighs of relief, gathered ourselves, and tried our best to keep our composure. After checking myself in the mirror, I patted my waves and headed toward the door.

We had only been in the bathroom maybe fifteen minutes, but that fifteen minutes seemed like forever. Meagan stood outside the door with a scowl on her face and her arms folded.

"What the hell were you all doing in there?" she asked.

None of my boys offered her an explanation, and just headed towards the sanctuary to take pictures.

"I just needed to talk to my boys for a minute," I said.

"It was just you and Sean in there. I had to send Don and Chuck in after you. I started to go in myself, but—"

"Sean was telling me what a lucky man I was to have you. Don came in too, of course, to talk shit. Chuck joined in on the fun, and I guess the four of us got carried away. I'm surprised you didn't send CC in, but it was good to hear that my boys support our marriage."

"They'd better, and I couldn't find CC because he's trying to holler at one of my girls. It's not going to happen, though, because CC is just a school teacher and *my girls* want more than a man with a B.A."

"Damn, baby, that's messed up. A man shouldn't be judged by the degree he has, should he?"

"And why not? I wouldn't be with you if you didn't have your MBA."

"Are you serious?"

Meagan didn't respond, but I already knew the answer to that question. My wife is fine as hell, but she is high maintenance and she knows what she wants out of life. Some days that is a good thing, and other days it's a bad thing. This wedding me back fourteen grand. Her ring was four grand, and our vacation cost me four grand too. The house we moved into is in Lynwood, Illinois, and just to maintain an affordable note, it cost me another twenty-three grand down. I knew what I was getting when I married Meagan. The thing I kept asking myself was whether she or any woman was worth all this.

"If the Toys 'R' Us kids are through playing around in the bathroom, can we take pictures now?"

"Sure, babe."

"I don't want any more damn distractions today!" She fussed as we went to the sanctuary to take pictures.

I don't want any more my damned self, I thought.

Chapter Five—Tiffany

Alicia held my hand all the way to her truck. It was as if she knew I was about to bolt, but I'm almost certain she couldn't imagine why. A million thoughts were running through my mind; *how did this happen? How did I not know and just how long have the two of them been together?* Again, I went back to the source.

"Alicia, they seem like a really cute couple, how long have they been together?"

"As far as I know, they've been together since Meagan's senior year of college. I want to say at least four years," Alicia responded.

Four fucking years! I screamed inside. My anguish had to have been written all over my face.

"Tiff, are you all right?" Alicia asked, looking back and forth between me and the road.

I wanted to tell her. Everything inside of me was screaming for me to tell her, but this was her cousin's man, now her cousin's husband. I still wasn't sure whose side she'd take, but I felt embarrassed because I'd been singing this man's praises for the last eleven months. I couldn't deal with telling her the truth right now. Actually, I couldn't deal with any of this shit right now. I knew I'd have to come clean about all of this, but not now. Right now I needed to find a way to get out of car and go home. *I can't go to their damned reception.*

"Alicia, I'm fine. I just feel a bit sick to my stomach. Can you drive me home?"

"Aw, come on, Tiff, you've put me off for your new

man long enough. Besides, there's nothing wrong with you. You want to go home and wait for him to call. He's out of town. I bet he's enjoying himself."

I don't know about that, I thought.

"You should have some fun tonight too. Deal with his bullshit tomorrow."

I didn't have the emotional strength to argue with her and I didn't want her to get suspicious. All the way to the reception, I prayed to God for strength to get through this evening. This was supposed to be my wedding to him, not hers. *Who does she think she is? I'm his woman. Or at least, I was. She couldn't possibly love him the way I do. I don't care how long they've been together. I can't believe that I'm going to his reception. I will go for just a minute and then find an excuse to leave. There is no way I can stay at their reception.*

The reception was at the luxurious Chateau Bu'che in Alsip, Illinois, which to me resembled the White House. The banquet hall sat in the center of a well-manicured lawn surrounded by a pond and a gazebo at the far end of the property. The front gates were also white. They opened to a cobblestone driveway that circled a stone fountain.

Once inside, the foyer was so beautiful it was breathtaking. There was a huge crystal chandelier in the center of the walkway, and cranberry carpeting covered the floor. The walls were painted a light shade of pink and the banister of the double staircase was gold. It was obvious someone had some money.

We were greeted and told that the reception was taking place in the upstairs ballroom. I was so anxious to get a drink that I left Alicia standing around talking to other guests. I rushed through the double doors and went right to the bar.

"Vodka straight up, please."

"Yes, ma'am."

Before the bartender could set the glass down, I grabbed it and sucked the drink up quickly. "Can I have another?"

Just as he gave me the second round, Alicia walked in. "Girl, why did you leave me?"

"I needed a drink."

"Tiffany, don't let the thoughts of your man get to you. I'm sure he'll be crawling back to you the minute he gets back in town."

By now, I was a little tipsy and all I could do was laugh. I grabbed the next drink and followed Alicia to our table, which was right by the door. After about thirty minutes or so, the bar closed, but not before I got a few more drinks. Soon, the music stopped and we were all asked to take our seats. Couple by couple, the wedding party was introduced as they came in and took their seats at the head table. Thanks to my friend Seagram's, I was doing all right until the newlyweds were announced.

"Ladies and gentlemen, I present to you Mr. and Mrs. Thomas Anthony Young."

Thomas Anthony Young? I had forgotten about his middle name. The invitations simply said "Anthony and Meagan." That was why things didn't initially click. Everyone there must have known him as Anthony.

Everyone stood, and as the doors opened, the couple was locked in a passionate kiss. I died a second death and gulped down the rest of my last drink.

"You wanna talk about it?" Alicia's mom asked and reached over to touch my hand. She was a cynical woman.

"Ma, why did you ask her that?" Alicia chimed in.

"A woman doesn't drink like that unless there's something on her mind and it's usually a man."

"Ma, stop meddling."

"I'm not meddling, I'm just saying."

I sat there listening as the two women bickered about what was on my mind. Neither one of them had a clue. They continued until Alicia's father silenced them both. As the toasts were made, I stared at the bottom of my empty glass, anticipating my next visit to the bar.

The food would be arriving soon, and although I wasn't hungry, I knew I would be spending a lot of time at the bar, so I had to put something in my stomach. I planned on nibbling a bit on the salad and maybe having two spoonfuls of soup. When the steak arrived, though, I planned to eat everything on my plate. That was my way of getting back at them for looking so damn happy. I would eat on their dime, not that it hurt them very much. It was obvious that the two of them had long money. Meagan looked like she was born to money. Here the two of them seemed happily married and the only revenge I could seem to plot was eating at their expense. Yeah, I know it wasn't really mature, nor did it make any sense. I thought it was either that, or show my ass up in there.

They had a brief dance before the food was served, and Thomas had finally seen that I was indeed at the reception too. I knew he hadn't planned on seeing me there and I hadn't planned on coming. For the time being, we both appeared to be stuck with one another. I'm sure we wished for the same thing, which was to be as far away from one another as possible.

The coordinator grabbed the microphone again and announced the happy couple. "So High" by John Legend played, and tears began to build up in my eyes as I watched the newlyweds have their first *official* dance. "So High" was a song that Thomas often played at my place to get me in the mood. It was so inappropriate for them to dance to that song. How could they—no, how could he? I stared at him with teary eyes, and when a tear rolled down my face, it caught his attention.

Chapter Six—Thomas

While holding my wife in my arms, my eyes connected with Tiffany's, but I quickly turned away. When I had first walked into the reception hall, I was nervous as hell. I wanted to ride with my boys to the reception, but I knew there was no way in hell Meagan would go for it. I rode in the limo with my new wife and my boys followed. I knew they were in Sean's truck, clowning me something awful. By then they were all telling CC what was going on and I knew they were having quite the laugh at my expense.

As we rode in the limo, Meagan was all kissy-face with me. Had it not been for Tiffany's presence, I would have been all over my wife. Instead, I was scared as hell and wondered if my sin and secret was written all over my face.

Before I'd gotten into the limo with Meagan, my boy Don signaled me to simply play everything off and be cool. I tried my best, but during our ride together, I felt as if there were a teleprompter over my head with an in-depth report of my activities for the past eleven months. Somehow, someway, Meagan knew something was wrong. I thanked God that she didn't know exactly what it was.

"Are you okay, Anthony?"

"I'm fine, babe."

"You don't seem fine."

"I'm just . . . just overwhelmed, that's all. It's a lot to absorb . . . being married, I mean. I'm just adjusting."

She jerked her head back. "Adjusting? You didn't have to do anything but show up!"

"Show up? This little party of ours is costing quite the penny."

"Is that what all this apprehension is about? Is that why you were really in the bathroom all that time with your boys? I know you're not tripping about cost. *It's just money.* Push comes to shove, you can simply make some more."

Is she fucking kidding me? She doesn't even work and she has the same damn degree that I have. Her family has money. She worked a few internships here or there but never anything serious. She was working for a fairly prestigious firm about a year ago, in Los Angeles while we were doing the long distance thing, but she quit that job to "find herself" and let her tell it, she wanted to be closer to me. She quickly found another job here in Chicago and just a few months ago, she left that job as well. She promised me that she would go back to work after we married. She promised that after we married we would immediately discuss kids. Now here we were getting married and she was putting us in debt fast and deep. So deep that I thought having kids might have to be postponed for a year or two. I wanted to start a family almost immediately.

I wanted to put her in her place so badly, but now wasn't the time or place to do it. Besides, I hadn't really thought about how much the wedding was costing me until now. Now that she brought it up, that contributed to my anxiety levels.

First Tiffany shows up and now this. How was I going to pay for this shit? *Meagan thinks I'm made out of money, but I had to cash in stocks, get a loan from my 401K and use a good portion of my savings for her special day. Not only that, but the tax bite at the end of the year is going to mess us both up for the next two years.*

If we were *white*, the father of the bride would have picked up the tab for the wedding. Meagan's father spoiled her to death, but he had made it clear that he was not picking up the tab for me to marry his little girl—his spoiled little girl. Her father never liked me much no matter how hard I tried to impress him. He felt as if his little girl should be with some-one better established. From what I have heard, her other suitors, though not as handsome as I, make close to a half million a year. Some are CEOs, some bank presidents and others are celebrities. Me? I make a meager one hundred thousand a year. Bank V.P.s make good money and have a lot of earning potential, but not enough apparently to compete with some of Meagan's suitors.

Her father didn't think I was good enough by any stretch of the imagination for his little girl. I swear if Meagan wasn't so damn fine, and I wasn't the envy of all my boys, there was no way I would have dropped all that coin for this *one day.*

I looked at Meagan and forced yet another smile. To cool the situation, I told her she made me the luckiest man in the world. I hugged her in the limo and held her tight. But during our cuddling moment on our way to the reception hall, all I thought about was Tiffany.

I didn't mean to hurt her. I never meant for our relationship to go where it had gone. I had known for more than a year that I was going to marry Meagan. I don't know what it was about Tiffany that made me approach her, but I had to. All I remember is that to me, she had a warming smile and she was the most down-to-earth and real woman I had ever met in my life. Sure she needed to lose a few pounds, but other than that, Tiffany in every other way was . . . the perfect woman.

As I danced with my wife, I tried to force the thoughts of Tiffany out of my head. I took another glance at her, and re-alized that even though she was a cutie, she wasn't the type of woman some men would marry. My boys expected more from me . . . I mean, Meagan's petite, educated, articulate, and a regular debutante. She can talk on any level, she understands finances the same way I do, and she can wear the hell out of a formal gown. She's so gorgeous that she's been asked to model for various charities, functions, and magazines. No doubt, my wife is refined and she's the perfect high-society wife. You know, the type of woman you can take to the Mayor's Ball or to Upper Echelon affairs. Or, the type you have on your arm when you're amidst VIPs, celebrities, and millionaire clients. On the other hand, Tiffany is the kind of woman you stay home and watch movies with or go bowling with. Taking her to Red Lobster or Houston's wouldn't be a problem, but only Lawry's or the Pinnacle would suit Meagan's taste. I liked them both, but the difference between them is night and day.

I enjoyed the times that Tiffany and I spent together, and we always had fun. In the beginning, we took long walks, and strangely enough, we had a lot in common. We had nice dinners (that were easy on my wallet). We always laughed and joked together, playfully wrestled, and watched old movies while eating popcorn at her place.

I never anticipated that my feelings would grow for Tiffany. The relationship between us sort of just happened. She always greeted me with a warm smile when we were at work, and the more I saw her, the more the idea of getting with her became more appealing. It started off as casual talk in the office. From there, it went to lunch and soon after, dinner dates and phone calls. The next thing I knew, every day that I didn't spend with Meagan, I found myself longing to speak to or be with Tiffany. We would talk on the phone sometimes for hours on end. Our constant talking, joking, and chatting on the Net soon after graduated to some of the wettest and best sex I had in my life. Tiffany had no equal in bed, which surprised me and solidified me as the new man in her life. Giving up her friendship would've been hard. Walking away from her sex was almost impossible. I was surprised with how much I cherished the time I spent with Tiffany and how great the sex was.

I went to my bachelor party on Tuesday, which is why I'd blown Tiffany off. I started the fight with her on purpose

Wednesday night, because I wanted her to break things off with me. I know it was juvenile, but I didn't see any other option at the time. I just got caught up, and each time I tried to break things off with her, she hit me with unconditional love, kindness, and understanding. Each time I tried to walk away from her sex, my body craved her like an addict. I couldn't stay away and kept coming back. Tiffany's sex was addictive. I wanted very much for our last night together to be memorable. I started to bring flowers and gifts. I started to confess my infidelity to her. When I lay at home at night some nights thinking about the two women, I often found myself thinking about how unfair I was being to *Tiffany*. Being unfair to Meagan never even crossed my mind.

I never meant to hurt Tiffany and never meant to lead her on. I didn't expect for things between us to last that long. In fact, the closer my wedding got, the harder I tried to end it with Tiffany. I don't know how, and I don't know why, but I kept showing up on Wednesday nights. Maybe it was her personality, or maybe it was indeed the sex. Whatever it was . . . it's over now, and I missed what we had. I wished I could somehow put Tiffany's personality in Meagan's body. I hate what I did to her, and losing her felt like losing a close friend or part of me.

Again, I snapped out of my trance and thought about where I was and who I was holding in my arms. "So High" was the song selected for our first dance. This was the song that Meagan loved most these days. I whispered to my bride how so very beautiful she was on her special day. Everybody watched us and I was deeply hurt, knowing that my lover's eyes couldn't stay off us and mine had traveled to her as well. Still, I danced with Meagan like a man in love. She held firmly on to me and we kissed, smiled, and enjoyed one another's presence like two graduates at an eighth-grade dance. The preacher walked over to us and whispered that the first dance had to wait until after everyone had eaten. I laughed and joked about wanting to keep my beautiful bride in my arms.

Meagan smiled a flattering smile. I looked at her and convinced myself that my doubts about our marriage were a good thing. It was okay to have doubts, and nothing in life was for certain. Just as I began to feel excited about my marriage, I felt another chill.

Meagan turned to greet all of our guests before dinner was served, and I watched Tiffany sit in the front row of tables with more tears pouring from her eyes. Several empty glasses were in front of her and she looked as if she'd tossed back quite a few drinks. I was speechless, and I wanted to say something . . . anything to her, but I couldn't. I smiled at the other guests sitting at her table, and they each held up their glasses to me, including Tiffany. My nightmare had now been extended, and it was obvious that my wedding day was turning into a disaster.

My groomsmen stood and raised their glasses as well. They were equally stunned to see Tiffany up front. All of our eyes roamed around the room, mainly in Tiffany's direction. I looked back at Meagan, and surprisingly, she was looking me dead in the mouth.

"What the hell is going on with you and your boys today?" she whispered softly enough so our guests wouldn't hear.

"Nothing, why do you ask?"

"I think you're hiding something from me."

"Something like what?"

"I don't know what is up with you today, but I don't want any bullshit on my wedding day. My sorority sisters are here, and I know they would like nothing more than for something to go wrong on *my day*. Many of them have trifling-ass men who are either blue-collar workers or men who cheat on them. Today, I am their envy and I expect things to stay that way. I don't want any crazy shit at my wedding, no practical jokes, no stepping, and no acting out like you and your boys sometimes do."

I stood in disbelief and sipped from the glass in my

hand. "Blue-collar?" I whispered. "What is wrong with brothers who work *real jobs* for a living?"

Meagan snapped her neck. "Is that all you heard me say? I'm talking about making sure that everything is perfect today. *Chicago Magazine* is here as well as *High Society* and other media people and—"

"Yeah, whatever, I heard you. I can understand you dogging brothers who might have cheated on your sorors, but *now* isn't the time to discuss this. Besides, like I said, there's nothing wrong with blue-collar workers."

"Like you know anything about manual labor, please." She continued to make her point and darted her finger. "Those brothers are working with their hands because they don't have the skills or the mental capacity to work with their minds for a living. Some of my sorors boyfriends have GED certificates. Can you believe that? I have no clue where they find these kinds of men."

"Meagan, let it go. I don't want to argue with you about this today, okay?"

"Then don't."

"Okay, but you need to lay off blue-collar workers."

"You work in a white-collar job, so what do you care?"

I huffed and noticed a lot of guests paying attention to our whispering words. Still, I couldn't help but go there with Meagan; her comments had sparked a nerve. "I may work in a white-collar job, but it was my father's blue-collar work that got my ass where I am today. I was one of those black men out there lucky enough to have a father who busted his ass to make sure I'm the man I am today."

"You sure he's your father?"

I looked at Meagan with a blank stare.

"I . . . I'm just saying. You all don't look alike, he's not articulate and he is poor with math. I don't see how he could be your father or you his son. I like your mother and all, but maybe you should ask her what was really going on back in the day. For all you know, you could be the product of some mad love affair."

This bit . . . woman is out of her fucking mind, I thought, but didn't let those words slip from my mouth. She was dangerously close to crossing a line that would make me contemplate putting my hands on her. She could see the pain and anguish on my face, and to soothe my nerves, she touched the side of my face and placed her lips on my ear.

"Baby, I didn't mean to offend you. I love you. You're my husband. Please don't make that face. If you cheer up, your little angel might be a little devil this evening. I have some toys, handcuffs, and a few outfits from Victoria's Secret. You play nice, and I will fuck you like there is no tomorrow."

"After how much this wedding has set me back, you should fuck me like there is no tomorrow anyway. Now, this conversation that we're having is over. Can we please get back to our guests?"

She smiled, and I thought about how my wife would look this evening in her lingerie. Right after she gave me a kiss, I gave her a hug and glanced over her shoulder. I saw Tiffany staring at us, and my eyes got big as saucers when she stood up at her table. During my disagreement with Meagan, I had forgotten about Tiffany being there. My heart skipped a beat and I tried to catch my breath. *Oh shit, my marriage is over before it ever got started,* I thought, and ushered my wife to the head table so we could eat. At the same time, I had to look at one woman and pretend that I was the happiest man alive, while hiding that happiness from another woman. We took our seats at the table. I was afraid to look up and see exactly where Tiffany was.

Chapter Seven—Tiffany

I couldn't take it anymore. Without a word, I grabbed my purse and took one last look at Thomas and Meagan who were whispering at each other and looking very much in love. I rushed out, leaving my shawl on the seat. I decided to take a stroll down Main Street, which was about a block from the main entrance, to get a bus. I prayed all the way that Alicia wouldn't follow me.

I sat in the bus shelter and waited nearly thirty minutes for the Pace bus to arrive. I kept looking back at the hall, hoping and praying that Alicia wouldn't come out looking for me. She must've had a fine man in her face because I had been gone a while and it appeared that she hadn't even noticed. As impatient as I was, getting out was better than watching my lover with his new wife. I stood up one more time to see if a bus was coming, and that's when I saw a cab approaching.

"Thank you, Jesus," I said aloud, and within thirty-five minutes, I was home.

Chapter Eight—Thomas

Tiffany left with pain and anguish on her face as she rushed out of the wedding hall. Dinner had just ended, and I had barely touched my plate. I surveyed the room to try to figure out where my wife's cousin was, and Alicia was at the bar which had re-opened. Some tall brother was trying to make a move on her, and I wasn't sure if she even noticed that Tiffany had left.

My groomsmen had been paying attention, and they all approached me to pretend as if they were congratulating me on my special day. We hoped this would prove as a good distraction for Meagan, but it didn't. She had seen Tiffany's abrupt departure too and I'm sure she wondered why Tiffany made the beeline for the door. As Meagan moved toward Alicia's direction for an explanation about her friend, I reached for her arm to stop her.

"Hey, hey . . . what about our next dance?"

"In a minute, baby. I need to know what that fat girl's problem that Alicia brought was."

"Fat girl? What fat girl? Baby, what are you talking about?"

"The fat girl Alicia brought just ate on our dime and left. She seemed choked up about something and I want to know what."

"That's her business. You know how some women get at weddings."

"But this is my day. Just as everyone was giving a toast, that heifer brought attention to herself when she got up and left."

"Well, I didn't notice," I said, trying to play it off.

"I did and she should have excused herself later. She brought all types of attention to herself and I still don't know what all the tears were for."

"So, this is about you, isn't it?"

"No, it's not, but what do you mean by that?"

"I'm saying . . . you're mad because of her *timing*. Her departure took attention away from you."

She rolled her eyes and pouted. "From us. She took the attention away from us, and I'm surprised that you didn't notice her."

"Whatever, this whole production is for you."

"Fine, it is for me. It's my damned day! Yeah, I'm upset that the bitch got a free meal and then got her fat ass up to leave. I don't think anyone needs any attention today, but me!"

Again, I tried to prevent my wife for blowing off steam at the wrong place and time. "The girl was obviously upset about something. Maybe she had a failed marriage. Maybe she lost her husband to some accident or something. All I'm saying is you don't need to jump the gun here. You don't know what that woman was going through."

That seemed to calm Meagan for a while, but I knew what had caused Tiffany to leave so abruptly. I didn't understand why she would subject herself to more pain and suffering. Why come to the hall rather than go home?

"You know," Meagan added with her arms folded, "I don't give a damn what her issue was. If she has personal problems, tragedy or whatever, she should've stayed her fat ass at home. If anything, she needed to have just the house salad when she was here, and instead of coming to our wedding, she needed to take her big rotunda butt in somebody's gym."

"Baby—"

"Or Jenny Craig . . ."

"Baby, that's not nice."

"Then, Weight Watchers."

"Stop, please."

"Or she could get on the South Beach Diet. The point is the bitch needs to push the damned dinner plate back."

She needs to stop. She really needs to stop. For whatever reason, it seems that I am not quite over Tiffany. I don't know why, but the more Meagan talks about her, the more upset I'm becoming. It's like watching two friends disrespect one another and talk behind the others back. Meagan doesn't even know Tiffany. There is no need to talk about her like she has a tail. There is no reason to be so damned mean.

"Okay, that's enough. I thought today was supposed to be our special day and you weren't going to let anything upset you. Remember, your sorority sisters are watching."

That stalled her from going into straight-up bitch mode. Some days, I thought my wife had mental issues because just as easily as she turned the evil on, she could cut it off. She cut me a phony but genuine-looking smile, took my hand, and led me to the dance floor. Instead of dancing to John Legend again, we began dancing to an Alicia Keys song. We danced, and my eyes stayed glued to the door and Alicia who was still at the bar.

Chapter Nine—Tiffany

I walked in the door and peeled off my clothes. My dress was tossed in the garbage; I knew full well that I could never wear it again. It reminded me of what had happened and I wanted no recollection of the hurt I'd experienced today. I kicked off my shoes, turned on the TV, and made a beeline for the kitchen. I pulled out all my favorite snacks: ice cream, oatmeal pies, and Pepsi. I grabbed my relief team and sat in front of the TV, switching channels.

"How could I be so stupid?" I cried out loud.

I flipped the channels, only to see movies about people in love or people cheating. There was no happy medium. I flipped, flipped, and flipped some more, until I became sick with the monotonous theme that played over the airwaves. I put the TV on mute and turned on the radio. That too seemed to play every song that reflected what I was feeling.

First, I listened to "I Should Have Cheated" by Keyshia Cole. Next was "Another Relationship" by Syleena Johnson. I started switching stations and that brought about more hurt. "How Could You" by Mario came on, then "If I Ain't Got You" by Alicia Keys, which had me near tears. When the new song by Mary J. Blige began, "No more Crying," I cried my eyes out while eating double scoops of ice cream cake I had made two days ago, and soda.

Mary could take me there. She knew what I felt. It was obvious to me that Mary had been through some shit in her life, and even though I was sad, her music helped me cope with my pain.

As the music took me to new depths and made me have a conversation with my soul, I looked back at the TV and a program called *Cheaters* was on. I left the volume on mute, but I could see clearly what was going on. A woman about my size was obviously brokenhearted, and she talked to the host, telling him why she suspect her man was cheating on her. It's clear that she knew, but was seeking confirmation or validation that the world she once knew was now upside down. I watched the program as the drama unfolded, and sure enough, her man was fooling around with another woman who was smaller, cuter, and had just as much attitude as the first woman. Of course, the second woman, *the other woman*, walked away, not wanting to be on film. The look on the would-be girlfriend's face was all too familiar to me. It was an expression of sorrow and misunderstanding that only a woman in love can know or feel.

"I feel your pain, girl!" I yelled to the TV. I walked to the bathroom, and when I finished taking a leak, I stood up to look in the full-length mirror that was on the door. I hated the sight of the woman I saw, and frowned at the fat bitch I wished never existed.

"Look at you. I wouldn't want your big ass either."

This was how self-hate started. I tried not to travel down this road that some women face at one time or another; the road to depression, because they can't seem to get a handle on their weight. I wanted men to want me, especially Thomas. I wanted people to look at me the same way they looked at Meagan. It's not that I felt she was better than me, but I wanted to know what it felt like to look like her. What was it like for so many men to want you? I got approached all the time, but not when I was with other women. I didn't get any attention when I would go out with Alicia. For once, I wanted to be the center of attention.

I looked at my reflection. I looked at my mid-section and became even more down on myself. I didn't have a gut, but I did have a slight bulge. I looked at my panty girdle and thought, "Meagan doesn't need anything to help hold in her stomach." I looked at the cellulite beginning to show on my thighs and the slight loss of tone in my calves. My arms were bigger than I would have liked them to, I could see ever-so-slight stretch marks on my breasts, and my shoes I had worn tonight seemed to be a little tighter than I remembered. Either my body was changing or I had gotten fatter since the last time I dressed up.

I pushed the door out of my way, almost as if I was pushing past my own reflection in the mirror. I stormed downstairs and gathered up all my sweets. I was just about ready to throw everything in the garbage, but then there was a knock at my door. I hadn't buzzed anyone in, so I figured it was one of my neighbors. I guessed that my music was too loud.

"Just a minute," I said.

The knocking became more insistent. I ran to the bedroom to get my robe. The knocking was again insistent, just like the police.

"I said just a minute, damn!"

I pulled open the door, ready to go off. To my surprise, it was Alicia on the other side. She stepped in and saw my shoes across the room, the snacks on the table and the dried-up tears on my face.

"Tiff, what's wrong? I knew something was up when I looked up and you were gone. I felt bad that it took me a while to notice. Girl, please tell me what's really going on with you?"

I wasn't going to tell her—I really wasn't. But I had no mother, no father, my brother would want to beat Thomas into a corner, and it seemed as if Alicia was the only person I had in the world. She was the person closest to me, and as more tears fell, I had to tell someone. She followed me to the couch and we turned to each other.

"It . . . it was him, Alicia. I don't know how to tell you this, but Thomas . . . I mean, Anthony . . . they're the same person. Your cousin married my boyfriend. I . . . I'm the other woman." I paused and took a deep breath. "This isn't coming out right. I . . . I thought he was single. I thought I was the one and I didn't know about her. I didn't know whose side you would take and—"

I was hysterical and my words made little sense. Alicia hadn't said one word yet, but she placed her hand on top of mine.

"Tiff, take your time. You aren't making much sense. Now, exactly what is it that you're trying to tell me?"

I inhaled. "My boyfriend's name is Thomas. His middle name is Anthony. I thought Thomas and I were seeing each other exclusively. As it turns out, the wedding that we went to today, was my boyfriend's wedding. Your cousin married my boyfriend. The man you know as Anthony is Thomas Anthony Young. He's my colleague, and up until the wedding, I thought he was my man and I was his woman."

There was a silence that fell between us and Alicia sat with her mouth wide open. For a while I didn't know whose side she would take. I didn't know how she would think of me. Would she think that I knew all this time? Would she lose respect for me? Would she ask me how I could have been so dumb? I didn't want to tell her, but I had to tell someone. I needed to get this off my chest. I needed to be heard. I needed to vent my anger, my frustration, and my pain. I blurted everything out and rolled the dice on losing my best friend. I couldn't help thinking this was one secret I should have kept. The silence between us was deafening.

I waited for another reaction and saw the moment when the light came on in her head. She shook her head in disbelief and leaned in to give me a hug. It was a hug that I desperately needed. The second she hugged me, I let the hurt flow out. As I cried on her shoulder, she backed away from our embrace and went over to the bar to pour me a stiff drink, Hennessey and Coke.

"Girl, I'm so sorry," she said, handing the drink to me. "Why didn't you say anything?"

"Do you know how difficult that was for me? He married your cousin, and I didn't know whose side you would take."

"Tiff, it's not about sides. It's about being there for one another. This had to be hell for you. You should've said something to me."

"But, I didn't want to lose your friendship."

"Our friendship would never end over something like that. If anything, I would've pulled out my nine millimeter and busted a cap in his ass!"

I smiled and sipped from my glass. It was such a relief to tell Alicia, and her support meant a lot.

"Alicia, I don't know what to do."

"Girl, let go and let God. Let Thomas have his witch, and I guarantee you that they won't stay married for long. Besides, you deserve so much better. I've known my cousin my whole life. I've known you almost as long. I love you like a sister and I love her like a cousin. No woman deserves a man who cheats on her, or betrays her trust, but if any woman did deserve such treatment, trust me, it's my cousin. She's family and I love her, but she's one blood-thirsty, gold-digging, spoiled brat."

I agreed, and we hugged again. I told Alicia everything that had gone on in the past eleven months, including my feelings during the wedding. For me, this was therapy and I had to get everything off my chest. She poured me yet another drink and had a double shot herself.

"Alicia, you don't want to hear all this."

"Yeah, I do. I let a fine-ass man go to find out what was wrong with you. The least you can do is share the dirt. Besides, we have to figure out what our next move is."

I told my girl everything there was to tell, and my best friend was there for me as I went through what had to be the worst day of my life. When it was all said and done, I felt relaxed. She was buzzed as ever and I was sloppy drunk.

"We need to cut off his balls and hang his ass by a yard arm!" Alicia slurred while lying back on the couch.

"What?" I said, laughing at her. Alicia was full of attitude, and although I liked her sentiment, she had to be joking. "I wish I could, but we can't do that."

"Then, we need to confront him."

"We can't do that either."

"What about my cousin?"

"I don't know, Alicia. Do you think we should tell her?"

"Yes. I think she needs to know."

"I thought about that too. But, here's the thing . . . what if he denies that it happened? What if she's happy with him? Do we have the right to say something to her? She's been with him for four years. She might turn on you and ruin your relationship. On top of that, you all might fall out over this and she'll end up staying with him. Then you have lost your cousin, your family, over some BS."

"You think that could happen?"

"I do, I see it all the time."

Alicia slowly sat up and widened her eyes to keep them open. "If . . . if you were Meagan, would you want to know?"

I closed my eyes and rubbed my temples. "Yes. Yes, I would."

"And, I would want to know too," she spat. "Hell, I think as women, we should stick together when shit like this occurs. I think when a woman is about to make a mistake with a man, and there is another woman with prior history with that man, we all have a duty to stand up and shout out his faults! I think the least we can do is forewarn one another, as sisters."

"And then where does it stop?"

"What do you mean?"

"I mean, do we really want to go around shouting

about each other's faults? It's good in theory but is that what you really want?"

"Hell, yeah! I think men should walk around with report cards and a letter from their last girlfriend in their wallets!" Alicia laughed and shot more Hennessey down her throat.

"Now, that's not a bad idea. I might want to know if a man has a nice body, but a little dick!"

We gave each other a high five and Alicia shouted, "Amen."

I darted my finger at her and yelled, "I want to know if he has a problem with commitment!"

"Preach!"

"I want to know if he's married, has a girlfriend, or a history of cheating!"

"They all do that."

"Right . . . and I want to know if he comes too quick, if he's uneducated, if he hits women, if he treats his mother nice, if he has a job, if he has bad credit, and if he's poor in bed!"

Alicia jumped for joy. "Girl, I feel you!"

We laughed out loud, and before I knew it, we both started to cry. I knew why I was crying, but I didn't understand why Alicia was crying. I looked at her, dazed and confused, while wiping my eyes.

"Okay, I know why I'm crying, but heifer, what's wrong with you?" I said jokingly.

She sniffled. "Tiff, have you ever wondered why it is that I never got married?"

"No, but why not?"

"Because every time I fall in love with a man, he breaks my heart. They all seem to lie, deceive, and hold back emotionally. Girl, I gave up on love so long ago that I forgot what it was like to be in a relationship. You know . . . a real relationship. Seeing you today and knowing your pain, it woke me up and reminded me of something."

"What?"

"It reminded me that I'm alone. Being in my late twenties, I often wonder if it's always going to be like this. Are there any good men left? I know it sounds messed up, but I was hoping that you would find somebody. When you called months ago and told me how happy you were, I was elated for you. I was also excited for myself because, if you found someone that made you happy, that meant there was hope for me. Hell, when we were younger I always thought we would be married long before now."

"Alicia, I don't understand why you feel that way. I mean, you're so pretty. You have a nice body, you're in shape, and you're intelligent. Men have to be coming at you every day."

"They do, but they only want to fuck me. It's been a long time since a man wanted to *get to know me.* I think men are intimidated by me."

"Shit, I would be too. You carry a nine millimeter!" I tried to lighten the mood by joking.

"You know what I mean. Men seem to shy away from me because I'm strong and I don't take any shit. Because of that, I'm looked at as a bitch or a feminist. I just wish that brothers understood I'm out here trying to do the same things they are. I'm trying to make a dollar out of fifteen cents, knowing that the deck is stacked against me! I don't know why some men can't accept me for who I am. Why can't they love us for us? Why can't they let us love them? Why are there so many MF questions between black men and women?"

"I think it's all by design."

"Is it? Or is it that men these days are weaker? Honestly, I want a man like my father. A strong man who isn't afraid of responsibility, isn't afraid to stand up for what he believes in, and is a man of his word. You know, one that will eat shit with a toothpick if it means that his family will be taken care of, and doesn't believe in making excuses. Where the fuck are the men who are cut from the *old-school cloth?*"

"They are being raised by new-school women who no longer share those values. Girl, many of them are tired, frustrated, and burned out. These young boys are being brought up by women who were disrespected, disenfranchised, and discarded. Thomas was probably raised that way."

"I'm afraid to believe that, but it is what it is. It's just like this whole down low phenomenon. My God, what is happening to the Black Family?"

"Like I said . . . I think all this shit is by design. All along, I think the plan has been to separate the family unit. You know the old saying, divide and conquer? That's what's happening to us, one family at a time. It's racial, economic, and again, by design."

Alicia nodded and I pulled out a joint from the drawer next to me. I knew Alicia would be tempted to smoke, but that might cost her a pension, a damn good job, and give her a record if caught. So instead, I set it aside and saved it for another day or time. Alicia tooted her lips and turned to me.

"Thanks for looking out for me, but let's go back."

"Go back where?"

"To the wedding."

"For what?"

"To confront that lying, bitch-ass nigga."

"On his wedding day?"

"Hell, yeah, on his wedding day! Let's go set this shit off! Now!"

Generally, I would be way too shy and reserved for something like this. I would just wallow in self-pity and let this shit go. But the Hennessey had been speaking to me and talked loud in my head.

Fuck that! Let's go have a talk with his arrogant ass. Who the hell does Thomas or Anthony, or whoever the hell he's calling himself, think he is? We have eleven months invested in his ass. If he wanted to fool around he should have said so up front. Instead, he wanted to get our feelings all involved and shit. So what if it's his wedding day? So the hell what? He wanted to play, well now, dammit, he has to pay! He got caught, and it's a penalty for being caught. That nigga needs to just tighten up his game. Besides, why should we be the only ones in pain? Forget him, let's go!

Chapter Ten—Tiffany

"That's right, let's go!" I said in a drunken stupor. Alicia thought I was talking to her but I was actually talking to the Hennessey. I put on a pair of jeans, gym shoes, and a top. My Tommy Hilfiger cap covered my messy ponytail, and once I stumbled to Alicia's truck, we headed back to the wedding to set some shit off!

We drove to the hall and almost hit a couple that was leaving. Alicia didn't seem to give a damn about anyone being in the way. We were on a mission and were about to snap Mr. Smooth the hell out.

My heart raced as we got closer and closer to the hall. I'd had quite a bit to drink, but being back here face to face with my demons was sobering me up quick. All day today, I had been faced with infidelity, self-hatred, self-doubt, and every other insecurity that I'd had since I was fourteen. I didn't want to hurt Thomas, but I did want someone to pay for my pain and suffering. I walked into the hall and surveyed the room. Both Thomas and Meagan had had a bit to drink and they were all smiles at one another on their special day. They were slow dancing to the newest R. Kelly song, and when Thomas looked up and saw me back and in street gear, he slightly backed away from Meagan. She turned and saw me standing in the doorway with Alicia, then stormed in our direction as if she'd known about me and Thomas. She came close to me, and before she could get close enough to strike, Alicia stepped in front of me. I knew they didn't like one another, and according to Alicia, Meagan always thought she was better than everyone else in the family. Regardless of what a bitch she was to Alicia, we both agreed that she didn't deserve to be done wrong by Thomas. That was what we thought—until she opened her mouth.

"Why are you back?" she snapped. "And why did you bring your fat friend?"

"Excuse me?" I snapped back.

"What did you just say?" Alicia said.

"You heard me. First you bring her after not sending me an RSVP. She ate on my dime, as did you, and neither of you gave us a gift! Then, just as I'm dancing with *my* husband, this heifer gets her big ass up and brings all the attention to herself!"

I couldn't believe what she'd said, and did my best to remain calm. "Miss Thing, I wasn't trying to take any attention away from you."

"You can't help bringing attention to yourself! Shit, when you got up, you looked like the back side of an SUV," Meagan said, folding her arms and rolling her neck.

"Meagan, what the hell has gotten into you?" Alicia shouted.

I balled up my fist and made up in my mind that I was about to drop this bitch, wedding day or not. Just one more crack about my weight and she had better pray to God for strength to get all 170 pounds of my ass off her.

"No, it's not about what has gotten into to me. It's about what has gotten into you. I know you're jealous because I found a worthwhile man and no one seems to want your gun-toting, dyke-looking ass. But there is no need to bring your *average*-looking, heavy-set girlfriend here to my wedding so that you can make yourself look good by comparison. Now, what the hell are both you heifers doing back here? Did you come to drink more liquor on my dime? And why isn't she at least still dressed up, did the seams on that dress finally give up the fight?"

Alicia and I looked at one another and then back at her. At this point, Thomas had walked up to of us.

"I came here to tell you something!" Alicia yelled while looking directly at Thomas.

He looked as if he were about to shit on himself, and his boys followed closely behind him. I just knew things were about to get ugly. Alicia reached into her purse, and although she didn't pull it out, I knew she had her hand on her gun. Meagan stopped talking when Alicia put her hand in her purse and Thomas was apprehensive as well. His boys, the groomsmen, were walking in our direction also, but the look on Alicia's face when she reached into her purse had everyone on pause, even me. The moment was tense and it took Meagan a few minutes to summon up the courage to speak up.

"What did you want to tell me, Alicia? What?" Meagan said.

Alicia began to pull her weapon out of her purse. I didn't expect her to shoot anyone, but she might have slapped someone upside their head with it had she pulled it out. I reached in front of Alicia and placed my hand on hers. Someone had to put an end to this madness. This wasn't me. This wasn't how Alicia and I get down, either. This was the liquor telling us how to conduct ourselves. We needed to regain control of the situation. I needed to regain control of the situation. I gently tapped Alicia's hand and let her know everything was okay. We didn't need to go there. I knew she would if we had to, but we really didn't need to go there.

I stepped forward, keeping my eyes on Thomas. At that point, I realized that we didn't need for this to get ugly—not today. Thomas looked at me, and if looks could speak, he would have had a Keith Sweat song tattooed on his face. His watery eyes pleaded for me to let this go, and that's just what I decided to do.

"We just wanted to say that you two . . . deserve one another. I'm sorry that we disturbed you."

I reached into my purse and pulled out a crisp one hundred dollar bill. I placed it in Meagan's hand.

"For our dinners." I also dug a bit deeper in my purse and handed Meagan a condom. "Here's a gift for your wedding night," I said sarcastically.

I walked up to Thomas and he shamefully looked down as I approached him.

"Congratulations," I whispered. "I thought it should've been me."

I cut my eyes at Thomas's friends who appeared to have his back, and turned to Alicia. "Let's go."

We walked off and Alicia's parents came up from behind and started fussing at Alicia. When I turned to glance at Meagan, she tooted her lips at Thomas and slid the hundred dollar bill in her bra. Her eyes floated in my direction, and then back at Thomas.

On the surface, she might not have known consciously, but subconsciously, *she knew.*

A woman always knows, but our minds and sometimes our hearts tell us differently.

The truth would be hard for her to face today, but tomorrow would be a whole new day. I looked forward to a new day, and I truly hoped that both of them got what they deserved.

Alicia and I headed back to her truck and took off like Thelma and Louise.

"We let them off too easily," Alicia said.

"Life will fix that shit. Life and God. Like my grandmother used to say, 'Keep on livin'."

Chapter Eleven—Tiffany

I went back to my life, such as it was. I went home that day and threw away all the comfort foods and removed my dress from the garbage. I hung it on the back of my bedroom door, where I would see it each night. Yes, it would remind me of this painful and hurtful night, but it would also remind me that some things are not always as they seem. It would remind me never to get so wound up into a man that I lose my identity, and it's okay to love a man, but never to let my guard completely down. It was one thing to take a risk with a man, but it was something all together different to be his fool or whore. Now that the light had shone, I knew that was all I was to Thomas. His "something on the side."

Looking back, I had time to reflect. It dawned on me just how stupid I had been. The minute his attention had started to wane was when I should've said something or at least questioned the change in behavior. I made the mistake of getting comfortable and complacent with my situation. I could feel that something was wrong with our relationship, but I refused to take action. All I cared about was how fine he was. I let his good looks blind me. Then I did the worst thing ever and started doubting myself. His great sex had me making bad choices, too, and I'll be the first to admit that, as good as it was what woman wouldn't fall to his bedside every time he came over? But, was it worth my self-respect?

Truth of the matter was Thomas knew how to hit my spot. There were times I let that moment of pleasure mask what was always bound to be an unreasonable and unprovoked amount of pain. Though I had been to Thomas's condo before, I was never there *consistently*. When he didn't contact me that Tuesday, I made another mistake of giving him the benefit of the doubt. After eleven months, he hadn't earned that much latitude yet. When he said he was out of town on business, he seldom called. I used to tell myself that he was busy, but for twenty-four hours of the day? No, I wasn't being naïve, I was being stupid.

When it got to the point where *I* was always cooking and always drawing his bath, and always giving him head, sex, and his every fantasy, dammit, I should have said something! No, I knew. I might not have known on the surface, but I knew.

My heart had told me.

My mind was in denial.

My body craved his sex.

My spirit told me over and over again that something was wrong.

This shit . . . was my fault.

Rather than cry about it, I had to force myself to let go. Slowly, I began to change myself from the outside in. I traded in my car for a brand new Cadillac CTS, exercised, and focused on my career. The spiritual and inner me would have to wait, because the outer me wanted to go shopping! I bought workout clothes and went to the Bally's in Countryside, Illinois. I got a premier membership and signed up for beginner aerobics, beginner step class, and paid for a personal trainer. I planned on losing some weight, but I was doing it for me, not some damned man. I started watching the cooking channel and learned how to better prepare my evening meals. My hair and nails took priority as well, and was my little way of "giving back to me." Everywhere I went, I pumped "Enough Cryin" by Mary J. Blige. That song touched my soul and I drove around with my head up in spite of all that had happened. I went to church on Sundays and slowly began to let go and to let God.

Almost two-and-a-half weeks after Thomas's wedding, I went back to work. I tried desperately not to look in the direction of his office. I figured he might still be away on his honeymoon, so I found myself taking more glances that expected. I couldn't help but think about how I'd been duped, and how we'd exchange messages and talk dirty to one another. It dawned on me again about how unfair he'd been to me and Meagan both. How dare he marry a woman knowing how he'd been carrying on with someone else? Again, I told myself that the two of them deserve, one another, and I had never met a woman more shallow and conceited as she was. Of course, I thought about what some women might have done in my situation, and I plotted revenge. *How hard would it be to simply print all of those e-mails he sent and give them to his wife? How hard would it be to give her copies of my phone bill with the hundreds of calls he made to me? How hard would it be to describe everything from his condo to the birthmark on the side of his penis?* I had intimate knowledge of her husband, and if I has wanted to, I could have turned her life upside down. I could have done all that, but again, I decided to do the right thing.

Matthew Tuskey, another V.P. in the bank, came to my desk as I sat deleting the previous e-mails from Thomas. Matt was a white guy who stood five feet ten inches and had ice blue eyes. He had blond hair, the build of a professional wrestler, and he could hang a suit. All the women in the office adored him, sisters and white women alike.

"Good morning, Tiffany. Are you okay?"

"I'm fine, Mr. Tuskey, why do you ask?"

"Well, I saw you at the wedding. I don't know if you saw me, but I was there. I had no idea you and Thomas were friends."

I had to play this off. I didn't want anyone in my business and I didn't want anyone talking about my closeness with Thomas.

"Actually, Mr. Tuskey, my best friend's cousin was

the one getting married. I went to support the bride. Meagan's cousin is my best friend, Alicia. I didn't realize that Mr. Young was the groom until that day."

"Oh, I see. Can I ask you about the ruckus that occurred at the end of the evening? What was going on?"

Shit, he saw that. Quick, think! Play it off!

"Oh, that. I . . . I think everyone just had too much too drink. As it turns out, my girlfriend and her cousin have had a rivalry since they were children. The two of them just kind of went after one another."

"It looked like she was going after you initially."

"Oh, no. Actually, Meagan asked me to make sure Alicia left earlier and she was mad that I had brought Alicia back to the wedding. When we came back, Alicia had a few too many."

I hated lying on Alicia, but this was my place of employment and I didn't need anyone all up in my business. I'd tell Alicia about this later.

"Well, if you don't mind my saying so, your friend is very attractive. Is she seeing anyone?"

No, he didn't! For starters, I can't believe he's asking me about another woman, and does he think Alicia would want to date a white man? Why do men always ask me about my girl rather than me? What's wrong with me?

"You know, I don't believe she's seeing anyone. I will ask her, just to be sure."

"Do you think she'll be concerned about me being white?"

"We've never talked about dating outside of our race before, but I'm sure that doesn't matter."

"Well, please tell her for me that I think she's beautiful and I would love to take her out sometime."

"Mr. Tuskey, if you have an interest in my friend, why didn't you ask her out?"

"Please, call me Matt. I didn't want to ask her out at the wedding because I didn't think the timing was appropriate. Besides, another man was attempting to make a move and I didn't want to crowd her."

"Oh, I understand. I will call her later and see if she's interested. If so, I'll let you know."

"Thanks. I appreciate it."

Matt said good-bye. I couldn't wait to call Alicia later and tell her about her new admirer. For now, though, I got busy with my work, and sent my resume to a number of different departments. I was serious about making some changes, and this evening, I planned to register for classes at National Louis University in downtown Chicago.

After a short lunch, I went back to my desk and turned my attention to Thomas's office where the blinds were still open. I could see inside and found myself reminiscing about the times that we made love on his leather sofa. My mouth watered from the thoughts, and as I started to think about their honeymoon, I closed my eyes and wished for my hurtful thoughts to go away.

Chapter Twelve—Thomas

After the wedding, Meagan and I took a plane to Beverly Hills, California for our honeymoon night. We didn't get a chance to consummate our wedding because we were both exhausted from the four-hour flight. The next day, we got up and made our way to the airport to get ready for our vacation in beautiful Cabo San Lucas. We had a room and balcony off the beach with an awesome view of the ocean. The sand was a rust color, and the tide came in with sudsy white foam that accented the hues of red and orange. Combine that with the sunset, and you have one of the most scenic places on the planet.

As I was waking up, Meagan straddled me and kissed my neck. She wore a black two-piece Lurex swirl baby-doll outfit with a g-string. My hands explored her backside, and I rubbed up and down her spine. I kissed my wife deep on the mouth and our tongues danced together. She grinded on top of me and I felt my manhood stiffen through my silk pajama bottoms.

She reached for my package, and as she massaged me, my eyes closed from her satisfying touch. I reached for the special place between her legs and could feel Meagan's moistness. She began to grind hard on my fingers and I had the pleasure of dipping into her.

Her scent, Attraction by Lancôme, was addictive, and when I undid the fastened Velcro that covered her crotch, I put on a condom and I worked my hardness inside. Meagan's body freely accepted me in. I loved the fact that she wasn't into a lot of foreplay and often just wanted me to force my way inside of her. This was something I guess a lot of men should be grateful for, a woman who wanted to get right into sex, a woman who didn't want to give or receive head. It was nice that she was always up for sex, but it was bad that she never wanted to exchange fluids. I always felt like this was a trust issue. There were times that I wanted her to taste me and vice versa. The only times we'd gone down on one another was if we had flavored condoms for me and dental dam for her. I didn't see what the big deal was. We had both been tested, but getting her to do what couples are supposed to do was like pulling teeth.

Meagan grinded against me and closed her eyes while sucking in her bottom lip. Her fingers ran through her long hair, and at times, she caressed her breasts. She was a beautiful specimen of a woman and I felt so lucky to have her. I was mesmerized by the way she touched herself and lost myself in her sex as she began to grind her pelvis against me. She bucked faster and faster and rode me like she was trying to win a race. I loved it when we had sex because, unlike a lot of women I'd been with, Meagan came vaginally. There was something about her being on top that stimulated the hell out of her clit and caused it to swell as it did. Her rosebud rubbed against the base of my penis, and her eyes rolled in the back of her head. She gained more momentum and assured both of us a good orgasm.

For me, watching a woman come ranks up there with fine art, a great movie, a great moment, a last-second touchdown, and a great orgasm. There's nothing more beautiful on the face of the earth, and men love that shit! Watching Meagan come made me harder, made me excited, and took me to a place that only she could take me.

"Oh, shit, I'm coming, oh shit, I'm coming." She purred. Her breathing became rapid, her ribs began to show and she pushed on my chest to get up off me. I held her firmly in place and began to grind back. I ground my pelvis against hers and worked her hard during her moment.

"Oh, shit, Anthony stop! Stop! Oh, shit, oh shit, oh . . . shit!"

She let out a sigh of relief and dropped her head on my chest. We were both sweaty like two prize fighters in the last round of a fight at the MGM. She felt so incredible and we struggled to breathe. My condom was full, and Meagan kissed my neck and began again, squeezing out the last of her orgasm like the last drop of toothpaste in a tube. I loved this but I hated it also. I loved the way she would grind on me to get the last of my seed out. I loved the way that she worked her vaginal muscles when I was inside of her. I hated, however, that she wouldn't let me feel her, truly feel her without a condom on. After all, we're married now. Before it was always about not having an unplanned pregnancy and taking every precaution. Now, well, now we were husband and wife and I expected some things to change; like planning for that family.

Soon after she was sure that I was completely spent, she immediately jumped up and reached for her clothes to get dressed. I was slightly put out. I didn't want to act like a chump but I wanted to hold my wife. I wanted some attention, and I'd hoped to stay in bed to kiss, talk, or continue what we'd just started. Surprisingly, Meagan had other ideas.

"Let's go shopping," she said while putting on low-riding jeans and tank top.

"Shopping? Why don't we lay here a little longer and talk."

"Talk about what?"

"I don't know . . . our future, the wedding, kids, and work."

She stepped up to the bed and asked me to stand. As we embraced, I kissed her cheek and she smiled.

"We're going to have a great future," she said. "The wedding was okay, but it could've been better. I don't ever want any kids, and I'm satisfied with you working at the bank."

I stepped back and my arms fell to my sides. I had to stop myself from going off.

"We talked about this before and I want kids. We also talked about you going back to work, somewhere down the line, so that you can help me purchase the house we want."

She threw her hand back and blew me off like I was speaking another language.

"We already found a house that fits our current budget. And, yeah, I talked about kids, but you aren't the one who has to have a child, nor are you the one who has to put in all the work to get your body back in shape. Let's face it, my body is my temple. Having a baby will do nothing but make me misshapen and disfigured."

"Meagan, don't even go there. You said that you'd consider it."

"Consider and concede are two different things. I've already considered it and the answer is no."

I sat back on the bed and shook my head in disbelief. "Did you even think about it?"

"I did. I also decided that it was not something that I wanted to go through."

"Not ever?"

"Not now."

"Then when?"

"Somewhere down the line."

"What about work? When do you plan to make use of your degree?"

She huffed and placed her hand on her hip. "I will look into working within the time frame that we decided on."

"Which is?"

"Somewhere down the line."

"Meagan—"

"Again, Anthony, you're not the one who has to carry the child, gain all the weight, risk your life, and then lose your figure. As for work, why are we discussing this right now? I have some shopping to do."

She looked around the room, and reached for her purse on the table. After she glossed her lips, she clutched the purse underneath her arm.

"Are you going with me or not? This is supposed to be our honeymoon and I had hoped we'd be able to spend some quality time together. Not sit around and discuss our disagreements."

"Look, Alicia, I'm not talking about having a child right now. I do want us to discuss that later on, as well as when you'll be returning to work. We're closing on the house the day we get back from this honeymoon. I'm going to need some help on that mortgage and that issue can't be put aside."

"Your salary covers the mortgage, doesn't it?"

"Yes, it covers the mortgage, but there are other things to consider."

"Like what?"

"The taxes."

"It's included in the mortgage."

"Insurance."

"Also in the mortgage."

"Heat, electric, food, cable, phones, cell phones, up-keep, maintenance, car notes, car insurance, health insurance, and . . ."

"Whoa! It's our honeymoon, remember?"

"It's the beginning of the rest of our lives, remember?"

She swallowed and looked away. Her look said to me that she didn't want to work—ever. I was in denial, but the look on her face clearly said that she never had any intention working again. It was almost as if to say her job was to be pretty and mine was to make the money. After taking a deep breath, she came over to the bed and sat next to me. "Anthony, why are you tripping?"

"Baby, I'm going to need some help with all of this."

"Okay, we will talk about it later. Right now, I want to enjoy our honeymoon. Now, get dressed, and once I freshen up my makeup, I'll be ready."

She dismissed me and I watched her ass sashay into the bathroom. My brain kicked in and I asked myself a serious question: *How is somebody with no job going to go shopping?*

I decided to ask that question out loud, just not with those words.

"Honey, how much money do you have?"

"We took in almost five thousand at the wedding in checks and cash."

"Good. I can use part of that money on bills."

"Uh, no you can't," she said, peeking her head out of the bathroom door.

"Why not?"

"Because I'm about to spend it."

"Are you sure that'll be enough money?" I asked sarcastically.

"If not, we always have your gold card, right?"

"No, we don't. And as for the five thousand, we don't have that to spend either."

Meagan came out of the bathroom with a frown on her face. "I wanted to buy some nice things for the house," she pouted. "And, I also wanted to buy some nice souvenirs for our parents and friends. I don't want to feel as if I'm on a budget, especially when we have a whole lot of money to spend."

I don't know . . . maybe I was being too hard on her. I knew she was high maintenance, and for years I wanted her like no man wanted any other woman. I chased her around like Dwayne Wayne chased Whitley Gilbert on *A Different World*. The thing is, just like Dwayne Wayne, when I got my girl, I discovered that she was fine, but she was also a piece of work.

Meagan clapped her hands together and interrupted my thoughts. "Are you ready to go?" she said, putting on her dark sunglasses.

"Yeah, I guess so."

I threw on an old pair of jeans, white on white Air Force Ones and a plain red T-shirt.

"You don't dress like a man who makes a lot of money," she griped.

"Then that must mean I'm not a man with a lot of money. So, be easy on my pockets and let's go."

Meagan made her way to the door, and all I could think was, . . . *Apparently, I will never make enough money to keep her happy.*

Chapter Thirteen—Tiffany

I had Pilates on Mondays and walked with Alicia on Tuesdays at the lakefront before and after work. Aerobics were on Wednesdays, Tae Bo on Thursdays, and Friday, Saturday, and Sunday I rested. Church was still on for Sundays, and it was time that I took my soul to the house of the Lord for a good cleansing. Sisters in the church who knew me whispered about how long I'd been gone. One had the nerve to ask me how long it had been and where I had been, and when I basically told her "none of her business," she walked away.

A few more Sundays later, I had everyone in check. This was my opportunity to make my connection with God, and I ignored much of the fakeness around me. I took Alicia with me and she felt the same way I did.

After church we went to lunch and then headed back to my apartment. Having Alicia around was a blessing. I'd forgotten how much I missed her being around. She kept me motivated, and if it were not for her, I would've cheated on my workouts and diet by now. Also, there is no way that I wouldn't have been crying every night on my pillow about Thomas. Alicia was a godsend, and while sitting on my bedroom floor looking at old pictures, I snapped my fingers.

"Girl, I almost forgot to tell you! There's a man interested in you at my office," I said excitedly.

"Really? I haven't been to your office in such a long time."

"I know, but he saw you at the wedding."

"Really? What's his name?"

"Matthew Tuskey."

"Tuskey? That's a weird name for a brotha."

"He's not a brotha."

Her eyes widened. "He's a white man?"

"Girl, yeah." I laughed.

Alicia cut her eyes at me and chuckled a bit too. "So who does he look like? Tom Cruise, Brad Pitt, Colin Farrell . . .?"

"If I had to say so, he looks like a combination of all three."

"That's interesting. Would you give him some?"

I held my prom picture and looked at the brotha, Dwayne, who I'd gone with. I had always dated black men and never really thought about sex with a white man. I shrugged my shoulders. "I really don't know. I guess he's cute but I haven't been into white men like that."

"Okay, pretend that you have. Could you see yourself having sex with him?"

"Like I said, I really don't know."

"Tiff, what's the problem?"

"The problem is I can't see you with a white man."

"You can't see me with a white man or *this* white man?"

"Any white man. I mean, you haven't given up on the brothers have you?"

"No, but I like to keep my options open. Besides, I don't want anyone to think I'm a racist."

"Wanting to date your own kind isn't being racist."

"That's the same script that the klan is pushing."

"No, that's racism."

"Why isn't it racism when we do it?"

"I don't know, girl, I'm just sayin' . . ."

"Tiff, stop beating around the bush. Is he cute or not?"

"Yes. Very cute."

"And he has a decent job, right?"

"Yeah."

"Drives a reliable automobile?"

"I would think so."

"No criminal record?"

"I can't picture him having one, but we know that anything is possible."

"Then, when can I meet him?"

"You really want to meet him? I mean, I can't believe we're having this conversation. If he were a brother, maybe, but . . ."

"If he were a brother, two of those four questions I asked you would've been no."

"That's so unfair. You were wrong for that."

"It may not be fair but in *some circles* it's true. Remember, I'm a police officer so I know what time it is. Now, when can I meet him?"

"I don't know; when are you off?"

"Tuesday."

"Then you and I can go to lunch at Flattops, and when we get back from lunch, I will introduce the two of you."

"Sounds like a plan to me."

Alicia smiled and we went to the mall to find some outfits. We wound up catching a movie, too, and gave thumbs up to nearly every white man in it.

I never asked Matt when Thomas was coming back from his honeymoon. Instead, I told him that Alicia was single and very much interested in meeting him. Ever since I told him that, he was as giddy as a school boy. He offered to buy me lunch on Monday and he also asked me if there was anything he could do for me. I took a forkful of my salad and placed it into my mouth. While chewing, I nodded.

"Well, now that you asked, Matt, please keep an eye

out for any other position in the bank that you think I may qualify for."

"You don't like being an AA?"

"I did, but I need to make more money and it's time that I did more for myself. I'm not asking for a handout or anything, but a reference from you could go pretty far in HR."

He smiled. "Let me see what I can do."

As soon as we got back to the office, Matt patted my back. "Hey, it looks like my guy is back. I'll talk to you later."

He headed to the elevators, and I knew he meant Thomas. I had temporarily forgotten about him, but my heart skipped a beat as I forced myself to look in his direction. Finally, I saw him. He stood in his office with navy blue slacks on, a white shirt, and a red tie with suspenders. He looked like a corporate mogul, and even from where I stood, he made me weak in the knees. Seeing him brought everything back from a few weeks ago. I instinctively changed my computer to my personal online account. I logged on to my instant messenger to let him know I was online. I didn't expect him to write or to e-mail me or to call. In fact, I knew he wouldn't. Still, a very small part of me wanted him to. I looked at my computer for minutes on end and nothing happened. I then got back to work, but glanced over several times at the other tower that housed his office.

By now, Matthew was in his office and the two men shook hands and laughed. A small part of me wondered if Thomas was laughing at me and not some joke Matthew had probably told him. I knew it was my self-esteem kicking in again, but it was all I could do to not go somewhere and indulge myself in an oatmeal cream pie or ice cream.

As soon as work was over, I rushed to Women's Workout World downtown and got in a quick twenty-minute workout. I then went to National Louis University that night for school. I had joined an accelerated program and was now pursuing a B.A. in Business Management. It felt weird going back to school as an adult, but according to the counselors at the school, it's easier after gaining "real world experience in the workplace."

No matter what I did that day, it didn't stop me from thinking about Thomas. All night long I wondered how his new life with his new wife was. I also wondered if he ever thought about me or about how I was doing. Who was I fooling? He could give less than a damn about me. Unfortunately, I wish I could have said the same thing about him.

Alicia and I walked our normal trail and talked about Thomas's return and her meeting with Matthew. Initially, she asked that I invite Matt to come along on our lunch date at Flattops. I explained to her that I wasn't playing third wheel and she was on her own.

I didn't understand why I was so against Alicia going out on this date with Matt, but maybe it was because he hadn't asked me out. It could also have been that I'd be jealous if Alicia found happiness. I definitely wanted her to, but I sure wasn't up to feeling lonely again.

When I arrived at work, there were a dozen roses on my desk. My heart skipped a beat when I saw them, and I thought they might have come from Thomas. However, the card read, "Thanks again for the hookup! Here's a little something for you." It was signed B765456. I looked at the signature and was like, "What the hell is this?" The flowers were obviously from Matthew, but what was with the odd-ass number signature?

Unsure, I got busy with work and set up appointments for the V.P. I worked for. After the appointments were made, I typed several letters for him, and then worked on my homework when I finished more of my daily duties. At 12:05 P.M., I left to meet Alicia for lunch and mentioned that Matthew sent me flowers. She was surprised.

"He sent you flowers? Shit, I know he must be a good man. That was very considerate of him."

"Wasn't it? I thought that was nice of him too." I looked down and fiddled with my fingernails.

"Girl, what's wrong with you?"

"I . . . I don't know. When I first saw those flowers, I kind of wanted them to be from someone else."

"You have got to be kidding me. Tiff, Thomas is a married man now. Yes, my cousin is a bitch, but please let her have him. You can do so much better, and not only that, you deserve better. Release him from your heart, girl, and move on."

"That's easy for you to say. You have Barry Manilow you're meeting in less than an hour."

"And even if I didn't, I'd still be saying the same thing. Now, does he really look like Barry Manilow? If he does, I'ma kick yo' ass."

We both laughed out loud.

"Don't worry. Like I said, Matthew is cute—for a white man."

"Could you please stop saying 'for a white man'? That shit is irksome. It's like saying, 'He's attractive, but . . .' Tiff, stop. You said yourself that he's nice looking, and seems like a good man who makes decent money. Can't you just be happy for me?"

"I'll try."

"Try hard."

Just as the waiter started to serve our food, in walked Matt and a number of men in white coats.

"That's her, gentlemen," Matt said while pointing to Alicia. He had a serious look on his face that was almost puzzling. Alicia and I were thrown off and looked at each other in confusion. The men left the restaurant, but Alicia met up with Matt by the door. I followed.

"Excuse me." She spoke with authority. "We were having lunch and you just interrupted us. Could you explain to me why you just pointed me out to those men?"

"I couldn't wait another minute to see you. You'll understand about the men in white in a minute."

Alicia's guard was up and she folded her arms with a mean mug on her face. She looked straight-up hood, and Matt's actions caused both of us to become defensive. We assumed that he was some type of stalker with security issues or something. And since we'd had our fair share of odd behavior from men in the past, this was rather bothersome.

"Listen," Alicia said. "I don't know who the hell you think you are, and there are laws against stalking women. I just happen to be a cop and you could find yourself in a heap of trouble."

Alicia looked like she was ready to kick some serious ass. We were about to make an ugly scene and I just knew I was about to lose my job. I definitely had my girl's back, but Matt just smiled.

"What are you smiling at?" Alicia said, tearing into Matt again.

Just then, the men in white coats were back. They brought in six dozen long-stemmed roses. The first dozen were red.

"Red roses signify love and respect," he said.

"It's a little soon for red then, don't you think?" Alicia snapped. She didn't seem flattered at all.

The second dozen were yellow. "Yellow roses are a symbol of joy," Matt said.

"Yeah, okay. We'll see," Alicia said.

The next color was pink. "These stand for appreciation or gratitude."

"Don't appreciation and gratitude mean the same thing?"

I watched everything unfold, and I could see Alicia's stance soften with each dozen that was brought in. The men placed the roses in vases that stood on tiny stands about two feet off the ground. Nearly everyone in the restaurant was melting with smiles. I had to admit, I was a little jealous myself, but was very happy for my friend. No man had ever done anything like that to me.

The next dozen were white. "White symbolizes both purity and secrecy," Matthew said.

"Well, you are late on the pure part," I joked.

"Secrecy, huh? You married?" Alicia asked jokingly.

"No, no I'm not," Matthew said, still smiling.

The next set was orange. "These stand for desire. And I definitely desire you."

Alicia smiled for the first time since Matthew had arrived.

The last dozen were pale purple, almost lavender. "Pale roses of any color symbolize friendship. I'd like to get to know you better. I'd like to get to know you a lot better, to be honest with you. But if nothing else, I definitely want us to be friends."

"You don't know me well enough to want to be my friend," Alicia said.

"Ain't that the truth," I chimed in while smiling.

Matt stepped forward and looked eye to eye with Alicia. "I know this . . . I know that you're beautiful. I also know that I want you in my life in any capacity I can have you."

"You talk a good game, but can you back it up?" Alicia asked.

"Games are not on my agenda. I'm sorry to have disturbed you and please feel free to get back to your lunch."

Alicia huffed. "How are we supposed to have lunch after the display you just put on?"

"You'll figure something out." He turned to address me. "Tiffany, you got your flowers, right?"

"Yeah, I did. I didn't understand the strange signature you left."

"I thought that might be a problem. It's a job posting. Send your resume to that department. They're waiting to hear from you."

Matthew left the restaurant without seeing Alicia and me glowing.

"So, what do you think?" I asked her.

"I thought I was going to have to bust a cap in his ass for a minute," she said, laughing.

"And now?"

She stared out the window and curiously watched Matt get into his car. "I think he's cute. Real cute."

"For a white guy!" we said in unison and high-fived one another.

I went back to the office and walked Alicia to Matt's office. The two of them sat down and immediately started talking. It appeared that although the first meeting was a bit odd, they seemed to hit things off very well. Not wanting to interrupt, I excused myself and headed back to my desk. I looked across the way at Thomas' office and lost myself for a moment while looking at him. I wondered what was going on through his mind and I also wondered if he'd been thinking about us. My trance was broken when Thomas stood up to close his blinds.

If that wasn't a message for me to get this man out of my head, then I don't know what was.

Chapter Fourteen—Thomas

I didn't know how I had gotten myself into this mess, but in just a few weeks of being married, I was seeing very little light at the end of the tunnel. I may have married who I considered to be the most beautiful woman on the planet, but I would be damned if she wasn't the most expensive woman on the planet as well. She changed her mind about the house we both agreed on before our honeymoon. When she said no, I lost it and went off on her. Again, I had to remind her that she wasn't working and she needed to contribute to the household. No, it wouldn't be forever that she had to work, but I could have used a little help for at least the first three to five years in our new home. She gave me the script about being able to "keep her in the lifestyle that her father kept her in." With every syllable that walked out of her mouth, I wanted to swift-kick her father's ass for spoiling her so.

Instead of staying at my condo, which was now for sale, or at her old apartment, she opted to live at her parents' home until we closed on ours. That went over really well with her father who already can't stand my ass. When he found out that his *married* daughter was staying with him, and her marriage wasn't even six weeks old yet, the first thing out of his mouth was, "What's wrong, son, having trouble making ends meet?" That burned my ass. Instead of saying something smart-assed like I thought about doing, I just explained to him that the situation was only temporary.

The house that Meagan decided upon was $274,900.

It was a four-bedroom, three full-bath house that was 2900 square feet. For someone not wanting and not expecting to have any kids, she wanted a significant amount of space. The house was beautiful, but it was forty thousand dollars more than I had planned on spending. It had a two-tiered deck, an above-ground pool, appliances, a newly remodeled kitchen, ceramic bath and foyer, a marble fireplace, central air, parquet flooring, vaulted ceilings, a three-car garage, and a manicured lawn. The down payment that I had to come up with was $27,500. That was for a $1700 mortgage at a thirty-year fixed rate. I thought the place was a palace compared to my condo. Meagan said, "It's a good *starter house*." I looked at her like she was out of her damned mind. A starter house? My parents are still in the same fucking house I grew up in!

I'd been back at work for one day, you hear me? One day, and already she had our lives in full throttle in the direction of the poor house. We had appliances. She went and bought new ones. She got a stainless-steel, double-wide freezer/refrigerator. She got an industrial stove with six burners. Her cookware was by AllClad, the dishes were fine china, and the silverware was sterling. She bought a ton of CorningWare, chef's knives, and had the countertops refinished with a different color marble, and that was just the fucking kitchen! What's worse? Meagan doesn't cook!

The living room was decked out in Italian leather sofas and recliners. The tables were all custom-cut glass with rosewood bases. Every wall had fine art, and the throw rug on the living room floor was pure mink. The only thing I didn't mind was the high-definition, 100-inch plasma screen TV in the living room. Unfortunately, she bought three of them. She bought one for the living room, one for the den or sporting room, and one for our bedroom. We had a Jacuzzi on each deck, a library put in one of the spare rooms, and she hadn't even started on the basement or the bedroom yet. I couldn't afford this shit. Sure, maybe I could get these things one item at a time, but all at once? I was in debt up to my eyeballs. What's worse was my *wife* didn't seem to give a damn. It seemed as if I would've been better off getting a call girl and simply paying for sex when I wanted it. I hurried up and took my ass back to work. It's the only way for me to make ends meet. I had my eye on some smaller banks and a few larger ones. With the right amount of mergers and hostile takeovers, I could afford to give Meagan the lifestyle she want. Thing was, I wasn't sure if her lifestyle was the same one that I wanted.

I had a headache and was stressing about money. My stomach was in knots, and rather than focus on work, all I could think about was what Meagan might purchase next. My neck was stiff and my muscles ached. I got up and closed the blinds to my office because the sun was glaring in and blinding me. All day long, people came in and asked me about my honeymoon, future plans, and whether I was ready to get back to work. I was ready, and since I needed the money, I didn't have much choice.

In addition to my issues with my wife, my heart was pumping like an oil rig in a desert. I was scared to face Tiffany. I just knew it would be a matter of time before she walked into my office and either slapped me, cursed me out, or told our sin to the world. I thought about her the whole time I was on my honeymoon and all the weeks that led up to my wedding day. She had no idea how much I valued our friendship. I valued our relationship, such as it was. *It's just that . . . well, she isn't Meagan. She isn't as pretty, she isn't as fit, and she doesn't have the education I would expect the woman I marry to have. I mean, I have an MBA. Tiff just barely has her high school diploma. I think she told me she went to college like a year or something, but she doesn't even have a B.A. I know that she raised her brother and I realize that college isn't for everyone. But I also know that my woman—my woman, needs to bring something to the table and the only way to do so is by obtaining a degree.*

I stood up and stretched my arms. Before I knew it, I

was punching the air as I thought about my wife not bringing anything to the table; *she is taking shit off the table. What kind of marriage do we have? I spend all my time at work, I haven't seen my boys since the wedding and Meagan constantly calls me throughout the day. If she were working, she would be too busy to call. And whenever I get home, she never asks about my day. All I listen to is gossip about her sorors or something that she saw on TV. Dinner is never on the table, but she always wants to go out to dine. For her, it must be nice.*

     I didn't leave my office at all and felt like I a prisoner in my place of employment. I was actually afraid of Tiffany's reaction. I dodged a bullet a few times on my wedding day, but didn't want to tempt fate anymore. Yes, I hurt my friend, and for that, I was sorry. I missed her, though. Missed her, a lot. I'd have to tell her just how much I did, but today, I didn't have the courage.

Chapter Fifteen—Tiffany

I came into work today and decided to act as if Thomas Anthony Young didn't exist. I would be lying if I said he wasn't on my mind, but I had to at least act like he wasn't. When I found myself distracted or thinking about him too long, I either called Alicia or took my behind to the gym across the street. That was my new thing. If I got angry, I went to the gym. Horny? I went to the gym. Depressed? I went to the gym. Fitness was becoming my drug and my cure-all for everything that ailed me. I decided that he had made his choice, and if anything, it was his loss. Yes, I was still mad and hurt, but I was at a point where I simply decided "fuck him." I started hanging out with Alicia more. I made friends in evening school and drove the hell out of my Cadillac—to the gym.

I still strayed and had the occasional fantasy. I found myself masturbating more often than I would like to admit. I don't know what it was about working out, but it felt like my endurance was up. It felt like I was better prepared for sex. I didn't crave sex like I used to, but if required . . . I could fuck a man all day and all night. I wanted to test that theory. So I decided, just for kicks, I was going to take on an outside lover or have a one-night stand. I had to get Thomas off my mind. I had to get my body to stop craving his sex. In order to do this, I felt as if I needed a backup man in my life, if only for one night.

After class that night, I got dressed and decided to go out and see if I could catch a man. I put on a tight black skirt, high heels, and a sequined top. I was starting to lose some weight around my midsection, but I didn't want to press things by dressing too young. I pinned my hair up and sprayed on some sweet smelling perfume. I went bare legged and decided to be a bit risqué and not wear any panties. I then jumped into my Cadillac while playing Alicia Keys *Unplugged.* As "Unbreakable" started blasting over the Jensen speakers, I headed to the south burbs to my favorite night club, Secrets, in Dolton, Illinois.

The best night to go to Secrets is Thursday. Tonight wasn't a bad night because they played some old-school cuts on Tuesday nights and the crowd wasn't as large as their Thursday night crowd. I went over to the bar and asked for a rum and Coke. The bartender gave me a stiff drink, and from there, I sat at one of the tables and surveyed the room.

I eyeballed many of the men in the room. I was looking for someone to sex me, but I had to be careful not to end up picking up a man with psychological issues. I didn't want a stalker. I didn't want a clingy man either, or someone who might put his hands on me. I wasn't looking for a boyfriend. Tonight, I only wanted one thing and that was to get laid.

There were numerous men, but some were too old and some too young. I noticed frat boys, college boys, or men who thought they were players. There were a few athletes there, but I knew there was no way they'd look at me. Their eyes were glued to the big-booty girls or the former cheerleaders. The types of men who looked at me were generally very plain, very married, or cute as hell with some major flaw. The scenery was quite interesting and I watched men laugh together, drink, and flirt with other women.

No one seemed to notice me, which added fuel to the fire. As "Atomic Dog" by George Clinton played overhead, I began to lose my nerve. I left the club and drove off with no destination in mind.

I jumped onto the Bishop Ford freeway and took it to Route 57. I then got off at Ninety-ninth and Halsted Street. I figured I would drive north to Eighty-seven Street and then west, taking side streets back to my apartment. I was mad and could've kicked myself in the ass for not gathering up the nerve to pick up a man.

I headed north on Halsted Street and stopped when I saw a bar on the east side of the street. It said the new 9705 Bar. I parked my car and decided to go in and have a drink. Maybe some liquid courage would give me the strength to do what needed to be done. I needed someone with me tonight. Not tomorrow, not the next day, but tonight and really soon.

I looked at the stained glass and noticed that it was sweating. I hoped it was because of the cool September night and not because it was hot or smoky inside. I knocked on the door and was buzzed in. Again, my eyes searched the room for men, but I connected with a smile by the woman pouring drinks.

"Hey, girl," she said. "Welcome to the 9705 Bar. I'm Adrienne. What can I get you to drink?"

She was a pretty woman with a warm smile. She looked to be in her mid-thrities and she had a way about her that said, "Welcome." I returned a smile, removed my coat, and took a seat.

"I think I'll have a stiff drink. What do you recommend?"

"On a Tuesday night? That depends on the problem and your mood."

"What makes you think I have a problem?"

"Sister girl, it's written all over your face. Let me tend to my other customers and I'll come back so we can talk about it. Meanwhile, try this drink."

She handed me a cola-colored drink that went down smoothly. I took it all in with one gulp.

"Easy girl! That's E&J, which is a sipping drink." She said, laughing.

"Can I get another one before you tend to the other customers?"

"Oohh, girl, you must have some serious issues if you

want another one of those. Here, sip on this. Be ready, 'cause in a minute that first drink is going to creep up on you."

After pouring me a second drink, she tended to her other customers. I surveyed the area and looked many of the people in the room. Some were bus drivers, others were cops, and most of the men looked at like they were about business. This surprised me because it was just a bar. In fact, it was like a well thought-out hole in the wall, but the people here seemed down to earth.

Several minutes had gone by and more people crowded into the small place. Virtually everyone who came through the door knew Adrienne by name. Those who didn't were greeted by the same warm smile that I was.

"What's up, babygirl!" The men shouted to Adrienne as they entered the bar, or simply, "Hey, Adrienne!" She saw to everyone sitting at the bar, and knew everyone's drink without them saying a word. She talked trash with the best of them before pulling up a stool and resting her elbows on the bar in front of me.

"Now, girl, tell me what's up with you."

I didn't know this woman. I had no plans to share my problems with her. But just like she said, within a few minutes, I'd be hit with a slow but methodic buzz that comes from a good drink. I looked at the bottles behind the counter and wanted to find out exactly what E&J was. When I discovered it was brandy, I knew that was the reason the intoxication crept up on me the way it did. It was a smooth but strong drink I imagined would put hair on my chest if I drank enough of it. My eyes became glossy and relaxed as I sipped on the second drink, which was just as strong as the first. Within minutes, I was feeling good and felt comfortable speaking to Adrienne.

I told her about what had happened to me a few weeks ago. I told her everything that happened at the wedding as well as how I thought Thomas was dating me exclusively. I also told her I was thinking about quitting my job because I felt used, hurt, and embarrassed. She explained to me that the last thing in the world I should be thinking about is leaving my job. I even mentioned what I was after tonight and how I lost my nerve at Secrets. When I said I had an itch that needed to be scratched, she shook her head.

"You must think I'm a ho, walking in here looking for a man to sleep with."

"Why would you say that? Shit, there are women who come in here every night looking for men. I'm not here to judge you. If anything, I might be able to help you."

"I have to be careful with who I leave with. I don't want any psychos, or men who want to call me afterward. I just want to be taken care of, you know?"

"I hear you. And, let me give you the rundown on these men in here. Most of them have damned good jobs, but some of them have some serious issues."

Adrienne went down the line and pointed out man after man and explained to me what was going on with each of them. She leaned in as if she were an informant and I was a cop getting the inside scoop.

"Okay, girl, this is what I know based on what I heard from various women about the men in this bar. That one has a little dick. That one has a big dick but doesn't know how to use it. He's married, that one is married, that one is gay, and that one is bi. The brother in the blue is unemployed. The brother in the leather just lost his job. All the guys at that table are cops and you don't want to mess with any of their crazy asses! Those brothers over there work for the Transit Authority and have good money and benefits, but most of them have a bunch of women. Any one of them will gladly hit it and quit it and none of them will be bugging you in the morning. Those are good brothers, I would start over there."

Those were just the single men. There were other brothers in the bar who were handsome as hell who also looked virile as hell, but they were with other women. I wanted to go talk with the brothers at the table that Adrienne suggested, but the brandy was telling me to be daring and try something different.

I looked across the bar at the last table where I saw a man about five feet, eight inches with a sharp razor-cut fade. He had muscular arms, a short torso, and glasses. He had a goatee like Method Man and his clothes were designer from head to toe. On his right hand, he sported a gold ring with five brilliant diamonds in it that you could see from clear across the room. On his wrist was a Kenneth Cole watch that must have cost about $1,000. The brother was put together nice and he was sitting at the table catching hell from a sister who obviously had to be his woman. He looked at her from behind his rimless Halston eyeglasses as if everything she said was something he'd heard before—many times before.

Her back was to me. From where I sat, I could easily make eye contact with him. He occasionally looked up from the verbal chastising he was getting and glanced in my direction. It was never more than a glance, but I could tell he was looking at me, and I think he liked what he saw. There was no way to be sure.

The woman he was with was pretty. She had long blond hair, a caramel complexion, she had light brown eyes, hooped earrings, and toned arms. She was wearing a pink Rocawear top, tight jeans, and knee-high leather boots that matched the top. Around her neck she wore a Rocawear platinum chain encrusted with diamonds, and on her wrist was a diamond bracelet. She was giving the brother the business and got louder and louder, almost as if she was trying to make sure he heard her more than he did the music that played overhead.

The more she fussed, the more it looked as if he was about to either yawn in her face or walk out. It was obvious that the only reason he put up with the woman was because she was beautiful. She looked like the video personality Free from *106th and Park* on BET.

"Girl," Adrienne said, noticing my attraction to the man. "I see you like to do things the hard way."

"Sometimes."

"What's wrong with the brothers I pointed out at the table over there?"

"I want him."

"As you can see, he has someone."

"I see that, but he doesn't look too happy with her."

"That may be the case, but that's still *her man*. Just looking at him like you were is disrespectful."

"Yeah, well, if that's the case, I've been disrespected by other women too."

"Maybe, but not by *that woman*."

Adrienne was right. I had no right lusting for him the way I was. I had just been the other woman and how dare I try to force my way into a situation where I would be the other woman yet again. I tried to clear my head and put the dirty thoughts out of my mind. But, I couldn't help myself. I wanted *him*. I think I wanted him because the woman he was with was much prettier than me. He was spoken for, but I felt as if I had to prove something to myself. I knew I was horny, but more than that, I wanted to make a point with someone else's man.

"So what is the deal with him anyway?" I asked Adrienne.

"Girl, that's Justin Davis."

"The writer?"

"Yes, the writer."

"What is he doing in here?"

"What is that supposed to mean?"

"I mean, why is he here rather than at some bar or club downtown?"

"Girl, any and everybody comes in this bar. He's here because this is one of the few places in the city he can get some privacy. Besides, he and I grew up together. We both used to live right down the street from here."

"He still lives here in the hood?"

"No, he lives in Lynwood. But this is where he comes to get his drink on."

"He's cute."

"He's spoken for."

"Can you help me test that theory?"

"What's in it for me?"

I looked at Adrienne and smiled. I reached into my purse and pulled out a crisp $100 bill.

"Will this do?"

"Make it another hundred and I will see what I can do."

"You will hook us up?"

"I will make sure that you both are in the same private space. The rest is up to you."

"How?"

"Let me worry about that."

Adrienne went back to tending bar. All the customers received refills on their drinks, the Rose Bowl was on the flat screen televisions overhead and the music was cranked up even louder. Adrienne talked trash with all the patrons, stroked a few egos, and then went under the counter and handed me a set of keys on a huge ring.

"Take these and walk in the back toward the bathroom. On the right-hand side is a door that looks like a closet with a padlock on it. Undo the lock and use the silver key to unlock the handle. Then go downstairs, turn on the light, which will be to the right of you at the base of the stairs, and wait there."

"Are you serious?"

"Shit, the question is, are you serious? You ain't getting the money back."

My heart began to race at the prospect of being naughty. I grabbed the remainder of my drink, and once again gulped the E&J. Adrienne poured me a third drink and I gulped half of it and tried to sip the rest.

"Okay, enough. Don't go and throw up on the brotha," she said jokingly.

"How will you get him away from his woman?"

"Don't worry about it."

"What if he doesn't like me? I mean, his girl is so much prettier and I don't think I really have a chance with him and—"

"Girl, you have already started talking yourself out of this shit. I see why your self esteem is so low, you talk too much. You want him or not?"

I looked over at him. He glanced in my direction and then looked down at his drink and smiled. His woman thought he was perhaps mocking her. I turned back to Adrienne.

"I do. I do want him."

"Then go downstairs. I'll take care of the rest."

"You sure?"

"I got you."

"Do you do this kind of stuff for everyone?"

"Nope, you're the first."

"Why me, Adrienne?"

"Girl, you need to work on your esteem. You need to be asking yourself why not you? Now here, take another gulp of this E&J and get ready to handle your business."

I took another hit of the E&J and walked past the couple as the woman continued to give him grief. Our eyes met and he smiled a courteous smile, then looked back at his lady who hadn't even noticed me. I went to the back, found the door that Adrienne had told me about and headed down the stairs. As I descended, I heard Adrienne's voice.

"Hey, Justin, can you come here for a minute? I need a favor!"

I heard a man's voice say, "I will be right there!"

THINGS THAT WE DO IN THE DARK

I went into the basement and cut on the light. I was hoping that there would be a bed down here; you know, someplace that perhaps Adrienne laid her head after work? There was no such thing. There were cases of liquor in large brown crate, like boxes, loose bottles of liquor, a large floor safe, and the furnace and water heater, as well as the plumbing for the bathroom. Overhead, I could hear lots of bass and the muffled sounds of Anthony Hamilton's song, "Sister Big Bones." My heart raced as I looked around the dark damp basement. What would I say to him when he came down? What if he didn't come down? What if Adrienne and everyone else was upstairs laughing at my expense? I know it all sounds like paranoia, but this is what went on through my head. Minutes later, I heard footfalls coming down the steps. With each step my heart beat faster and faster. I backed away from the door like a woman in a horror film. I have to admit that I was scared. I have to also admit that I was excited as hell, too. Seconds later, I was face to face with the man I desired (for only this night). It was out of character for me. It was a strange and scary ordeal for me, but it was something I felt I needed to do. I don't know if it was because of the hurt that Thomas put me through, or the fact that in all my life I have never really done anything that could be considered risqué. Perhaps I was just horny. In either case, I needed to see how this thing played out.

"Hey," he said seductively with a smile.

"Hey," I replied back.

"So . . . what's up?"

"I don't know, what's up with you?"

"Adrienne said that you wanted to see me."

"I did . . . Did she, um, tell you why?"

He smiled. I felt so embarrassed and so dirty, but that didn't change my desire for him.

"Yes, she did."

I fidgeted with my hands and was mortified. "What did she tell you?"

He was blunt. "She said you wanted to get fucked."

"And your response was?"

"That you're a cutie, and yeah, I have no issue with fucking you."

My heart raced a hundred per hour. I couldn't believe this was happening. I wanted him but I stood in place paralyzed with fear. He walked in my direction, and as he got closer, I took a single step backward.

"What about your girl?"

He stopped in mid-stride. I kept telling myself to shut the hell up, but for whatever reason I needed to know.

"What about her?" he shrugged.

"How can you, I mean . . . why . . . um . . . is she . . . should we . . . well . . . I . . . um."

"You weren't too concerned about her while you stared at me during our conversation."

"No, no, I wasn't."

"And, you weren't too concerned with her when you told Adrienne you wanted to fuck me."

"True."

"So, your reason for being concerned now is because . . . what?"

"I just . . . I don't want to be caught. I mean, I don't want to hurt her. I don't want anything long term. I was just thinking out loud and well, I don't want you to think that I'm a ho or anything. I just wanted you real bad. I don't know why but . . . well, tonight I just have so much going on. I'm horny and Adrienne said you were a decent guy. I just um—"

He smiled and rubbed his hands together. "You just want to be fucked."

"Yeah."

"Then say it."

"I . . . just want . . . to . . . be . . . fucked."

"Say it again. This time with conviction."

"I just want to be fucked!"

He walked closer to me, but this time, I didn't back away.

"I don't want to be caught. I don't want any drama. As far as your girl is concerned—"

"Fuck her!" he said while grabbing the back of my neck, pulling me closer to him, and kissing me deeply on the mouth.

Our tongues danced together. I wanted to undress him, so I reached out to remove his clothes, but he stopped me. This wasn't about to be a romantic session. This, if anything, was about to be some thugged-out shit. He kissed my lips, and neck, then he reached out for my ass and palmed it. We continued to kiss like teenagers in the car at the beach. I could taste the rum and Coke on his breath and I'm sure he tasted the E&J on mine. Together we became intoxicated by the taste of one another. Together we became primal.

The small storage room was filled with the sounds of our kissing and the erratic panting of my breath. I ran my hands up and down his muscular arms and became lost in the moment. For a brief second, I imagined that he was Thomas. This was the same ritual that Thomas and I had during our prequel to sex. To break the routine, I reached out for his package and began to vigorously massage him through his pants. He reached between my legs and felt that I had on no panties. He became harder in my hand and I could now feel his heart rate increasing. He fingered my clit, and in virtually no time at all, his finger was glistening with the juices of my wet sex. I let out a moan as he ran circles around my clit before sticking his finger inside me.

"Right there . . . hell, yeah." I purred.

"You like that?" he whispered.

"I love that."

"Then you'll love this."

He turned me away from him as if he was a cop and I was under arrest. He then placed my hands on the wall in front of me.

"Spread your legs," he ordered. "Arch your back, and let me see that ass."

I loved being told what to do. This shit was turning me on.

I arched my back so he could get a good look at my backside. Some brothers thought I was fat, he obviously saw me as being thick. I do have a nice ass if I must say so myself. I moved it back and forth and in a circular motion, almost daring him to take me from behind. I heard a tearing noise that made me pause. I looked back and was grateful to see he was tearing open a condom wrapper. I had condoms with me, but almost got caught up in the moment. Perhaps I was being too risqué.

"You came prepared," I said.

"Adrienne gave me this."

I smiled to myself. This girl Adrienne thought of everything. She was like a female ghetto fabulous Mr. Roarke from *Fantasy Island*. I looked back to see how far he was rolling back the condom. I was happy to report that one of my favorite authors was about to write his name and place his stamp on my ass.

He hiked up my skirt and exposed my ass. He smacked it a few times to watch it jiggle. I was pleased to know that he liked what he saw. He used his longest digit and went back to teasing my clit again. He quickly ran circles around it and my eyes rolled to the back of my head, very close to coming. The excitement of his fine ass taking me down here while his woman was upstairs turned me on. The prospect of getting caught got my nipples hard. Just when I started to tell him that we didn't have a lot of time, he grabbed a fist full of my hair with one hand, and smacked my ass with the other while simultaneously entering me.

My sex took most of him. I felt full as he entered me slowly, pushing past the limits of any other man. He was both long and thick, a combination I hadn't had before, but one that I could get used to. He started fucking me with slow methodic strokes. My mouth was open and I strained to take all of him inside me. With each stroke, he went deeper, and each time he went deeper, my legs trembled and my lower back shook. Again, he smacked my ass and the smack on my ample behind was a pleasant distraction from the stabbing that he was doing. He began to pick up the pace, but not too fast and not too slow. He hit my spot and he hit it just right. I took one hand off the wall and cupped one of my breasts. I pinched and tweaked my nipples as he picked up speed and began to stroke me faster, coming all the way out to the tip and driving back in as far as my vagina would let him.

"Oh, shit, right there!" I yelled.

Smack! was the sound of his hitting my ass.

"Oh, baby, I love that shit."

Smack! He hit me again, this time assuredly leaving a mark.

"That's it, baby, put your name on this shit!"

He held my ass, bent me completely over, and I grabbed my ankles. I fought to keep my balance as he stroked me harder and faster. The storage room was filled with the sounds of our bodies slamming against one another. I thought that I might come, and just as the sex became near orgasmic, he pulled out of me, turned me forward to face him and backed me up against the wall.

"Raise one leg up," he directed.

I did as he instructed and where my knee bent, he hooked my leg with his arm. His biceps began to bulge through the material of the shirt he wore.

"Now the other one," he said.

"You have to be kidding," I said, thinking there was no way he could handle my weight.

"You're running out of time."

Remembering that we were on the clock and someone would be expecting us soon, I complied. I raised the other leg up and he used the wall as leverage against my back. He grabbed my ass with his hands as his elbows supported my weight and he re-entered me. My sex was still wet and I freely accepted him. I kissed him deeply on the mouth and wrapped my arms around his neck as he began to rock slowly back and forth inside of me. We kissed over and over again, and as he picked up speed, he began to really pile-drive me.

"Oh, shit baby, that's it!" I screamed.

He grinded hard and sweat starting to form on his forehead. "You like that shit?"

"I love that shit."

"You want that shit."

"I need this shit."

"What is it that you want?"

I strained to talk as the feeling was so good. "I . . . I want to get fucked!"

"Say that shit again."

"I want to get fucked!"

"You like how I fuck you?"

"Ohhhh, I love how you're fucking me!"

"Good. Then, keep on saying that shit!" He began to poke harder and really get his stroke on. The next thing I knew, he was hitting my spot so well that I felt the juices running out of me and all over him. I didn't think I could initially accommodate his girth, but now all bets were off. I was getting fucked—well, and this was the type of dick I had hoped for. I had been fighting the orgasm that was welling up inside of me. I wanted to come. I *needed to come*. After all I had been through, the hurt, the heartache, and the drama with Thomas, my body needed to release the stress and take in a good hard orgasm. I kept telling myself, *Look at him. Look at his ripped muscles. Look at his bedroom eyes. Watch his expression of pleasure as he moves inside of you.* I looked at him and saw ferocity and lust in his eyes. His breathing was heavy, my breathing was heavy, and together we were all into each other. During this encounter, we were both as one. He went deeper inside of me, filling me up. He felt *so good* inside me that I had to let loose. I held firmly on to his neck and bit down on his shoulder though the material of the shirt. That's how good he made me feel. That's how much my pussy loved him. My eyes rolled in the back of my head and I thought about Thomas. At the same time I looked at the man that was inside me. I then thought about every man that had ever pleased me in my life. I also thought about every man that had let me down. Six weeks I had gone without sex. Three weeks I went without masturbating. For longer than that, I had this stress building up inside me, this thing building up inside me that I was ready to let loose. I began to rock back on top of his dick and began *fucking him.* I fucked him to get back at Thomas. I fucked him to please myself. I fucked him for the let down of every man who ever hurt me. I allowed myself to feel good. I allowed myself to go there again. I let this man please me, and I in turn tried to please him. Over and over again he went inside me, and after a few more long and methodic strokes, we both came hard. I was dripping wet with sweat and my hair was disheveled like Saddam Hussein's was in that damned hole they found him in.

Justin slowly put both my legs down. He then kissed me on the lips and then withdrew from inside me. He left me satisfied, so much so that I just slid down the wall and waited for my orgasm to subside. He pulled up his pants and tried his best to fix himself up. I pulled down my skirt and we both didn't say a word for a full minute. He broke the silence first.

"I'd like to fuck you again, without the time con- straints."

"I didn't come here for that. I just came to get fucked."

He reached in his wallet and I became incensed think- ing that he might offer me money like some whore. I was relieved that he handed me a card and not a crisp bill.

"Here's my number. This is for the next time that you want to get . . . fucked."

I gave him my card for my type-styling business that I used to run out of my apartment. The business was no longer running, but the number was still the same.

"Here's my number. Use it when you have some free time."

He grabbed two cases of Hennessey from behind us and took them to the stairway.

"Wait ten minutes before you come upstairs again," he said.

"Adrienne's suggestion?" I quipped.

"Yeah."

"She certainly thinks of everything."

"That she does."

He went upstairs and I looked at the wall where we had just been sexing each other up. *Ten minutes, he said, hell after that build up I'm going to need ten hours.* I waited twenty minutes before going upstairs. When I got upstairs, I was surprised that Justin and his lady had left. I slipped Adrienne back the keys that she gave me.

"So where did he go?" I asked.

"He took her home."

"She doesn't know what happened, does she? I mean we were only down there about sixteen minutes."

"You were down there thirty-eight minutes."

"Shit, are you serious?"

"Yeah."

"Did she know?"

"She might have acted like she didn't know. But she knew. A woman always knows."

That sent chills down my spine.

"What do I do now?"

"Have another drink—and tell me how it was!"

We laughed. I told Adrienne how Erotic Author Justin Davis broke me off proper in the basement of the 9705 Bar. I gave her every gritty detail and went back to talking about how badly Thomas had broken my heart.

"Girl, you need to stop worrying about this married man and fall in love with yourself all over again. You can't love anyone else or be of any use to anyone else without first loving yourself."

"So, you are saying that I shouldn't have fucked Justin tonight?"

"No, maybe you needed that. I'm just glad it was him and not some other strange man. You can't let a man take you to the point where you're having self-destructive behaviors. You could've come in here and fucked the wrong man and ended up on the news tomorrow. If that happened, where do you think this guy Thomas would be? How would his life be any different?"

I thought about it and came to one conclusion. "It wouldn't."

"And he'd still be married. My point exactly, girl, move on and move up."

"I . . . I will."

Adrienne wiped the bar with a towel, while I finished my drink. Afterwards, I headed toward the door and heard her laughing.

"What is so funny?"

"Did he fuck you up against the wall?"

"Yeah, I forgot to mention that. But, how did you know?"

"Look at your back."

I looked at the back of my top in the mirrored wall and it was covered in the red clay from the wall downstairs. Also, my ass had two dirty handprints on them. I felt so embarrassed that I quickly put on my coat and made my way to the door.

"Girl, I will see you another time, I gotta go."

"Make sure that you come back again."

"I will."

I went home, showered, and went to bed . . . satisfied.

Chapter Sixteen—Thomas

I know it was wrong as hell, but only after the third Wednesday I got back from my honeymoon, I worked late. All day Tuesday, I avoided Tiffany and refused to let myself look in her direction. I did the same thing today. The problem I had was that the more I tried to push her out of my head, the more she seemed to invade my thoughts. I saw less and less of her, in the office and that should've been a good thing. Instead, I found myself thinking about her off and on, night and day.

I wondered what her thoughts were. I wondered if she hated me and if she had been thinking about me as much as I had been thinking of her. Of course she hated me, she had to. Didn't she? I found myself thinking about her smile, thinking about her sex and thinking about all the fun we had together. I tried to go back to work and focus on something else, but nothing seemed to come; nothing—but her. When I got off work that third Wednesday back; I found myself going to the Flower Bucket in Hyde Park, as I had done many Wednesdays before. I found myself driving west to her apartment, and before I knew it, I was in the parking lot of her complex.

I didn't know where her car was. In her space was a Cadillac CTS. I sat in my car rubbing my temples as I figured the car in her space must be her new man. Could she have moved on that quickly? Who was I to talk? I had led her on and cheated on her the entire time we were together.

I walked in behind someone going in her building. I pretended I lived there, and went up to her door. I tried to get the nerve to knock, but it just wasn't there. I laid the roses down at the base of her door and walked off. I shook my head in disbelief at the fact that I let such a good woman get out of my life. I thought about how I should've told her there was someone else.

I should've asked her if we could open the relationship and just be lovers. Naw, that wouldn't have worked. She would've walked away, which is why I lied to her to begin with. That was why I kept her in the dark. I did it for the same selfish reasons that all men lie to women. I wanted to have my cake and eat it too. I stood in front of her door for some time trying to figure out what I was going to do about her. I wanted to write or send a card saying that I was sorry, but that would be evidence of my infidelity.

I wanted to knock on her door and tell her in person, but I was sure that I was the last person she wanted to see right now. I let out a heavy sigh as I stared a while longer at her door. I could smell her perfume from where I stood. Just then, my cell phone rang, while I was right outside Tiffany's door! I quickly opened the phone and headed down the hall and out of the building. The phone call was my *wife* wondering where in the hell I was.

Chapter Seventeen—Tiffany

I was surprised as hell to see flowers outside my door when I got ready to leave for work the next morning. There was no card, so I assumed they were from Justin. The card I gave him had this address. I guess he thought it was too soon to be knocking on my door, so he simply left flowers. That was sweet. It was unexpected, but sweet. I could still feel him inside of me. I could still smell his Burberry Touch cologne. The only thing I regretted about last night was how much I drank. As far as my tryst with Justin, I thought that could blossom into a regular thing sexually, or at least I hoped so. I enjoyed my encounter with him. I was quite impressed with him as an author. I have always loved his books and also always wondered if he as anything like his characters. As it turned out, he was. I had to admit, I couldn't wait to read his next book to see anything if resembled the primal sex we'd had at the 9705 Bar. *I'd also like to end up as one of the oversexed leading ladies in his next novel.*

I brought the flowers in and cut the stems at a 45-degree angle. I then placed them in a vase of water and set them on my dining room table. I smiled at the prospect of a man sending me flowers again. *I wish he could've been more creative than red roses, but it's early on and he doesn't know me well enough to use variety.*

I jumped in my car and headed to work. Today was going to be a long day because I had to work, then go to class and then hit the gym. I was drinking nothing but water these days, hitting the gym every other day, and working hard in and out of class to better myself. I have to admit, I thought college would be harder as an adult. It was actually easier. I did all of my assigned work that my boss gave me and jumped right in to doing my homework. After that was complete, I started working on a long term paper. I was just about to go to lunch when Alicia walked in. I figured she had just left Matthew's office. I hadn't seen or heard from my girl since she'd started seeing him. She came toward me with a huge smile on her face. If I hadn't known any better, I would've sworn she was glowing.

"Hey girl, what's up?" Alicia said.

"I don't know, you tell me. You've been missing in action for some time now."

"Yeah, I know. I'm sorry, girl, I've been busy."

"Been busy or gettin' busy?"

"Both." She laughed.

"Ooohhh, girl, you are kidding me. So how are things with Eminem?"

"Very funny. Things are fine. In fact, things are good."

"They must be good, it hasn't been a month yet and you already gave him some ass? What has gotten into you?"

"He has."

We both laughed and gave each other a high-five.

"So, okay, don't leave a sister in the dark. How was he?"

She leaned in close to me and whispered, "Girl, did you hear me from your apartment last night?"

"Damn! Was he that good?

"Surprisingly, yes."

"And are all the myths about white boys true?"

"Myths, what myths?"

"You know, size, oral skills, would you go back for seconds?"

"Size was okay, I've had better, but he knew what he was doing and he was very attentive. His oral skills are on point! He should be the one they call superhead, and seconds? Yes, I've already gone back for seconds, thirds, and eighths."

"Shut up! You're kidding me."

"Girl, Matt is like the damned energizer bunny."

We both said in unison, "He keeps going and going and going!"

"So, where did the two of you knock boots at?"

"The Hilton."

"Downtown?"

"Vermont."

"What!"

"Matt took me to Vermont. We initially just went out to dinner and we had such a good time that he later asked me if I wanted to do something spontaneous. I said yeah, and the next thing I knew, we were in Vermont."

"What the hell did you do in Vermont?"

"We went skiing, hiking, and of course had breakfast, lunch, and dinner out there. Then, we had each other for dessert."

"Skiing? Sisters don't ski!"

"Shit, I do now. Matt taught me."

I folded my arms and gave my lips a toot. "What else did he teach you?"

"Believe it or not, he taught me some new positions. I thought I'd been around the block a few times, but he opened my eyes."

"I thought you'd been around the block more than a crackhead looking for her dealer."

We both laughed. There were a lot of people passing by us, so I suggested that we go to lunch together and finish our conversation. We went to the cafeteria, and as soon as we took our seats, I continued.

"So, where were we? I think you were about to tell me all that he taught you."

"Believe it or not, he came up with all kinds of positions. My favorite was missionary, with my arms underneath me. Girl, Matt took both my forearms, and pulled downward while he was inside of me. It was like a jerking motion, while he penetrated me deep."

"Deep? How deep?"

"Like the X-Clan used to say, 'deep, deep, deeper than Atlantis, deeper than the ocean floor traveled by the Mantis'."

"He went *that deep?*"

"Yes, that deep. Shit, I thought I had found buried treasure when Matt got through with my ass. I even talked into the microphone like I was an MC on Freestyle Friday."

I burst into laughter, as Alicia really had a way with words. She seemed to really enjoy herself with Matt, and even though I was a bit jealous that I didn't have that kind of story to tell, I was pleased to hear things was working out between the two of them.

"You know," Alicia said, "it's not just about the sex for me. I mean, yeah, the shit was good and I'm very surprised that a white man or any man could get my body to respond like that. But, the thing is I had a really good time. I could picture myself having more really good times with Matt. Tiff, I think I can grow to really like him."

"Because he's paid?"

"No, but because he treats me nice. He knows how to have a good time, he compliments me, he calls to see how my day is going and he listens. He actually listens."

"That's because it's new. They all do that when it's new."

Alicia cut her eyes at me. "Tiff, you sound jaded. Are you still upset about Thomas?"

I let out a deep sigh and apologized for raining on her parade. "A little. I'm sorry, Alicia. If Matthew treats you right, then that's all that counts. I'm happy for you."

"Thank you. But remember, you hooked us up. We owe you."

"Yeah, but just remember that in the event you get

married and go and have a little mixed baby or something. If you have a little girl, be sure to name her Tiffany."

She agreed, and as we dove into our salads, I couldn't help but think about Alicia and Matt. Maybe it was time I started exercising my options and stopped putting limits on myself. Maybe going white was all right. I started to ask her if Matt had any friends, but she asked me a question that shook me back into reality.

"So, what did you do last night? I called but you weren't home."

A little embarrassed by what I'd done, I picked at my salad. I didn't feel as if Alicia would judge me so I came out with it. "You wouldn't believe what I did last night."

"What did you do?"

"I . . . I went to a bar to get Thomas off my mind and I slept with a man."

Alicia dropped her fork on her plate and her voice rose. "You did what?"

"I slept with a man I met last night."

"Tiff, that's dangerous. You could've been hurt . . . or worse."

"It's no different than sleeping with Matthew."

"Are you crazy? It's very different. You knew I was seeing him, I know where he works."

"I didn't know the two of you went to Vermont."

"I called you to tell you."

"That was after the fact."

"That's not the point."

"Why not? You could've called me and Matt could've killed you right after you hung up the phone."

"If he would've you would know who to look for. And, you'd have enough info to put his full bio on *America's Most Wanted.* I don't know anything about the man you were with last night."

"Yeah, you do."

"I do?"

"Yes, he's one of your favorite authors."

Her eyes widened. "Who?"

"Justin Davis."

"Shut up! Girl, stop playin'!"

Alicia's mouth hung open as I gave her all the details about how Justin and I got down in the basement of the 9705 Bar, in spite of his woman being right upstairs.

"Girl, you are scandalous! What if his woman had caught you?"

I shrugged. "I don't know. But that was the thing; the thought of possibly getting caught excited the shit out of me."

"Has Justin called you since?"

"No, but he did leave me flowers outside my apartment door."

"Scandalous. I bet this shit ends up in his next book."

"It better not. I'd sue his ass if it does."

"You would sue him for how much?"

"No girl, not money, sex!"

"Was it that good?"

"It was a'ight."

Again we laughed and joked about our recent escapades. The only thing I wasn't happy about was how our roles had reversed. Generally, it was Alicia telling me about some mad affair she was having, not the other way around. I was happy for my girl, but feeling sorry for myself. Just then, Matt walked up to both of us and we were so busy laughing and joking that we hadn't seen him.

"Hey, you, I thought you were leaving?" he said to Alicia.

"I was, but I decided to have lunch with my girl," Alicia said.

"Hello, Tiffany, how are you?"

"Fine, Matt, how are you?"

"I'm great. I came to see you, just so I can thank you

for this wonderful woman here. Also, I wanted to tell you we reviewed your resume, and since you're in school, there's an opening in acquisitions and treasury. The job is yours if you want it. It means a raise of eight thousand dollars for you and a corner office on the next floor."

I was excited about the news and spoke anxiously. "So, the person I'd be assisting is on the next floor?"

"Assisting? The position is for a manager trainee."

I was shocked. "A manager?"

"Yeah, it means you'll be training the next eight weeks, and if successful, you'll be given your own AA. Didn't Alicia tell you?"

I looked across the table at Alicia and folded my arms. "No, she didn't tell me. I guess because we were talking about *other things*."

"So, how about it, Tiffany? Are you game?"

"Matt, I don't know what to say."

"Well, say yes. You took a chance on me and hooked me up with your friend and now I'm taking a chance on you."

I was blown away. A management position? Was I up for the challenge? Did I want to just leave the position I'd held for so long? Then I thought about Thomas and the words he'd spoken to me that night in my apartment. That made me focus again; that made me think. I'd made my decision.

"Matt, I will call them right now. I'm going to take the manager trainee position."

"Good for you."

Chapter Eighteen—Tiffany

I made the phone call to the new department, and off of Matthew's recommendation alone, I was in the management training program. I felt guilty as hell as I looked on at the other trainees. Most of them were younger than me and many of them had recently graduated from college. The HR rep told me to keep my mouth shut about not having a degree. The HR rep's name was Olivia Beauregard. She was a nice looking black woman, who wore expensive suits and looked like an older version of Serena Williams.

"So, how long have you known Matt?" she asked.

"Just a few weeks, why?"

"He's never called in a favor like this before, so please don't mess this up. Who knows, if you get a chance, this may be an opportunity for the bank to open up more doors for more of us."

"Don't worry, I won't mess it up."

"You know if you get through the training program, you'll get another raise, right?"

"No, I didn't know."

"Not only that, but you'll get another raise in a year and there are all types of bonuses and commissions that come from staying under budget in your department."

"That's really great news."

"And, there's a comprehensive 401K plan, stock options, money market accounts, six weeks' vacation, and a good pension and medical plan."

"Wow, I'm surprised. I've been here for years and I don't have all that."

"I do, but it was very hard to negotiate. How do you know Matthew that you could pull such a favor? Did you sleep with him?"

I thought this was unprofessional as hell, but we were in sister-girl mode, so I satisfied her curiosity.

"He's dating my best friend."

"A sister?"

"Yeah."

"Well, keep telling your friend to keep on doing whatever she's doing. On another note, just make sure you don't tell anyone that you don't have a degree yet. There are haters everywhere in this building."

"I'm ashamed of having to lie like that."

"Don't be. All you have to do is learn the same things everyone else in the room has to learn. How do you think all these white folks do things? Half the people in this training program were recommended by other V.P.s in the bank, executives, and department managers. You will probably be the only person of color in the program who hasn't slept their way in or was a relative of someone. In this field, many times it's not what you know, it's who you know."

"I know that's the truth."

"Tiffany, this is an opportunity. You need to look at it that way. I know you need the money, who doesn't?"

"I do," I laughed, and extended my hand to hers. "Thanks for the chat session. I need to get myself ready. When can I expect a call about a second interview?"

"There is no second interview. You start Monday."

"Really?"

"Really. Congratulations, it seems that you might be on your way."

"Thank you."

I went back to my desk and started clearing things off. Shit was happening so fast that my head was spinning. I finished my work for the day and told my boss I was transferring to another department. He'd already known because Matt had shared the news with him while I was in HR. He said that he would be sad to see me go but wished me all the best. I thanked him for the opportunity and he gave me the next day off *with pay.*

Later that day, I went to class then to the gym. I was losing about a pound-anda-half a day, now that I was working out regularly and eating right. In my heart and in my mind, I was starting to envision a new me.

The next day, I drove to Chicago Ridge Mall and bought two suits, a few blouses and shoes for the training program. I had to bring my A game to the table and I didn't want anything to stand in my way. On Saturday afternoon, I hit the gym again. I was up to a mile-and-a-half running, rather than walking on the treadmill, and getting stronger each day. Sunday I went to church and gave thanks to the Father for this opportunity. Sunday night, I hit the books hard and got all my assignments done that were on the syllabus. I didn't want school to distract me from the task at hand.

I got up bright and early that Monday morning. The training program was from nine to five, but I was so hyped that I was up at six. I caught the train in to work and read a small handheld Bible that I kept in my handbag for encouragement. After I read a few verses, I turned my MP3 player/ radio to V103 where I heard Justin Davis giving one of his on-air speeches. Hearing his voice made me tingle on the inside. I thought back briefly to that night at the 9705 Bar. As I reminisced about our one-night stand, I listened to the words he spoke over the airwaves. Today's message was about the power of blackness.

"Good morning, Chicago! This is your boy Justin Davis from the south side of Chi bringing you, my brothers and sisters, words of encouragement on this fine Monday morning. I am asking everyone that can hear the sound of my voice be encouraged and not discouraged because today—God has given you a chance to take charge and take your life, the life he has given you, in a new direction. I'm asking each of you to be blessed today and to bless one another, to uplift one another, to take pride in being black, to take pride in being strong; to take pride in being God's chosen. I'm asking each of you to change your mindset today as you head into work to make someone else some money. I am asking you to look at the world through black glasses, not rose-colored glasses as many of our counterparts would have you do. I am asking you to ask yourself a question this morning. Instead of saying why me, as many of us do, I want you to ask yourself *why not me?* I want you to take note of the pep in your step. I want you to take note of the glide in your stride. Many people look at black men and women and wonder why we talk funny, why we walk funny, and do we have problems with our knees and our legs because we each walk with a little more bounce than they do, a little more jiggle than they do, and yet a little more wiggle than they do. Some people look at us funny because we seem arrogant to them, misunderstood to them and yet, a mystery to them. Well, today I'm here to tell you that it's okay to let them know the reason why we do the things we do is because there is power in being blessed. There is power in being God's children. There is power in being black. Yeah, being black ain't easy, but the *power* that is in each one of us gives us that extra pep in our step. It's the reason why sisters walk with a little more jiggle. Sisters . . . are blessed. It's not easy being a black man in the white man's world, which is why it sometimes looks like we're doing what they call 'pimp walking.' Today I am here to tell you that again, it's okay to let them know that the reason we walk the way we do is because the power that is *within us* is sometimes heavy. It ain't easy being black! It ain't easy being this beautiful! It ain't easy being this powerful. It's a heavy burden but you know what?

God never gives us more than we can stand! And we have stood it, haven't we, Chicago? Honk your horn out there if you hear me. Honk your horn if you have financial trouble. Tap your foot if you have had relationship trouble. Clap your hands if you have ever been tired. Stomp your feet if you have ever been lied on, cheated on, discriminated against, talked about, faced with eviction, faced with conviction, or had a time where you didn't know where your next meal was coming from. Yeah, Chicago . . . Black people . . . my people . . . we have been there, haven't we? But you know what? Better yet . . . you know who? Someone had our back! Someone had our back when that person hurt us! Someone had our back when we were lied on! Someone had our back when the lights were cut off! Someone had our back when that man touched you in the wrong way! Someone was there and had your back when you were raped! When that man beat you! When that woman had another man in your house! When you found out the baby wasn't yours! When you found out that he was really gay! When they laid you off! When they put you down! I am here this morning to tell you that someone has your back! That person is God and he is inside each and every one of us. Today, I want you to go to work with a smile on your face. I want you to stride today. I want you to glide today. I want your spirit to rise today! I want all my black people that hear my voice to uplift one another today. Don't feed off anyone else's negative energy. Each time that you see someone of color today, when they say good morning or hello or good afternoon, I want you to say when they inquire about you today that *Justin Davis says, today I'm blessed.* This is just a small experiment, but I dare you to try it! I want you to see how many people approach you and say today *Justin Davis says today I'm blessed.* I want you to see how powerful being black is. I want you to see that we can uplift one another. We can, be there for one another. We can and most certainly do, make a difference. As you bless one another today, I want you to take note of how many people hear my voice. I want you to take note of how much you and everyone that you know make a difference. I want you to think about how powerful we are and how powerful we can be . . . if we just came together. Think about this: ask yourself how much purchasing power you have with your present credit and salary situation. Now, when you get to work ask yourself how powerful you would be if each person that greets you today gave you a dollar, or five dollars, or ten dollars! Alone we are each great in our own right, but *together, we are indeed powerful!* That's my time for today, family! Remember, you make a difference, as do your prayers. This is your boy, Justin Davis, and I'm out!"

It was a small, sixty-second slot, but it was powerful. I couldn't believe that just days earlier, this was the man who had been inside of me; who tossed me against the wall. This was the man who recently *fucked me.* He did a lot of motivational speaking around the city. I was hoping that he might call me soon so he could motivate me in other ways.

A few minutes later, the train let me off downtown, and as I got off I said hello or good morning to various people. There was the train conductor, the regular people who rode with me each day, and cops on the streets. I spoke to each of them as I did every morning and I was stunned at how many people said, "Justin Davis says that I'm blessed." I smiled as I thought about the impact this brotha had on the city and the people he met. Most of all, I was delighted by the impact the brotha had on me.

My heart began to race as I got closer and closer to the building. I noticed a lot of white people heading toward the revolving doors, and I wondered whether they were heading to the training program. My palms were sweating and, started to call Matthew and tell him thanks but no thanks to the position. Then I thought about Justin's words and decided to put a bit more stride in my walk. The closer and closer I got to the elevators, the more my fear seemed to fade. With each black person who walked by me, I greeted them and they greeted me back.

I took the elevator up to the twenty-ninth floor and got off where I saw about thirty young white men and women sitting in the conference room where there was a sign pointing out the manager trainee session. I also saw two Hispanic females, three sisters, and four brothers. I sat in what was naturally created by us as the colored section and felt a bit uncomfortable being around all these degreed young people. Either way, I spoke to nearly everyone and began an intense training session.

Day one was hard as hell, but I got through. Day two was equally hard, but we uplifted one another and made it through. Day three was a little bit easier—that was, until Wednesday night.

Chapter Nineteen—Thomas

I went into work this week and every day I glanced in Tiffany's direction to see what she was up to. When I looked over, I noticed she wasn't there. I wondered if she was on vacation or something, so I decided to be nosy and checked the H drive in her department for her schedule. Strangely enough, not only did I not see PTO (paid time off) next to her name, but her name was no longer on the schedule.

"Had she been fired or did she quit?" I thought.

That Wednesday, I went to Matthew Tuskey's office. He was a V.P. in that department and I knew he'd know where she was.

"Hey, Matt, how are you? How have you been?" I asked. He shook my hand and invited me to take a seat.

"I'm doing well, Thomas, what about you? How's married life?"

"Draining." I laughed, and he did too.

"You aren't supposed to be saying that for like another five years or so."

He might have thought I was joking or being facetious, but Meagan was driving me crazy. I was having sex virtually every night, but it was always missionary and there were never any oral exchanges. On top of that, she was spending money like we were printing the shit in the basement of our house. We were about to go into the month of October and she had the nerve to be planning for a Halloween party at our house. She wanted a bunch of grown-ass people to play dress-up like we were twelve. Then there was the fact that she still hadn't budged on the children issue. She was taking birth control pills and we were using condoms. This was my wife and she wouldn't even allow me to go in her raw, which is what she had been promising we would do after we got married. We went raw once and that was the day after we got married. She shopped every day with the other women in our neighborhood, and I guess they all thought they were the black version of *Desperate Housewives*.

"Matt, I can honestly say that my wife is already driving me insane."

"Unfortunately, sometimes, that's what pretty women do."

"Yes, she's very pretty, but I would be lying if I told you that was all that she really had going for her these days."

"What do you mean by that?"

"I don't want to elaborate on all of that right now, but truthfully, Matt, I think I made a mistake."

Matt looked shocked. He got up to close his door, which gave us some privacy. "A mistake? Already? It might be too late to realize that, Anthony, and you know what they say . . . it's cheaper to keep her."

"Yeah, I wonder about that. In my case, that might not be so."

Matt clinched his hands together and placed them on his desk. "So, how are things in your department?" he asked, quickly changing the subject.

"They're fine. How are things over here?"

"Couldn't be better."

"That's good. And how are things going with your personal life?"

"It's funny that you ask. I have a new lady in my life and I found her at your wedding."

I almost choked when he said that and swallowed hard. Was he talking about Tiffany? Jealousy hit me out of nowhere, and as hard as it was to keep my composure, I had to ask this new woman's name.

"Her name is Alicia."

Aw shit! Alicia knew what went down. I wonder if she told him and how much information he might have shared with other people. How the hell did the two of them get together? Damn! I can't seem to catch a break.

"Alicia?" I said, playing it off. "She . . . she's my wife's crazy cousin?"

Matt smiled and placed his hands behind his head. "Yeah, that's her."

"Wow . . . that's um . . . good. I mean, that's great! How did the two of you hook up?"

"I asked her friend Tiffany to hook us up."

"Tiffany . . . Tiffany. Oh, you mean the cute, heavy-set sister who works over here somewhere?"

"She used to work here. She's gone, but yeah, that's who I'm talking about."

"Oh, okay. So, she hooked you two up? Great. How's that working for you?"

"Truthfully speaking, things couldn't be better."

"That's great, Matt. I'm really happy for you."

"Thanks, Thomas. Who knows? We might be related one day. Alicia is a special kind of lady . . ."

"That she is," I said as Matt continued to ramble on about Alicia. I wanted to inquire about exactly where Tiffany was, but I didn't want to draw attention to myself by asking too many questions. Instead, I quickly wrapped up our conversation and headed back to my department.

On the one hand, the news about her no longer being here should've been good news. On the other, I'd miss her. I hoped that the age-old adage applied here, "Out of sight, out of mind." Still, I wasn't sure how I was feeling. It was a cross between hurt and separation anxiety. I couldn't explain it, and I couldn't help but feel that Tiffany no longer being here was my fault. I felt sorry for her, sorry for us, and sorry for what could have been. I wanted to see her. I needed to see her. I wanted to get this heavy guilt off my chest. I thought I'd made a mistake marrying Meagan, and the woman I should've married was the woman who just walked off this job and out of my life. What was I going to do about it now?

Chapter Twenty—Tiffany

I was tired as hell from working out at the gym. I went home, took a nice long hot bath, and fixed myself a smoothie. I then booted up my new laptop so I could start doing my homework. I lit some scented candles, poured the smoothie into a cup, and crossed my legs as I sat on the couch in my robe. It was 11:00 P.M. before I started to unwind, and my long workout gave me the energy I needed to get my homework done. After my homework, I still had to go over the work given to us in the training class for tomorrow's class. I'd just completed reading about twenty pages of my economics book, when I was interrupted by a knock at my door. I wasn't expecting anyone, so I placed my pen in the middle of my book and yelled from the couch.

"Who is it?"

I didn't have the time nor the energy to deal with one of my neighbors today, and I wasn't up for some begging-ass crackhead trying to say their car broke down and needed a few dollars for gas. Since no one responded to me, I tossed my hand back and placed my book on my lap. There was another knock at the door, this time a little bit more insistent.

"Who the hell is it?" I said, slamming my book shut.

A soft-spoken voice replied, "It's Thomas."

I must be hearing things. "Who?" I said, lowering my voice.

"Thomas," he repeated.

I was frozen in time and couldn't move. My head ached and my soul hurt. In just seconds, the pain that I thought was just beginning to diminish was back again in full force. My bottom lip quivered and my eyes scanned the room. I don't know why, but I eyeballed the butcher knives sitting in the butcher block on the counter. For a millisecond, I plotted a homicide in a small town in an even smaller apartment complex. In two milliseconds, I envisioned killing the man I once thought to be my boyfriend who turned out to be my lover. I pictured him bloody, begging for his life, and crying that he was sorry. That brief fantasy faded as he knocked on my door a third time, this time softly, breaking me out of my trance. *He has some damned nerve bringing his ass here; his married ass here.*

I started to call Alicia because I needed some support—quick. The reason that I didn't call my girl was because she was on patrol tonight and I was afraid that she might have come over here and busted a cap in Thomas's ass. I prayed to God for strength. Just then, my cell phone went off.

I know he ain't calling me on my phone.

I looked down at the caller ID on my cell phone and it said "Justin."

He'll have to wait tonight too. I waited all this time for him to call and he waits almost a week? I took in several deep breaths, walked over to the door and opened it. My only thought was, *Why in the hell are you at my front door?*

Chapter Twenty-one—Thomas

I knew that going to Tiffany's house was wrong, but I couldn't help myself. It was Wednesday, and in a way, I felt like it was still *our day*. I had some nerve coming here, but I needed to see her. I needed to get some things off my chest, and wanted to know if it was really over between us.

I was willing to admit that men are some strange and primal creatures at times. Our behaviors can be very unpredictable. Women, however, are easier to read (when we have been sleeping with them). Every man knows that when he is in a relationship he is generally allowed one indiscretion. I know that it's wrong, but that is how we feel. We know that we get one time to cheat on credit and the woman will take us back. Many men are serial cheaters. Meaning that they cheat until they get caught and when they do get caught, that is when they settle down. Men know this. Women can argue until they are blue in the face, but in their hearts they know it to be true. My situation with Tiffany was a little more . . . unique. But for the most part, it's the same scenario. I hoped to pull this off. If I didn't think I could, I wouldn't have been here. It wasn't about right or wrong, or being arrogant. It was about limit testing and whether I could have my cake and eat it too. I talked to my boy Don about this, and according to him, I had nothing to lose at this point and everything to gain. I was following his advice to the letter and was about to find out whether I still had any chance at salvaging my relationship with Tiffany. I'd have loved to repair our friendship, and almost equally important, I wanted her back in my bed.

When she opened the door, I just stood there. I didn't smile and didn't say a word. I needed to simply gauge where she was, and what she was feeling and process from there. We stood there like chess masters and waited for the other to break the silence.

"Thomas," she said flatly.

"Hello," I said in an equal but humble tone.

Her move, I thought.

She pursed her lips, and without asking me to come in, she stepped aside.

My move, I thought and stepped inside. From that moment, I knew this chess game of life, betrayal and heartache had begun.

Tiffany gathered her robe to cover up and didn't look at all happy to see me. "So, why are you here, Thomas? Or is it Anthony? Which do you go by these days?" she snapped.

"Okay, that's fair. I deserved that."

She darted her finger at me. "No, what you *deserve* is for me to go upside your damned head with something solid, like an iron!"

I wasn't expecting her to be this mad; this strong. I mean, I knew to expect something, but the fire in her eyes, the hurt, I just . . . Well, never mind, I had to press forward; feel her out.

I nodded and remained calm. "Okay, I understand how you feel and I can see that you're upset."

"That's putting it mildly. Now, what the hell are you doing here? Why are you at my house and where is your wife?"

Wife? Hearing her say that word caused my heart to skip a beat. She could bring my world crashing down on top of me. I was taking one hell of a risk here, but I had to see her, I had to know. Don told me she might go there. He said even if she did to stand my ground. Physically, there wasn't a whole lot Tiffany could do to me, but for whatever reason, I was scared.

"She . . . my wife . . . is at home . . . sleep."

"Does she know you're here?"

"No, of course not. She thinks . . . she thinks I'm working late tonight."

"Uh-huh, sure she does."

I stepped closer to Tiffany, but she backed up. "Look, I came over here to . . . apologize."

"Yeah, well, you're eleven months and weeks too late on that shit!"

I looked down at the floor. Maybe she was right. I had no business being here and at least I got a chance to apologize to her. "This . . . this was a bad idea. I'm sorry I came. I'll just leave."

I turned to the door to leave, taking the advice of my friend Don. He told me earlier that any woman worth her salt wouldn't let me leave. She would at least want an explanation for what happened. Basically, he advised me to head toward the door and wait for her to ask me something, . . . anything, and that would be my chance to explain myself and sell myself hard to her. As soon as my hand touched the door, Tiffany spoke.

"Four fucking years, Thomas!"

I turned to her. "I'm sorry. What did you say?"

"I said, you have been with Meagan four years!"

"Yes, unfortunately, for four years."

"Could you answer something for me?"

"Anything."

"Why the hell did you start up with me? Why didn't you just tell me what was up from the beginning?"

"Because I didn't think you would have gotten involved with me if you knew the truth."

"I wouldn't have, but shouldn't I have been given that choice?"

"Yes, but I wanted you so badly. I was feeling you so much and I had to have you."

"So, because you were feeling me, you lied to me?"

"I'm not happy about it, but yes. Yes, I lied."

"Why?"

"I just told you." I reached out and held Tiffany shoulders. "Look, I don't know how we got here. All I know is we shared good times together. You were an amazing person to talk to, a good friend, and an even better lover to me. Somewhere along the line, I started caring for you a whole lot. I admit, I got in it with the worst of intentions. Initially, I got in it just to hit it and see what you were like. I was just looking for something sexual with you, but I got to know more about you. In getting to know you, I started to care for you."

"You couldn't have cared too much; you went and got married on me. You had to have been planning the wedding four or five months before we got together. How the hell do you think it made me feel to find out that my boyfriend was getting married to someone else?"

"I'm sorry, Tiffany. I can't begin to imagine how you must have felt."

"No, no, you can't."

"Please know that I never meant to hurt you."

"What did you mean to do then, Thomas?"

"I just . . ."

"You just what?"

I let go of Tiffany's shoulders and paced the room. "I just wanted to get to know you better. But having these feelings for you wasn't in my plan."

"So, you never intended to have feelings for me?"

"No."

"And saying that shit is supposed to make me feel good?"

I halted my steps. "Yes, I mean . . . no. I don't know what I mean."

Tiffany folded her arms and jumped on the defense. "I don't know what you mean either, but I'd like for you to get the hell out of my house."

It was time for me to put up or shut up. I looked deep into her eyes and spoke with sincerity. "Look, baby, I miss you."

She cut her eyes and looked away. "Yeah, right."

"I do. I really miss you."

"You got some damn nerve, you know that?"

"I know, but I'm just being honest."

Tiffany moved away from me and took a seat on the couch. She crossed her legs and folded her arms again. "So, I have more questions for you."

"Fine. Whatever you want to know, just ask."

"How were we able to have all those dinners and walks in the beginning if you were in a three-or-four year relationship?"

I let out a sigh. I could've lied, but if there was any chance of me getting with her again, Don told me that I would have to come clean. So . . . I did.

"In the beginning, Meagan was in Los Angeles. After she got her master's degree, her father sent her to L.A. I had to work, so while she was out there, I was here—with you."

"And when my time started to get cut back, you weren't working were you?"

"No. I was with her."

"And the times that we had sex in your office, where was she?"

"At home, she lived with her parents up until we got married."

"Just where did she think you were on those nights?"

"Working late. Work always seemed to be a good excuse."

"So you took risks by screwing me in your office? She could have walked in on us at any time and killed us both."

"No. She would never do that."

"How do you know?"

"Because I know her."

"You never know what one might do in a situation like that. Don't be so sure of yourself. Also, I've been to your condo. Where was she when I was there?"

"Probably shopping or out with her girls."

"And there was no danger of her coming to your condo?"

"No, there wasn't."

"Why? Let me guess, because you know her so well."

"No, because she hated my condo. She'd been there only a handful of times."

"So when you all had sex, you slept together, where?"

"Hotels, her place . . . wherever."

"But not your condo."

"Very seldom would she go to my condo."

Tiffany was silent and seemed to be in deep thought. Her voiced had calmed, which was very good news for me. I waited for her next question, and I looked at how toned she was. Obviously, she'd lost some weight.

"You've lost weight. Have you been working out?"

"Working out, crying, and throwing up; all because of you."

I let out a heavy sigh. "What else can I say other than I'm sorry."

"Yeah, you are very sorry. Can you tell me again why you're here?"

"You asked me that already."

"Well, I'm asking you again."

I hated that she'd taken a new tone with me. All I could do was stress the truth again.

"I miss you, Tiffany. More than you will ever know."

She stood up and tears welled in her eyes. "Fuck you, Thomas. You hurt the hell out of me, and how dare you stand there and repeat how much you've missed me."

"Get as angry as you want at me, but it's not going to stop me from feeling the way I do. I want us to be friends again."

"Is your wife okay with that?" I didn't say a word so Tiffany continued. "You broke my heart, Thomas. Do you have any idea what that feels like?"

"Sort of, baby, but breaking your heart was never my intention."

"I'm not your baby."

"To me you are, and I've told you how I feel. How we move forward . . . that's up to you."

"What is that supposed to mean?"

I walked up to Tiffany and left no breathing room between us. "Baby, I'd like to start seeing you again."

She moved her head back. "To be the other woman? To be your mistress? Is that what you're asking me?"

Per Don, I needed to man up here and stand my ground. This would be simple. The answer would be either yes, or no. I couldn't lose here. If she said no, there would be no harm, no foul. I would go home to my beautiful wife and life would go on. If she said yes, I'd get to have my cake and eat it too. I was scared to do what needed to be done, but I had to know where I stood. I had to give it a try.

"Yes. I'm asking you to be the other woman. I'm asking you if we can be friends again as well as lovers. I miss what we shared. You may not believe it, but I do. The choice . . . is yours."

She stomped away from me and headed for the door. "I don't have time for this shit. I don't have the energy for this foolishness, either. Get the hell out of my house! I'm not your whore!"

Checkmate. She made her move, and although it may seem like a draw, I am the one who feels like he lost—big.

I made my way to the door. "Sorry for disturbing you this late evening, but thanks for hearing me out." I opened the door, but before I took another step, I turned to her again. "Oh, I forgot. I do have one question for you, Tiffany."

"What, Thomas?"

"Why didn't you speak up at the wedding?"

She didn't hesitate to answer. "Because I didn't want to hurt your wife. No woman should hurt as badly as I did that day. Not even that bitch you call your wife."

I shook my head in agreement, then walked out of her apartment, quite possibly out of her life. Once I closed the door, I heard her cries. I had no right to come here tonight. All I did was open old wounds. It hurt me that I'd hurt her and I was deeply sorry for what I'd done.

I walked slowly to my car, and had a moment of pause as I held the steering wheel. I hadn't even started the car yet because it felt as if I were in mourning. Twenty minutes had gone by before I even started my car, and I sat there thinking how I'd lost such a good friend. I felt my phone vibrate and assumed it was Meagan. I picked up, getting ready to tell her I was on my way home.

"Yeah," I said dryly.

"The only day I have available is Friday night," Tiffany said.

There was silence, and I couldn't believe she had changed her mind. I was glad to hear the news, but my Fridays were often spoken for.

"Meagan will be expecting me home on Friday nights."

"Take it or leave it. Eight o'clock on Friday nights, or forget it."

"Done. I don't know how, but I'll make that happen."

Tiffany hung up and I was glad that she was willing to see me. I smiled the whole way home and thought about what Don had said would be the final result. He was right.

I guess I do get to have my cake and eat it too.

It was wrong. I knew it was wrong on so many levels, but hey, she could've said no, but she didn't.

Chapter Twenty-two—Tiffany

I hated giving in to him, but I couldn't help myself. I hated that he had such a profound effect on me. I hated that I missed him so damned much. Here I was just starting to get over him, and as soon as I started to heal, here he came again walking into my life. Why do men have to do that shit? I didn't know, but Thomas disrespected me by coming here tonight. Worse than that, I just disrespected myself by allowing him back into my life in any capacity. Mentally and spiritually, I was kicking myself in the ass. Here I was putting myself in a position to be his other woman. I might as well have put a sticker on my head that said boy toy or whore. I felt guilty. I felt guilty for disrespecting his wife as well as disrespecting myself. I went to bed and cried myself to sleep. I felt like all the self-esteem issues I'd had were back in full force.

I woke up and went to work the next morning. The training program was just starting to get easier and easier, and it became apparent to me that in spite of my esteem issues, the people in class knew as little as I did, even with all their degrees. The HR rep was right, all I had to do to be successful in this program was come and learn everything that the facilitator taught me.

That day, I spent hours trying to keep Thomas off my mind. All day long, as the facilitator taught, I had fleeting thoughts of all the sex-capades we'd had. I found myself thinking about how good he felt between my legs, how good he ate at the "Y," and how much in love with him I had been at one point. I replayed in my mind a hundred times his asking me to be the other woman. I also kept playing in my head my telling him that he could now have my Fridays. From this point forward, I was just as at fault as he was for anything that happened. Now, I was a willing participant in an affair. How could I have stooped so low? How would I feel if I were a wife and this was being done to me?

When I got out of my training class, Matt was in the hall waiting for me. I was wondering if something was wrong because he asked me if he could speak to me, and although he was dating Alicia, I didn't really get down with him like that. I mean, we didn't normally have a world of conversations before, and I didn't expect to start now just because he and Alicia were together. I was grateful he got me the hookup, but at the same time, I wondered what he wanted. He pulled me aside from everyone else and spoke in a whisper.

"Hey, Tiffany, listen. I have a friend I would like for you to meet. I was wondering if you had time this weekend, and would be willing to come to my house for a small party? I'm introducing Alicia to all my friends."

"Oh, okay. . . . yeah, I can do that, when?"

"Saturday at two o'clock in the afternoon. Here's the address."

"Thanks for the invite, Matt, I'll see you there."

I thought it was odd that he'd ask me out to his place, but because of my girl, I figured I'd go. I didn't really feel like being around a whole bunch of people and have them smiling at me, but I wanted to support Alicia. I wanted desperately to tell her that I was seeing Thomas tomorrow night, but I knew if I did she would talk about me like I had a tail. I didn't want to hear that. I didn't need to hear that. I did need to talk to someone though, so after work, I headed back to the 9705 Bar.

I walked into the bar and the first thing that came

to mind was my sexual tryst with Justin. My eyes instinctively looked toward the back room that looked like a closet. I looked across the bar and there was Adrienne stocking the shelves with liquor. As usual she was all smiles.

"Hey, girl, it's five-thirty. You getting your drink on kinda early, ain't ya?"

"Not too early, it seems." I sat on a nearby barstool and looked around at four other men and two women. "What about these other people?"

"Girl, these people are my regulars and all they asses are alcoholics." She laughed. "So what's up with you?"

"That man."

"What man?"

"The man I told you about before."

"The married man?"

"That would be the one."

We headed to the bar and she poured me a drink of E&J. This time, I sipped on it.

"So, what is it about you and this man that you just can't seem to shake him? Was the dick just that good?"

"I don't know if it was the dick, or because he is so fine, or just the fact that I want him to want me. All I know is the shit hurts and now he wants to be back in my life."

"As a lover, right?"

"Yeah, how did you know?"

"Because I see it all the time. That fool is looking to have his cake and eat it too. I can't believe he had the nerve to come at you like that."

"Well, he did."

"And what did you say? Other than welcoming him back?"

I gave a long pause and sipped my drink. "I told him that he could have Fridays."

"Okay, I can see that."

"You can?"

"Yeah, I can. I think every woman has been here before."

"So, Adrienne, what do you think I should do?"

"You know he's married and that nothing good can come of this. It's your call as to what you want to do."

"I want to leave him, but I don't think I have the strength to."

"Why do you think you lack the strength to leave him?"

"Because he's the most attractive man I've ever met and the only one to pay attention to me like that." I smiled. "And, the sex being good has a lot to do with it, too."

"That's good where it's got you considering being the other woman?"

"Yes, that good. The kind of sex that makes your toes curl good."

"Well, then, that means you only have one option."

"What's that?"

"You need to figure out a way to wean yourself off of him."

"Wean myself?"

Adrianne leaned in closer to me to make sure I understood what she meant. "Yeah, wean yourself. You see, the reason you can't let him go is because you're still hurting, you are down on yourself for being duped. You want him and you think that you will never get anyone as good-looking as him again. You're wrong about that shit, but until you see that, no amount of lecturing or fussing is going to get you to change. You need to see for yourself that this man may be fine on the outside, but on the inside he ain't shit. If anything, he needs to be chasing you and not you chasing him."

"So what do I do? How do I wean myself off of him?"

"By beating him at his own game."

"I don't understand."

"You will when I get back."

Adrienne stepped away from me at the bar and wait-ed on two other people. I sipped from my glass of E&J and couldn't wait for her to get back and continue. It felt good pouring my feelings out to someone, and Adrienne didn't seem like the type to judge me.

When she came back, she wiped the spot in front of her with a towel, and placed her elbows on top of the bar. "Now, as I was saying . . . you have a lot going on right now, don't you?"

"Yeah. I have a new job, I'm going to school, and I'm working out three times a week."

"How has that been working for you?" "Very well. I mean, look at me."

I stood up and turned around a few times so that Adrienne could get a look at me. I had dropped several pounds since she'd last seen me and it was very noticeable.

"Okay, I see . . . you're working it and it looks good on you. So you gave him Fridays, why?"

"That's my only day off."

"Fine, then. He wants to sleep with you, you want to sleep with him, he's good in bed . . . so I say go for it. Be the best woman you can be, enjoy your time with him, and keep doing what you're doing. Keep going to the gym, keep going to school, and keep bettering yourself."

"And then what?"

"Oh, you'll see. The more you take care of you and the better you feel about yourself, the more people will see you in that same light. Before you know it, men will be com-ing at you right and left; real men."

"And Thomas?"

"If my hunch is right, and I'm seldom wrong, he'll see you for the queen that you are."

"And you think he'll want to be with me?"

"I do. But by the same token, by the time he decides he wants to be with you, I'm betting money you won't want his trifling ass anymore."

"You think so?"

Adrienne slapped the towel against her hand and winked. "I'm willing to bet my mortgage on it." She leaned in close to me again. "Now, let me tell you how to play this."

Adrienne went on to tell me how to play Thomas. She also told me to keep my options open, continue doing what I was doing, and gave me pointers on how to dress. I thought the way I dressed was fine, but she apparently saw me in a totally different light. She suggested that I transition from JC Penney and Sears to shopping at New York & Company and Marshall Fields. I had a few drinks, a few laughs, and then went to the restroom.

When I came out, Justin Davis was sitting at the bar having drinks. The last time I'd seen him was that night I'd had a few drinks, and my back was against the downstairs wall as I gave him my goodies. Seeing him in the daytime while he was in a suit and while I was in a suit made me feel a little ashamed. At the same time, I felt a slight tingle between my legs. He looked up, and when he saw me he welcomed me with a smile and a huge hug.

"Hey, you. How are you?" he asked.

"I'm fine. How are you?"

"I'm blessed."

"Yes, you are," I said, smiling and taking a seat next to him.

"So what's up?"

"I don't know, you tell me."

"I just stopped in to have a drink. Why don't you stay for a while and have a few with me?"

"Only for a little while, okay?"

"That's cool."

I was expecting him to say something crazy like, "Do you want to fuck again?" but he didn't say anything crass like that. He was a gentleman, and for a short while, we sat at the bar and discussed politics, the war in Iraq, movies, and current events. He didn't bring up that night and neither did I. He also didn't bring up leaving flowers at my door which led me to believe they weren't from him.

"So . . . I called you the other day and you never returned my call," he said.

"Sorry, but I was busy."

"Well, I was calling to ask you out to the Al Jarreau concert next week, you game?"

I looked at Adrienne as if she were my agent or something.

"Girl, what the heck are you looking at me for? That man asked you a question," Adrienne said.

We laughed and I nodded with pleasure. "I think I can do that," I told Justin.

"Great. I'll call you with the details later."

He put money on the counter for our drinks, and after giving me a kiss on the cheek, he headed toward the door.

"Hey . . . um . . . Justin." I said nervously.

"Yeah, what's up?"

"Do you have time to, um—"

He put his hands in his pockets and smiled. "Finish that conversation we had earlier?"

"Yeah."

"When?"

"Now?" I smiled while looking at the closet door.

He looked at his watch. "How much time do you have?"

"How much time do you need?" I shot back.

"I think this next conversation is going to be a long one."

I flirted and sipped from my glass of E&J. "I hope so. But, how long do you think?"

"Hours. We'll have to go somewhere else."

"That's fine with me. I guess we should get started then, shouldn't we?"

I winked at Adrienne and headed toward the door.

"I'll follow you in my car," I whispered to him.

"No, I'll follow you."

"Okay."

"Girl, things are looking up already!" Adrienne laughed.

I left the bar and Justin followed me in his BMW 5 Series. We went back to my place, and this time, I didn't need brandy in me to do what needed to be done. I asked Justin to have a seat in the living room while I freshened up. He walked over to my stereo and started going through my CDs. He apparently didn't see anything there he liked and reached into his jacket pocket for a custom CD of his own. I changed out of my work clothes and slipped into something sexy. I heard "The Hush" by Maxwell blaring over the speakers as I changed into the delicate material and sprayed on some Vera Wang perfume.

I checked myself in the mirror and walked into the living area. I was surprised that Justin wasn't on the couch. I turned to my right and there he was with two glasses and Chardonnay in hand. I was a little put out that he raided my fridge, but glad to see he was creative. He stood in the dining area in nothing but boxer briefs and a smile. The Chardonnay was there for Thomas, but for the moment, I decided, fuck him, he could have Kool-Aid if he got thirsty.

"You want a drink?" Justin asked.

"Yeah, that'll be nice."

"Do you want anything else?"

"You know exactly what I want. Do I need to simplify it for you?"

"Oh! I see we've gotten over our shyness, huh?"

"I'm working on it."

"Okay. Well, my queen, how else might I serve you this evening?"

"I don't know, I think I'll leave that all up to you."

"Then, why don't you have a seat over there on the floor and let me take care of you."

If sitting on the floor was his way of serving me, then I was all for it. I did as he asked and he poured me a drink, lit one of the scented candles on the living room table, and sat behind me on the couch. "Purple Rain" by Prince played as I sipped my drink and Justin began to give me a nice slow shoulder and neck massage.

"You're tense," he said.

"It's been a hell of a week."

"You wanna talk about it?"

"What, are you a therapist or something?"

"I am."

"Really?"

"Yeah, so if something is on your mind, you can tell me about it . . . if you want. If not, it's no pressure."

"I think it would be awkward to talk to you."

"Why, because we fucked?"

"Maybe."

"Okay, then I won't pressure you to talk. If you want to, though, I'm a good listener."

He continued to massage my neck and shoulders. My eyes closed and I allowed myself to relax as I took in the guitar riffs by Prince and the electric touch of Justin's hands. Over and over again he began to knead my flesh, rubbing away the pain that was on the surface and getting to some of the pain that was going on inside. He rubbed my neck with his thumbs, gently rubbed my shoulder muscles, shoulders, and upper arms. He then moved my hair to the side and gently planted warm, wet kisses on my neck and the back of my shoulders. He reached in front of me and began to squeeze my breasts. My nipples were hard and pointing ahead of me like the unannounced erection of a pre-teen. I let out a sigh as he played with my nipples, fondled my breasts and continued to kiss the back of my neck.

"Angel" by Angela Winbush started playing, and as she sung I moved my head back and forth, allowing Justin to kiss more of my neck and shoulders. His kisses were so soft, so warm, and so very welcome.

I could feel his erection on my back. The more he kissed me on my neck and back, the harder his erection became. I leaned my head back and he reached around, cupping both breasts as we slowly tongue kissed and rocked back and forth to the music. We then stood up to dance while kissing each other intensely. We danced close, pelvis to pelvis. His hardness was calling to me and me to it, but Justin seemed to be in no rush to take me. He smiled and held me like I was his woman. And in that moment, I felt like his woman. He pecked me on the lips and moved my hair out of my face.

"You're beautiful, you know that?" he said.

I shyly looked down at the floor. "Do you really think so?"

He placed his finger underneath my chin and lifted it. "Yeah, I do."

"I'm glad someone thinks so."

He placed both hands on my ass and I wrapped my arms around his neck. I kissed him again and together our bodies rocked to the slow sounds of the music. I felt like I was in high school again, dancing in the foyer at Percy Julian High School. We danced for two or three songs before Justin asked me to find him some body lotion. I went in the back and got some lotion that Alicia got me for my birthday from the Bath & Body Works. I brought Justin the bottle and he held my hand.

"Let's go to your bedroom." We walked into my bedroom where I turned to face him. "Lay down and turn over on your stomach."

I did as he asked and he began to peel off the teddy I wore. I felt a little self-conscious laying there naked in front of him, but all my fear subsided as he poured lotion across my back, shoulders, and buttocks. I was in another place as Justin began to give me a light and sensual massage. He hands roamed down my spine, across my ribs, down to my ass, thighs and calves, exploring the entire backside of my body. His touch was strong and sensual all at once. He then went from a light massage to a deep tissue massage and I felt myself drifting, almost floating as I began to take a light nap.

I found myself dreaming about a sloe gin fizz on a rust-colored sand beach in Cabo San Lucas. I pictured that I was walking along the shore and everything in my life was right. The sun was setting, the sky was filled with orange, red, and yellow hues, there was a gentle breeze coming off the ocean, and as the waves washed over my body, I knew nothing but peace and serenity. I smiled in my sleep as I slowly began to awaken. Where there were once Justin's hands, now his lips were planting soft, sweet kisses across my backside. I felt his tongue run up my spine and plant soft kisses on the back of my neck. From there he began to kiss down my body and planted kisses all across my back. My body was so relaxed that I moaned in bliss as I felt myself almost float away. I purred like a kitten as he kissed the back of my calves, my thighs, my ass, and then . . . my special place.

"Oooohhhh," I purred.

"Shhhh," he said.

His tongue was long and warm. As he kissed my kitten, my legs opened up to him, inviting him to feast and to taste more of me. He obliged and the next thing I knew, my ass was hiked in the air and I was clenching the sheets as his tongue teased me, explored me, and penetrated me. My juices began to flow and I held firmly onto the sheets, almost ripping them as I began to come. I came so hard that I didn't realize how loud I had squealed while he licked me well past climax.

I tried to catch my breath after coming so hard. I released the sheets, and found myself grasping them again as he entered me from behind. Once again, he began to stretch my vaginal walls and I freely accepted him. He took one hand

and placed it on the back of my neck, and he used the other to hold me firmly by my waist. He took long and deliberate strokes over and over again.

"Damn, baby . . . you feel so good. You feel so good . . . you are so beautiful."

My eyes closed as I not only felt him deep inside of me, but I also felt his words. It might have been a lie. It might have been just the way that he got down, but this man . . . this man . . . made me feel good. I moaned a gracious moan as Justin began making passionate yet slow love to me. No doubt, our first time together we fucked. This night was something all together different. This night—I enjoyed every minute that he commanded my body. Tonight, Justin made me feel like a woman.

Thirty minutes into the session he picked up the pace. As he increased his pace, both of our heart rates increased. He placed my legs on his shoulders as he gave me all of him and I gave him all of me. He came for the first time and I came for the second time. We collapsed in each other's arms and then he held me. It was 7:00 P.M. when we had arrived at my apartment Thursday night. It was midnight when we finished making love for the third time and definitely a night to remember.

In the morning, I smelled breakfast cooking. Justin had spent the night in my bed, holding me in his arms. I got up and headed to where he was.

"Hey, you," he smiled while placing a sausage patty on a plate.

"Good morning," I said, unsure of what else to say or do because it had been years since a man other than Thomas had spent the night at my place.

Justin poured some orange juice in a glass, and my eyes searched the neatly decorated table with delicious-looking breakfast food served on one plate. "As you can see, I made you breakfast." He pulled back the chair for me. "Have a seat."

"Thank you," I said. "Everything looks and smells delicious."

"It will be delicious." He looked at his watch. "I already showered. I'm headed to work in a minute at the radio station to promote my new books. I'm then headed to Waldenbooks in Calumet City to do a book signing. I would've showered with you this morning and woke you up, but you looked like you were sleeping peacefully. So, do I need to ask how you slept?"

"No, I slept well," I joked.

"Well, I have to get out of here. Here's your plate, I hope you like the food. In the meantime, I have to figure out what I'm going to tell my girlfriend. When I woke up this morning, I had ten messages on my phone."

His girlfriend? That was a reality check. I knew he had a woman, but got caught up in the moment. Yet and still I made a mistake by reading more into last night than what it was. He was sensual, romantic, and attentive. The dick was good and the foreplay was phenomenal. But somehow, I had gotten things twisted and thought last night was special, whereas Justin obviously thought of it as just sex. It was good sex. It was great sex. The thing I needed to keep telling myself is what some men want us to know: *it was just sex.* I was disappointed, not with Justin, but with myself. Once again, I was number two and was the stand-in, part-time lover. Worse than that, I willingly walked into this situation.

I let out a heavy sigh. "Hey, Justin, listen. I don't want you to take this the wrong way, but last night was a mistake."

"Why do you say that?"

"Because you have a woman and I don't feel right about you being here. We . . . we can see each other anymore."

"Okay."

"Is that all you have to say?"

"What else do you want me to say?"

"I don't know . . . something else."

He removed his jacket from the chair. "I'm sorry you feel that way, Tiffany. I respect your decision. If you should change your mind, give me a call. You take care."

He kissed me on the cheek and made his way to the door. When he opened it, there was Thomas standing in the doorway. I was blown away because it was 6:30 in the morning and Thomas was the last person in the world I expected to see. He and Justin looked each other in the eye and Justin extended his hand.

"What's up, player?" he said.

"My First Love" by Rene and Angela was playing on the stereo.

"Hey, um . . . man . . . what's up?" Thomas shook his hand with a bewildered look on his face. Justin gave him the head nod and headed down the hall. I was in my robe, and for whatever reason, I felt naked and immediately covered up. It was obvious what had happened and I wasn't going to deny it. Thomas stepped in and looked at me almost as if demanding an explanation.

"Was that . . . Justin Davis?" he asked.

"Yeah. What are you doing here? You're not supposed to be here until tonight," I said as I began to eat the food that Justin prepared.

"I . . . um . . . came to see you before you went to work. You know, to say hi."

"At 6:30 in the morning?"

"I didn't think the time mattered."

"Well, as you can see, it does. I don't do unannounced visits. Don't come over here unless you call first or I'm expecting you."

"You were expecting me."

"Not until tonight."

Thomas sighed and looked at the closed door. "What was Justin Davis doing here and why aren't you dressed?"

I laid my fork next to my plate and wiped my mouth with a napkin. "I'm sorry, who are you talking to?"

I didn't know where it came from, but I felt more and more confident. I didn't know if it was because I had some great sex last night or because of the reality check Justin left me with this morning. In either case, I wasn't feeling Thomas this morning, nor was I about to be questioned in my house by a married man. I was now feeling more in control and completely understanding Adrienne's point about weaning myself off Thomas. I wasn't over him, but getting over him wasn't going to take as long as I had thought. Thomas had some good dick, but so did Justin. I knew now that I could get good dick whenever I wanted. In fact, I planned to use Justin as my ICE contact (in case of emergency). Meanwhile, I was on a new quest, looking for good dick with a single, unattached man who wanted to be with me. Until I met this fictional character, Thomas would have to do—with a few rules attached.

Thomas's voice rose and he sternly spoke. "I want to know why Justin Davis was over here."

"Thomas, what you *want* is irrelevant."

"If I'm correct, he has a girlfriend. I think she's a model or something. Her name is Rachel."

"So?"

"So, he's attached."

"I knew that."

"You knew that?"

"Yeah. Being with men who have women seems to be the 'in' thing these days."

He shut up for a second and finally took a seat at the table with me. "This . . . this thing with you and him, how serious is it?"

"Why?"

"Because I want to know."

"How serious is your marriage?"

Again silence.

"Tiffany, all I am saying is . . ."

"All you're saying is nothing. I told you that you can have Friday nights and that was all. You have no right to question me, judge me or to bring your married ass here unannounced. Now, if you can't handle a little competition then perhaps you need to go home to Wifey."

"Wifey? Tiff, when did you start talking like this? When did you start acting like this?"

"When you broke my MF heart, that's when."

"Are you doing this to get back at me?"

"Back at you? Please. You give yourself too much credit. You might be the reason that some of this foolishness kicked off, but I'm a grown woman. Any decision that I make is mine to make. That includes messin' with Justin Davis, messin' with a white man, or even messin' with you!"

"A white man? What the hell is up with that? Who said anything about a white man? Are you going to start going outside of your race?"

"Don't go there! Please, don't go there! If I did decide to run into the arms of a white man it would be because a *black man* pushed me into his arms!"

The only reason I said anything like that was because meeting up with one of Matthew's friends tomorrow was on my mind. Initially, I was against the idea, but every time I heard how happy Alicia was, that softened my stance on interracial dating considerably. I've heard nothing but positive things from the sisters I know who've crossed the race line. Many have found love, others have found peace. *If nothing else, I might just find financial security.* I hated to sell out brothers like that but it appeared that if you're heavy, didn't look a certain way, and weren't sucking them, fucking them, and feeding both their bellies and their egos, brothers would trade you in for Barbie in a damned heartbeat.

"Look, just because your friend is dating a white man doesn't mean you have to."

"Really? What should I do then, date your married, lying—"

"I'm just sayin'."

"I'm not tryin' to hear what you're saying."

I got back to eating my food, and when I finished, I turned up the music playing on the stereo and went into the shower. I smiled as I stepped into the water and thought Thomas's jealousy was cute. By the same token, I felt bad about sleeping with Justin earlier and would most likely sleep with Thomas later on. I felt like such a whore. Then it dawned on me that men do this type of shit all the time. I washed Justin's scent off my body and with that scent went away my guilt.

I dressed in the bathroom and put on my makeup. Afterward, I walked back into my bedroom and looked for a pair of shoes to wear. I went into the living room to see if Thomas was still there, and sure enough, he was looking at a photo of him and me together that was on top of my TV. I watched as he observed the photo. If I didn't know any better I would say that he was reminiscing. I had forgotten the photo was even there. *Note to self; remove anything that reminds me of him from plain sight.*

Chapter Twenty-three—Thomas

What the hell was Justin Davis doing there? I couldn't believe that Tiffany had another man in there. Had she replaced me already? I had to admit, I was hurt seeing someone else there. I know I didn't have any right to say anything, but when I saw him leave her apartment, I can't lie, I wanted to take a swing at him. I couldn't believe how casually she'd dismissed me. She acted like having another man there meant nothing to her. Could she have changed that much in such a short time? Was I at fault for that?

She went to shower, and as she did, I walked around her apartment. I peeked in her bedroom and the sheets were all over the place. It was obvious what had taken place last night. I looked at the counter and there were two plates with breakfast food on them. I figured he'd spent the night, and I wondered how close they were. Full of jealousy, I walked back to the living room and made note of the music that played. It was all slow music and quite the selection. I was sure the music had set the mood. I couldn't tell, but I would have almost said that this relationship was serious. I never would've imagined Tiffany getting so serious with another man this quickly after our breakup.

With my stomach in knots, I looked at a bookshelf that still had a picture of the two of us in a frame. We took the picture at one of those photo shops that has photos ready in an hour. I held the photo in my hand and looked at our expressions in the picture. We looked happy. We also looked good together. I had pictures of my wife and me and we didn't look as happy as Tiffany and I once did.

The reason that I had come over so early was because Meagan and I were up all night arguing. I came home last night and there was an interior decorator sitting in the kitchen telling her about all the things he wanted to do with our house. I'd had a long-ass day at work, and without asking her what he was doing there, I simply told the man to get the fuck out of my house. I told Meagan that we were not spending another damn dime without the consent of both of us. Even then, we weren't buying anything else unless she was working a job full-time with benefits. That enraged her but I didn't give a damn. I hadn't been married six months yet, and was already more miserable than I'd ever been in my whole life. I was broke, stressed the hell out, I had no money in my savings, and nothing to show for my marriage; nothing—but debt. She called me a weak-ass man. She told me to quit whining about money. She had me so pissed off, that again, I was *this close* to smacking her ass á la Ike Turner style. Well into the night we argued about money. Not only did we argue about money, we argued about the fact that her father never liked me, who she could've married, and what her other suitors did for a living.

There was a quarterback for a pro team who was interested in her, a few pro basketball players, CEOs of big companies, and the occasional celebrity or two. I told Meagan if she was that fucking miserable with me, perhaps she needed to move on. She actually had the nerve to tell me that I should be grateful she married me, and if anything, I needed to compete with the other men who were interested in her.

When she said that shit, it was 5:00 in the morning. I hadn't slept a wink. I had jumped in the shower, jumped in my car, and headed out of the house. I was glad that we'd had that argument; it made me feel less guilty about hooking up with Tiffany again. I headed toward Tiffany's house, thinking that I might be able to get some. You know, start both of our days off right. It appeared that while I was up arguing all night, she was getting her freak on—with someone else.

She walked out of the shower dressed for work but without shoes. I still had the photo of us in my hand.

"So, I see that you've moved on," I said scornfully.

"Did you come over here to argue with me?"

"No, actually, I came over here to start our day together early."

"You mean that you came for sex."

"Not just sex. I wanted to see you. But, yeah, I was hoping we could maybe get with each other. But I see you've had your fill already. Tell me, was he good?" I said sarcastically.

She put her hand on her hip and gave me a look that said, *No, he didn't!*

"Since you asked, he met and exceeded all my expectations!"

That hurt. "What is that supposed to mean?"

"It means I'm not sure you can follow what happened last night."

That hurt even more.

I put the picture back on the shelf. My forehead was lined with wrinkles. At this point, I was frustrated. Tiffany had pushed my buttons. "What the fuck has gotten into you?"

"I'm just tired, that's all."

"Tired?"

She pointed her finger at me and spoke as if she meant every word she said. "That's right, tired. I'm tired of men disrespecting me, tired of men who don't want to grow the fuck up and tired of men who don't know what they want out of a woman, or life, for that matter."

I pointed to myself. "You mean me? I know exactly what I want."

"Yeah, right. I'm tired of the bullshit, Thomas. I'm tired of the games men like you want to play, so I've decided to play too. The other day, you made it clear that this is about sex and you having what you want, when you want it. You made it clear that what I want is of no consequence to you. You made it clear that I'm good enough to fuck . . . but not good enough to be your woman. So, you came over here to get some ass this morning, well, I don't have time this morning. To be honest with you, I'm feeling quite satisfied right now. But if you want to still come over tonight, you can. I'll see you then. Meanwhile, you need to leave. I'm on my way to work."

Quite satisfied? What kind of shit is that to say to a man? Who does she think she is? Okay, so I get that she's upset, maybe she has a right to be. By the same token, shouldn't she be happy that I am more focused on her now? I mean, come on, let's keep it real. Tiffany is cute, but she's no runway model. I expected her to be happy to see me. I expected her to try to go all out to win me back. I expected her . . . to now play the role of the dutiful mistress. Maybe it's just her anger talking. Maybe she just needs more time to adjust to all this.

No doubt, my feelings were bruised, but I wasn't up to arguing with Tiffany this morning. I needed to switch gears a little; I needed to know where the hell she had been.

"I . . . I asked Matthew where you were he simply said that you didn't work there anymore. Where are you working now? You didn't quit because of me, did you?"

"Don't worry about where I work. Don't worry about how I live my life. All you need to worry about is whether or not I'm available for you on Friday nights."

She grabbed her purse and slid on her shoes. I had to admit, she looked good as hell. She switched to the door and motioned for me to walk out. I couldn't believe how cold she was being. She walked out to her parking space, and to my surprise, the Cadillac that was in her space was her car, not Justin's. It seemed as if she was making major changes in her life, and I wondered how these changes were going to affect me.

Chapter Twenty-four—Tiffany

The training sessions were getting easier and easier. All day long I thought about how good I felt, as well as how interesting it was that the prospect of having someone else made Thomas jealous. I couldn't believe he had the nerve to ask me questions knowing damned well he was married. When I saw how jealous he was, there was shift of power in our situation. I was now the one who was more in control, whereas he was, simply, about to become the sex in my life. I thought about seeing Justin again but decided against it. I didn't want to see numerous men. I only wanted to sex one man until the right man came along. Both men were dynamic in bed, but Thomas was the one who had jaded me. I guess that old saying about "the devil you don't know is worse than the devil you do know" was true.

All day long in training I took notes. I paid attention to what was being said and I knew midway into the day that doing the job would be easy. Managing people would be the problem. Not with me, but just dealing with other people's bullshit was going to be the main reason that we got the salaries we deserved. While I took my notes, I found myself wondering how I would play things with Thomas that evening. After much thought and deliberation, I decided that although I was still hurting on the surface, on the inside I was actually beginning to heal. What I decided to do was treat Thomas as if he had never hurt me at all. I would treat sleeping with him the same way that Justin treated me, as if it were just sex.

I got off work and headed to the gym. I got my workout on in step aerobics and grabbed a salad and water to go. Following my normal routine when I got home, I showered, changed into my silk robe, and poured myself a drink. By the time I started my homework, the doorbell rang. I buzzed Thomas in and quickly got back to doing my homework. Thomas peeked in the door as if he were a criminal looking for the cops.

"Can I come in?" he asked.

"That's why the door is open."

"Usually, you greet me at the door with a kiss."

"A lot has changed since then."

He came inside and closed the door. "Is this going to be a problem? I mean, do you have an attitude? If so, I can leave."

"I don't have an attitude. My door is open. You can stay or you can leave. Whatever you do is up to you."

I never looked up. We had this whole conversation as I studied my econ book. He placed his coat on the back of a dining room chair and sat next to me on the couch.

"What are you doing?"

"Reading."

"Yeah, I can see that. What are you reading?"

I held the book up for him to see and went back to reading.

"You're doing homework?"

"You sound surprised."

"I am. When did you start going back to school?"

"A while ago."

"What are you majoring in?"

"Business."

"What do you plan to do with a business degree?"

"I don't know, I guess I'll join the circus."

"You sure you don't have an attitude?"

"Maybe so. But only because you're asking me a lot of dumb questions. I'm going to apply the business degree to my job."

"That sounds like a plan, but I thought we were hanging out today."

"We are. I just want to finish up this last chapter."

"Is that going to take long?"

"It will, as long as you keep interrupting me."

Thomas leaned back on the couch and placed both of his hands behind his head. "You know, you've become quite cynical lately."

"Really," I said sarcastically. "I wonder why?"

"And you are sure you don't have an attitude?"

This time I snapped. "I will if you ask me that shit again."

He backed off. I finished the chapter and put the book away. I grabbed a few DVDs to watch: *The Wedding Crashers, Two for the Money, and Mr. & Mrs. Smith.* After popping some popcorn, I sat next to Thomas and watched the first movie.

"Is there anything here to drink?" he asked.

I pointed to the kitchen without looking his way. "Check the fridge."

Thomas huffed. "What?" I said, now looking at him. "Oh, you thought I was going to get up and serve you, huh? Naw, player, those days are done. Get up and handle that. You ain't my man, and I don't consider you a guest, either."

Thomas looked at me with a bit of fury in his eyes. That made me think. I got the impression that the reason I got messed over by this man was because I was too nice to him and gave him his way. Now that things were even, he was the one with the issue and I could take it or leave it (his attitude, that is). I was curious how things would be when we had sex. I was wondering if he would have the same power over me that he had had before.

We watched the first movie and then decided that the other two were too long to watch. After all, one of us was on the clock. We then watched *Comic View* on BET and started laughing our asses off. After that, I played some new CDs that I had bought, Anthony Hamilton, Mary J. Blige, and Jamie Foxx. We tripped hard on the song by Jamie called "Extravaganza." We talked about the job, but I didn't tell him about my training program, my promotion, or what I was doing with my life. All of that was none of his business. We talked about things that we were familiar with. I didn't ask him about his wife or what was going on between them. That wasn't my business. About 10:00 P.M. was when he made his move. He leaned back on the couch and wiggled around to get comfortable. "So, can I get some special attention?" he asked, and placed his hands behind his head again.

I knew that was code for a blowjob. Inside I laughed at him, but on the outside I slightly tooted my lips.

"Maybe later, but you can give me some special attention."

That threw him off, but I was now flipping the script. He smiled at me and then leaned over to kiss me. At first, I was a bit repulsed by him. I had to force myself to kiss him and clear my mind of him being a married man; the same married man who had played me and broken my heart. Instead, I stayed focused and allowed our kiss to continue. I loved the way his lips felt, and when they lowered to my neck, I dropped my head back. He undid my robe and started licking my breasts. From there, he went down my midsection and straight to the place between my legs. I tapped him on the head to speak to him just as he was about to devour me.

"Where is the fire?" I said, looking down at him. From between my legs he looked up and spoke.

"I'm pressed for time," he said.

"I'm not," I said without a smile.

With that being said, he took his time and pleased me orally. I made damn sure that I didn't allow myself to come for at least a half hour. When I did let loose, though, I came hard. He got up, sat on the couch, and waited for me to reciprocate. I went into my bedroom and came back with a flavored condom. I passed it to him and he looked at me with a raised brow.

"What is this?"

"What does it look like?"

"It's a flavored condom."

"You want some head, right?"

"Well, yeah."

"Okay, then put on the condom."

"We never used these before."

"In case you haven't noticed, Thomas, things have changed. I don't know where your dick has been."

"I just ate you out without any dental dam or anything.

"I know where my pussy has been."

"I don't."

"Well, I guess that's the chance you take when you sleep with someone for more than eleven months. Come on now, you're wasting time. You want some head or not?"

"It doesn't feel the same with this damned balloon on my dick."

"Take it or leave it. Wifey will be looking for you soon."

That snapped him back to reality. He tore open the package and I smiled at the control I now had over him. Yeah, I was classified as the mistress right now, but he was the one putting his whole life and career at stake.

He slowly rolled the condom back and I knelt between his legs. I massaged his manhood, then licked up and down the shaft. I deep throated him a few times while taking in the strawberry flavor that was on the condom. Over and over again, I deep-throated him, jacked him off, and massaged his balls. Pretty soon the room was filled with nothing but my slurping sounds and his moans. Moans that inspired me to go faster and faster, and caused me to moan myself as if I were getting something out of it. The next thing I knew, Thomas was coming, condom on and all. I kept sucking him past climax, which was driving him crazy. He tried to get away from me and I held on more firmly to his dick as if I were trying to get every drop that came out of him. His moaning went to screaming and eventually screaming went to squealing and begging.

"No more, no more . . . no more," he whimpered.

"Not bad for head with a condom on, huh?"

"No, not bad at all." He grinned.

"You want some ass now, or are you spent?"

He took several deep breaths. "I'm spent."

I didn't believe that he was spent, but again he was on the clock.

I stood and swiped my hands together. "Then, I'll see you next week."

"Next week?"

"Yes, next Friday."

"Can I call you before then?"

"I wish you wouldn't, at least not until Thursday."

Again, he hit me with a bewildered look that I was starting to see quite often. He got up, got dressed, and looking as if he'd lost his dog, he headed to the door.

"Next week I want to go skating," I said. He stopped in his tracks and turned to me.

"Skating?"

"Yeah, skating. I want to go out on dates. Tonight was cool, but you aren't going to be coming over here just to get your roll on. You need to treat me like a woman. That means dates. I think that is the least you can do." I went over to my bag and pulled out an itinerary that I had written at work. "Here."

"What's this?" he asked while looking at it.

"Things that I want to do on Friday nights for the rest of this year and part of next year."

"I can't guarantee you that I can get away every single Friday night."

"Remember, you aren't the only one with the list. If you can't make it, I need to know the day before or else it will be two weeks before you see me again."

"What do you mean I'm not the only one with the list?"

I lied. He was the only one with the list but he didn't need to know that. He needed to know that I had options.

"If you don't take me out, someone else will. That's all that I'm saying."

Thomas placed the list in his pocket. "Tiffany, you've changed so much. It's like I don't know you anymore."

"Yeah, well, apparently I *never knew you*."

"Are the shots ever going to stop?"

"I don't know, we'll see now, won't we?"

Thomas looked at his coat and there was a buzzing noise coming from it. As he took a glance at his watch, he looked at me with guilt. We both knew it was Wifey wondering where he was.

I looked away as if I didn't give a damn, although it was tearing me up on the inside.

"We'll go skating next week."

"Can't wait. See you then."

I opened the door and let him out. I didn't cry when he left, but I did feel hurt. I opened my books and went back to doing my homework. Soon, I started wondering how long this would last between us, or if being with him was still worth my time.

Chapter Twenty-five—Tiffany

The next morning I got up and went to the gym to walk two miles on the treadmill. From there I had a light breakfast at home and then got dressed in a pair of pumps, jeans that accentuated my curvier ass, and a sweatshirt. I tied my hair in a ponytail, and as I looked at myself in the mirror, I was proud of all the hard work I'd done. My body was shaping up nicely. So far, I had lost about fifteen pounds. It may not have been much, but it's a damned good start. My clothes fit better and there were even a few pieces that had been in my closet that I absolutely refused to throw away, that I could get into now.

I also bought a few new things. I knew I still had a long way to go, and perhaps I should have put off shopping until I got to my ideal weight, but in the meantime I needed to reward myself for my progress. I'd been reading a lot of magazines as well as watching programming tailored to more full-figured women. This helped me with my new wardrobe and the new me. I gave myself a makeover, and my new wardrobe suited me well.

With the slow and subtle changes, I found myself smiling more. For whatever reason, when I smiled, people tended to notice me more and that alone made me feel more attractive. I'd been watching new fashion trends, asking sales women whose styles I admire for fashion advice, and I went to stores like M·A·C® and Ulta® for free makeovers to learn how to mimic certain makeup styles myself.

I never put my hair in a ponytail anymore. I either went to the salon and got it done or maintained it myself to the best of my ability until my next appointment. I used to shy away from certain designers because their clothes never seemed to fit me, whereas now I was just trying on a bigger size for that designer; only now I wasn't ashamed to pick up a bigger size. If I liked the style, I brought the style, no matter what the size tag said.

Because I'm top heavy, I made sure to wear something that complimented my bust, rather than hid it. I have nice full breasts and I have come to believe that there is nothing wrong with giving "the twins" a little air every now to then and show them off.

I wear heels now which make my legs look longer, I wear colors that better compliment my complexion, and I am completely done with stripes which tend to make me look wider, and totally done with floral prints that used to make my behind look like a small couch. I know a lot of girls my size who are confident and believe that they can wear any and everything, but I'm of the impression that everything is not for everybody.

I got in my car and headed to Matthew's house in order to attend this affair he was throwing for Alicia. During our previous phone conversation, she told me Matt had mentioned hooking me up with someone. She didn't say who, but she did say that Matt had some very nice and intriguing friends. At first, I was apprehensive about meeting someone white, but after seeing how happy Alicia and Matt were, I began to soften my stance.

I drove to Matt's suburban home in Countryside, Illinois. I was in awe of the six-bedroom, three-full bath house with a three-car garage. There were a bunch of people out front eating, talking, and having a great time. It was late October in Chicago and cookouts at this time weren't rare. It depended primarily on how the weather wanted to act. I walked around back where people were playing simulated golf, cooking, talking business, eating, and listening to music. Inside, there were professional men of all races watching ESPN on Matt's plasma screen, while others sat at the dining room table discussing everything from the Chicago Bears' recent loss, to how the White Sox will do this year, to the stock market. I walked around the vast house looking for Alicia. Minutes later, she found me and tapped my shoulder.

"Hey, girl, how are you?" Alicia said, giving me a hug.

"I'm okay."

"How's the training session going?"

"It's going okay."

"It's going better than okay," another voice interrupted. I turned around and it was Matt. He handed Alicia and me two glasses of wine.

"Matt, hi. I didn't see you there."

"Hello, Tiffany. I've heard nothing but wonderful things about you in the training program. I hear they're going to permanently assign you to treasury."

This was news to me so I was excited. "Really?"

"Yes," Matt said.

"Looks like things are starting to look up for you," Alicia said.

"Well, it's about time." I laughed. We clinked our glasses and sipped the wine.

"Oh, before I forget, Tiffany, there's someone here I want you to meet."

Matt looked behind me, and without warning, I turned around to see who he was looking at.

"Tiffany, this is William Alexander."

I expected that Matt would introduce me to a white man. Instead, there stood a brother about six feet tall with dark black twists, bedroom eyes, a goatee, and a million-dollar smile. He was light caramel in complexion and had a huge chest, chiseled arms, and a nice bulge between his legs (yeah, I looked!).

"Hello, how are you? I've heard nothing but positive things about you from Matthew."

"I'm fine, thanks for asking." I looked at Matt with astonishment, as he had definitely gotten it right.

"After so many good things being said about you, I couldn't wait to meet you. Now that I've seen you, I'm sorry but I must have a few more minutes of your time so I can get to know you."

"What are you sorry about?"

"Monopolizing *all* your time."

He extended his arm and I took it with a wide smile on my face. I looked over my shoulder and waved good-bye to Matt and Alicia. They hugged each other and were pleased by the connection William and I had instantly made.

"So, where are we headed?" I asked him.

"To the bar."

"What if I don't want to drink? What if I'm hungry?"

"Then we'll eat. I'm up for whatever you want."

"Whatever I want may not be here on the menu." I covered my mouth. "Oops, that didn't come out the right way. What I meant was, they may not have what I want to eat here. I can be a picky eater."

"Then we'll leave and get you whatever your heart desires."

"Careful now, my heart desires a lot."

"Whatever it does, I'm sure I can handle it."

Arm in arm, we headed outside. I spotted Alicia talking to some other people, and when she saw me, she mouthed the words, "He's fine." I nodded. She then mouthed, "You lucky MF," and I shrugged. We smiled at each other and my attention went back to William.

"Is there a bartender in the backyard?" I asked.

He looked around, but didn't see one. So for now, we took a seat on two lawn chairs. "I'm sure there is because my boy Matt knows how to throw a party. He's the best. How did he end up with your friend?"

"He didn't tell you?"

"Nope, we never talked about how they hooked up. All he said was that he had an equally fine sister for me."

"Matthew said that?"

"Yep, he said that you were a good woman who was going places. He said you had a good head on your shoulders, a nice body, and a great smile."

I smiled and made a mental note to thank Matt later. "Okay, you've expressed how Matt feels, but tell me what you honestly think and don't hold anything back."

He chuckled and bit down on his bottom lip. "I'll answer that once you stand up, turn around, and let me see what I'm working with. I think I already know, but I just want to be sure."

Being playful with him, I turned in several circles for him. My body was coming along well so I felt confident and proud of it.

I put my hand on my hip. "Well, what do you think?"

He nodded and looked pleased. "I like what I see. I'm good. It's obvious that you work out. I might have to get back into the gym myself."

"Where do you need to lose weight?" I said, astonished because William was well built.

He patted his stomach. "I could stand to lose a few."

"You look like you're packaged pretty well to me."

"Trust me, it all looks different outside of clothes."

"Ain't that the truth?"

"So, what do you want to eat? Would you like to go somewhere else?"

"Naw, I was kidding about that."

"Well, I'm not. If you could have anything in the world to eat now, what would it be?"

I started to say, *Your fine ass on my bed— I will eat you up!* "I wouldn't mind a good steak."

"Okay, then steak it is."

Just like that, and after we said good-bye to Alicia and Matt, we left the party.

"You don't mind taking off with a complete stranger, do you?" Will said, opening the car door for me.

"My best friend is a cop. I'm not worried about you."

"You sure? You never know about people these days."

"I have a feeling I'm in very good hands."

"Thanks for your confidence and you are."

"Besides, I never leave home without a stun gun in my purse."

"Good to know." He laughed.

We went to Lawry's Steakhouse in downtown Chicago. I had a filet mignon with baked potato and asparagus and Will had the same. We talked about my training program, my desire to get in better shape, and our love for sports. I talked about all my favorite movies, people in history I would like to meet, how I would live my life differently, if given the chance to do things differently, and my favorite places to shop. William shared with me how much we had in common. He was two years older than me, but he went to Percy Julian High School in Chicago just as I did. He went to U of C for college and did graduate school at Northwestern. I asked him what he did for a living and he said that he was a V.P. like Matthew. I figured he wasn't doing as well as Matt because he drove a Hyundai. It was a nice Hyundai, and was fully loaded. I just expected that a V.P. would be driving something a little more on the high end.

After we left the restaurant, we went to a movie, then to the Field Museum for a jazz session that was going on at the promenade. The jazz session concluded, then we went for a long brisk walk downtown along beautiful Michigan Avenue.

Will told me that he was raised by his mother and stepfather. He never knew his biological father. He had a half brother who was an attorney, a half sister who was a chief financial officer in a large corporation, and an adopted younger sister named Stephanie who was mildly retarded. He explained that with the exception of Stephanie, all of his siblings had gone to college. They never knew how they were going to do it, but they each knew that their mother and stepfather would find a way.

Will was the oldest. When he finished college, he helped his mother and stepdad out. As his brother and sister got older, they helped out as well. Stephanie, from what he said, was spoiled to death because everyone helped with her. Just from what he said, I could tell that Will was a good man. He glowed when he spoke of the love that he had for his mother and I knew that he had a great deal of respect for his stepfather, just in the way he talked about him.

William explained to me that although he never knew his father, he didn't miss not having him in his life because of the man that his stepfather was. His stepfather taught him how to pursue realistic dreams and not set himself up for failure. His mother taught him how to treat and respect women. They were both old school and they made good partners when it came to teaching William how to be a man. I asked him a million questions that night. I asked him how he felt about kids and he said that he wanted at least four. I shied away slightly at that because I never really thought much about kids. I always knew that I wanted at least one, but after raising my brother, that desire had faded some.

We talked about AIDS, sex, using contraception, and what he would be doing if he weren't working at the bank. I asked him how he felt about interracial dating and every topic that I could think about. William didn't shy away from anything I wanted to know and it was as if we'd known each other forever. I could see that he was handsome, but he was also articulate and seemed to really know what he wanted out of life. I enjoyed his company immensely and never wanted the night to end.

Before I knew it, it was time to say good night. My car

was still at Matthew's so William drove me back there. When I got back to my car, he gave me a peck on the cheek and told me to have a good night.

"Can I call you sometime?" he asked.

"You may," I said, smiling. I gave him a copy of my new business card and told him how much I enjoyed his company and looked forward to seeing him again.

I walked toward my car, thinking about the great time I had had tonight. I turned around before William pulled off and waved for him to stop.

"William . . . what are you doing tomorrow?"

"I'm going to church in the morning, to the gym, and after that I have to make a stop at my parents' house. What did you have in mind?"

"I'd like to see you again. I mean, tomorrow if you aren't busy."

"Do you want to go to church with me tomorrow?"

I did, but I was going to my church tomorrow, I would invite him there, but I wasn't ready for all that yet.

"I'll have to pass on church, but I'd be more than happy to go to the gym with you."

"I think that'll be great. I'll call you for directions to your place."

"Okay."

"Tiffany?"

"Yeah?"

"I really had a good time with you tonight too."

"Thank you. Maybe next time you'll let me pick up the tab for dinner?"

"Never," he said, smiling. "Take care."

"One more thing," I said. "Do you go to bed early? I mean, is there a bad time to call you on your cell phone?"

He started laughing.

"What are you laughing at?" I asked.

"Tiffany, look at the card I gave you. You have my

home number, my cell, and my office number. You can call me anytime. I'm not married, not playing games, and you can call me anytime."

I couldn't stop blushing and silently thanked God for moving me in the right direction. William winked and drove off. I sat in my car for a while thinking about him. He may not have been rich, but from what I saw, he had a lot of potential. He was fine; fuck that, I mean "Foine," and seemed to know how to treat a woman. Just as I was getting more excited about the potential of me and William, my cell phone rang.

"Hey, girl, you're getting back pretty late."

"Alicia? How the hell did you know my date was over?"

"Look at the window."

I looked over at Matt's house and in the window was Alicia. It was obvious that she was spending the night at Matt's house. I continued to talk to her on the phone.

"Where's your car?"

"In the garage."

"So you're spending the night over I take it?"

"Every other night until I get tired of it."

"Is the lovin' that good?"

"If it wasn't, I wouldn't be here."

"Okay. So Eminem has some serious skills."

"Hey, lay off that Eminem shit, he just hooked you up with a damn good brother."

"Speaking of which, what do you know about him?"

"Come in for a few and I'll tell you."

I cut the engine off and headed into Matt's house. I didn't get to see too much of it when I had been there earlier, but it looked even nicer without all the people, and clean. I walked into the kitchen where Alicia made us coffee. She was in a pajama top with no bottoms. Her hair was all over the place and it was obvious they'd just finished doing the dirty deed.

She poured us a cup of java and started blowing on hers to cool it off.

"So, how did your date go?" she asked.

"It was great. He took me to lunch downtown, then a movie, and a long romantic walk. We also listened to some jazz at the museum. He's a family man, treats his mother right and even goes to church. Is he the missing link or what?" I said, laughing.

"Yeah, he is. He's not without his demons though."

"Aw shit, I bet the other shoe is about to drop. Is he gay, bi, or used to be in jail?"

Alicia started laughing. "No, nothing like that. But, according to Matt, he used to be a player back in the day."

"For real? He doesn't seem like the type."

"From what Matt told me, he was. Not just any type of player either. For a while he was on some Bruce Wayne type of shit."

"That bad, huh?"

"Worse."

"So, why should I think that he's a reformed man now?"

"Life has been kicking his ass, God has been talking to him, and his last girlfriend tried to cut his ass in half."

"Girl, stop playing."

"I'm serious. I'll know the day you all sleep together because you're going to call me."

"Call you? Why?"

"He's self-conscious about something, and I have a feeling when you see it, you're going to want to tell me about it."

"What happened? Did she cut off his dick and it doesn't work anymore?"

Alicia almost spit out her coffee. "No, but she did cut his ass like I said—almost in half."

"How?"

"I can't say. I promised Matt that I would let William tell you his side of the story."

"Girl, fuck that . . . spill it."

Alicia leaned in and whispered to me. "About four years ago, he was living with his last girlfriend and she was supposed to be at work. She got sick and came home one day and heard him in the bedroom with another woman. From what Matthew told me, she crept back downstairs, grabbed a fucking samurai sword from over the fireplace, and went into the bedroom swinging."

"Girl, get the hell outta here. You're lying, right?"

"Nope. His ex cut the woman he was messing around with across her midsection and fucked her up really bad. He tried to subdue her, and she cut his ass like a goddamn filet. She got him from his right shoulder blade across his body to his left hip. Matthew says that the scar looks like the way you cut sandwiches diagonally for grilled cheese."

"That's what he meant when she said that he looks different outside of his clothes."

"Yeah, well, anyway, his ex is still in jail. He paid for her legal defense. He didn't press charges because he knew his shit was out of order. The woman he was with though pressed charges. She can't have kids and has gastrointestinal problems as a result of her injuries."

"Damn!"

"Yeah, well, William still sees his ex in jail. He visits her monthly, apologizing for his behavior. She's doing twenty years downstate, but he's working on getting her sentence reduced. He's paid for her first appeal."

"So what makes you think that I want to be with him now?"

"He fucked up. But trust me when I say that he has learned his lesson. I don't think cheating is ever going to cross his mind again. And like you said, he's a good man."

"Good man or not, I don't think I can deal with someone with drama like that."

"That was years ago. Besides, his ex was the one
snapped. William was just caught being a man."

"Yeah, well, I'm going to have to sleep on that shit."

"So when are you seeing him again?"

"I was going to say tomorrow at the gym, but shit. I'm
not sure after hearing all that."

"Girl, stop tripping. I think it's a good thing that the
bitch almost killed him."

"Alicia, how can you say that?"

"I think all these fools need to meet one jaded sister
who has been cheated on just one too many times. That way
they'll know we ain't playin' with their asses."

I laughed at Alicia. "Well, at least you don't have that
problem. You have a white man."

"What the hell is that supposed to mean?"

"They don't cheat as much."

"Shit, where did you hear that bullshit?"

"That's how it seems."

"Girl, that's the TV lying to you. If they have a penis,
cheating is a possibility. It's not a black thing, white thing, or
Hispanic thing. *Men cheat.*"

"So you have to worry about Matthew cheating on you
too, huh?"

"Oh, hell naw."

"Why not?"

"I tell Matt all the time, he better remember what happened to his friend. Plus, I don't need a sword. I carry a nine
for a living. He better recognize!"

We both broke out laughing.

Just then, Matthew came in wearing nothing but pajama bottoms. He kissed Alicia on the lips and spoke to me.

"So, was my friend the perfect gentleman?"

"He was."

"Cool, he's a good guy."

"Yeah, as long as I have a Ginsu nearby."

Matt looked at Alicia surprised.

"You told her?"

"She was going to find out eventually," Alicia said.

"You should've let Will tell her."

Matt smacked Alicia on her ass. He then smiled as he felt the jiggle. She smiled back at him and I knew immediately where this was going.

"You're bad," Matt said.

"You're right, I should be punished. I think I need to be spanked."

"I'm ready whenever you are" Matt said smiling.

"Okay," I interrupted. "Maybe I should go before you two lovebirds get started and begin going at it right here on the counter."

"It wouldn't be a first," Matt laughed.

I shook my head and Alicia walked me to the door. We hugged. "Bye, girl," Alicia said.

"Have a good one."

"You too," Matthew said from a distance while looking over Alicia's shoulder.

"'Night, Matt, and thank you for everything."

"No problem, Tiffany. Anytime."

SUNDAY AFTERNOON

I slept in late and got dressed for the gym at about 1:00. I called William and had him meet me at the Bally's in Countryside. I was going to let him pick me up, but after hearing about his previous drama, and the issue he used to have with cheating, I decided to take my time with getting to know William.

We went to the gym and I was surprised at how incredibly built William was. He came out of the gym in a Lakers jersey, but I couldn't see the infamous scar because he wore a T-shirt underneath. The T-shirt was sleeveless, but it still covered up all signs of the injury. As it turns out, William was a health and fitness guru. He showed me a simple workout that required me to do many of the same exercises that I was already doing, but with lighter weights and a different style of lifting. We worked out together and talked about diet, cheating days (on the diet), burning calories, and how we're both going to work on our fitness together.

We spent the rest of the day at the dollar show, then a local bar, and later that evening we went to a health food store where we shopped for various items. I went back to my car and gave him a soft gentle kiss on the lips. Today was tame compared to yesterday, but I wanted to take things slow. I didn't want to make any more mistakes with men than I had already.

The next day I went to work. The training was almost done and William called me every day to give me tips on the training program, and also help me with my homework. It wasn't long before our everyday conversations led to us seeing each other more. We started working out every other day together, and the days that I had to go to school, he met me at the school library. What started off as a casual interest began growing into something very special, very quickly. To make sure that things weren't going too fast, and I wasn't getting ahead of myself with William, I continued to see Thomas every Friday as I always did. I spent the week with William and I told him that Friday nights were the nights that I spent with my brother, Kyle. William had no idea where I stayed, and right now, I wanted to keep things that way in the event that Thomas decided to stop by one day unannounced, just as he had that morning he saw Justin (whom I hadn't heard from since) that morning.

I asked William if he had any objection to not know-ing where I lived and he explained that I would invite him over when I was ready. I asked him about his place, and although he was available by phone every day at anytime, he explained that he wasn't comfortable with my coming to his place yet either. That threw me off and again made me think he was either married or his girl in jail was com-ing home one day and I was just the other woman. He never brought up the scar, and I still hadn't seen it, so I didn't press. I liked the way things were going. William and I weren't hav-ing sex, but we had everything else. I loved being courted. By not having sex, we were getting to know each other on a com-pletely different level. When William and I went out, we held hands, watched movies, went skating, and did anything that our hearts desired. We ate at soul food restaurants, high-end restaurants, and sometimes just hung out with Matt and Alicia. On Fridays, I had my physical needs met by Thomas. I enjoyed the time that I spent with Thomas. Our friendship was going back to the way it had been in the beginning, and I became less and less upset about his marriage. In fact, I was almost glad that Thomas had fooled around on me, because otherwise I would've never met William.

Eventually I didn't really care if Thomas came over anymore or not. I mean, the sex was still on point and I loved him giving me oral sex each week (I insisted on that or he got nothing that Friday). But as far as loving him, that shit was becoming less and less intense each week. These days William seemed to hold my interest, whereas Thomas was just some-thing to do. From time to time I still felt guilty about messing around with a married man, but the more time flew by, the easier that became. Between the two men, Thomas and Wil-liam, all my needs were being met. It was like I was taking two men and building one. I wondered if this was the feeling men got when they dated more than one woman, and I thought about the consequences of continuing both relationships. I found myself falling in love with William and in routine with Thomas. That's when I began to feel bad again. That's when I began to think of myself as a whore. That's also when I decided that I was using Thomas as a safety net; in case it turned out that William, like Thomas, was just not was into me. I needed to take a chance. I needed to take a risk on love and the new me. Perhaps it was time to cut the safety net loose. A few days later, I began getting sick. One day I began throwing up violently and had to take a few days off from work.

"This better just be the damned flu," I said while on my knees in the bathroom.

Chapter Twenty-six—Thomas

I think I might be in love with Tiffany. I don't know how or why, but I really think I love her. She's looking good as hell these days. Why is it that some women wait until they're no longer seeing a man to start looking their very best? I wish I had known that Tiffany was going to start shaping up the way she has. Maybe I would've tried to stay with her and might not have married Meagan. Meagan still has supermodel looks, which makes me the envy of many of my boys, but I am really wondering if all the drama is worth it. I mean, is it enough to simply have a woman who is super fine, or does that even matter in the long run? Tiffany is just getting over the flu, and these past few days without her while she recuperates have had me thinking how much I think I love her, and how much I think I despise my wife.

I hated to use condoms with Tiffany. Before, Tiffany had been on the pill and that was enough. I guess I couldn't blame her for wanting to use a condom now. I did kind of let her down with the whole marriage thing. I didn't realize it before, but Tiffany seemed like the perfect woman for me. She likes sex (a lot), and she loves sports, a good movie, and I didn't have to break myself financially to please her. She wanted to go out every now and then, but she was also satisfied just being at home and being in love.

When we first started dealing again, she asked me to start taking her places. We went skating, shopping, and kicking it on the other side of town where no one would see us. She even stopped with those demands, and now didn't want to leave the house ever. *That's fine with me because by not leaving the house, that lessens my chances of getting caught by Meagan.*

I feel bad about having an affair. Technically, I'm still a newlywed.
Cheating seems wrong, but I just can't seem to get enough of Tiffany.

Meagan started to make some major changes that I couldn't deal with. She gained weight, looked thick, and her ass got more round. She gained twenty-five pounds in virtually no time. It looked good on her—but what if she kept gaining? My fear was that she may gain another fifteen pounds and cause her butt to go from perfectly round to square. I wasn't supposed to see that middle-aged spread women put on for quite a few more years. And, with all the money I was shelling out, she needed to keep herself well preserved for life.

I was halfway cool with the weight gain. There wasn't a tactful way to mention it, so I hadn't said a word. But then, this heifer went and cut off all her hair. She could get away with her new look, but I really loved her locks. I think a woman should sign a contract on her wedding day to go with the vows, stating that she'll never get a breast reduction, never withhold sex, and never cut her goddamn hair!

The other thing we'd been fighting about was her getting a job. She took a part, time job with a travel agency that caters to a lot of celebrities. She brings in a decent penny, but the only thing she had offered to pay was the phone bill. I tried to explain to her that I really needed her to handle the utilities while I picked up the mortgage. We argued about that shit until I was blue in the face. She got mad as hell, but for my own good, I now had her on an allowance. That made me wonder what kind of fucking idiot I was. I gave her an allowance and she had a job. So the money that she gave me on the phone bill was really nothing but her giving me back part of the money that I gave her to begin with. I had some relief with her working. At least this way she didn't ask me for as much money as she had.

In addition to that, we stopped having sex. Scratch that, we didn't have sex as often as we had. We used to average three to five times per week. Now it's once a week. I hated that, but it's a good thing Tiffany was giving me some on the regular; otherwise, I might have lost my mind.

I had to sneak just to masturbate. If Meagan caught me masturbating she made me feel dirty as hell. Now I had to wait until she's gone or sneak around and do it like a twelve-year-old. When we did have sex, it's pretty much missionary only, and Meagan acted as if she's simply obliging me. When I had sex with Tiffany, that shit was off the chain! We did missionary, doggie style (my favorite, because Tiffany knew how to back that ass up!) side by side, woman superior, rock the cradle, vertical joyride, and anything the two of us could imagine.

It used to be that Tiffany and I would put off sex until the end of the night. Now when I came in, some days she's like, "Strip, nigga, a sister needs the dick!" I mean, Tiffany talked dirty, she got foul with it, played with herself, and even role-played. She's breaking me off proper on Fridays, to the point that every Wednesday evening, I started getting excited about the weekend!

I'd been telling Meagan that I was working late, trying to take my department in a new direction. She hadn't tripped once about my not being home until late on Friday nights. Until she did, I planned to milk this shit for all it's worth. I bet she spent Friday nights spending my money at the shopping malls.

Lately, though, she'd been spending a lot of time traveling with her job or shopping with her mother. The more she's away from home, the better things seemed to be for me. I'd asked Tiffany for more time, but she would not increase my time with her beyond Friday. I knew that she was in school and working at some damn mystery job she wouldn't tell me about, but damn, I would have really liked to add another day of the week with her.

I remember when she used to sweat me about taking her out, but these days when I want to take her out she says no. Her excuse is she's tired and, "our Fridays are meant for fucking!" Fridays are meant for fucking? When she said that, I felt like I was the luckiest man in the world. Every week she seemed to be re-inventing herself. Every week she seemed to make me want her more and more. It's like wine: the pussy just keeps getting better with age.

      Either I was in love or I was just pussy whipped. Lately, she'd been down to earth, easy to talk to, and didn't want for anything. Although I had attacked her intelligence, she was smart as hell and bodied up nice. Before, she was fat, then she went to being thick. Now she's just like BLAM! I loved the feel of her thighs, her taut stomach, her firm breasts, and her long free flowing hair. It's like she and Meagan had done a complete reversal. Every week Tiffany had a new lingerie outfit on. She must have had stock in Victoria's Secret and Frederick's of Hollywood. *I'm also wondering if she's taking vitamins because she has some endurance out of this world. I can hit that ass two or three times when I'm over there and she just keeps going on and on like she never gets tired.*

      I'm starting to miss her at work also. One day last week I was thinking about her and sent an e-mail to her Yahoo! account. Awhile ago, all we were doing was sending each other nasty-grams. I guess she stopped shortly after I did. I sent her a really nasty e-mail detailing all the things that I want to do to her this weekend. She never responded, and I must admit, that hurt.

      If that weren't bad enough, people at the job started talking about her. I had to be in her old department more and more these days because of some changes the bank was going through. We started consolidating and merging various departments and I was given more staff to oversee, as were all the V.P.s in my department. I often heard people talk about how much easier things were when Tiffany was here. Although I dogged her out by saying that she was "just an AA," she was apparently very important to her department. V.P.s and workers alike were all saying how she was irreplaceable. Upon hearing that, I was beginning to think she wasn't just irreplaceable in the workplace, but in my life as well.

Eventually, I knew I shouldn't have done it, but I started telling Tiffany about my problems with Meagan. I knew it was disrespectful, but Tiff was such a great listener. She gave me advice on how to save my marriage, rather than tell me to shut the hell up. I thought she'd be glad about my shaky marriage, but instead, she seemed to say all the right things and encouraged me to do what I could to make things right. I could tell how concerned she was about me, and it was little things like that that made me think about her at work. There were many times that I found myself looking across the way from my office and looking at the spot where she used to sit. Now, there was a huge Jamaican woman sitting at her desk. She was a temp, and didn't have what it took to take my baby's place. At this point, nobody was filling that void, and I started to think about how I could involve her in my life on a full-time basis. Maybe some changes with my marriage had to be made.

Chapter Twenty-seven—Tiffany

After I completed my training, the job sent me to a managers' course in Las Vegas. It was a two-week training where we each stayed at Circus, Circus and went to seminars during the day and kicked it hard at night. The first three days away from William were hard. I was really starting to care for him and I think I was falling in love with him. Dating a man with no sex, I truly got a perspective on what it was that he liked about me.

William was constantly complimenting my smile, my ambition, and my progress in the gym. I was missing him by day four of the training. We talked on the phone twice a day, and I told him how much I missed him, his arms around me, his kiss, and his scent. No doubt, I was anxious to get back to him and he was ready for me to come back as well.

On the fourth day of the training, my phone rang and the front desk asked me to come down and pick up flowers sent by William Alexander. The message brought a smile to my face and I hurried to the lobby to get my bouquet. The bell captain looked around for them.

"I'm sorry, ma'am. I seem to have misplaced them just that quick." He looked around and I couldn't help but feel irritated. He saw the frustrating look on my face. "I'm sorry, ma'am, they were just right here. I will tell my manager and have him reimburse you for the cost."

"Reimburse me? Are you kidding me? My man sent those flowers and reimbursing me isn't going to suffice."

I was upset and he didn't want to see me snap the

heck off up in here. I was about twenty seconds from acting my color. The bell captain looked worried and spoke in a nervous tone.

"I think I saw one of the other guests pick up your bouquet of flowers."

"What? Who?"

"The gentleman behind you," he said, smiling.

I turned around and there stood William, my William.

He smiled and handed the bell captain a fifty spot. They both had played me.

"Sorry, ma'am, he made me play along."

"No, let me apologize for my attitude. Sorry I acted out like that."

I punched William on the arm, softly of course.

"I can't believe you played me like that. What are you doing here?" I said, smiling.

"You said you missed me. I took that as a hint to come down here."

"You traveled fifteen hundred miles to see me?"

"Baby, I'd go anywhere just to be near you."

"Aw, that's so sweet."

"Now, just let me check into my room and then we can go and get something to eat."

"Check in? Where?"

"Here. I'm going to stay for two days and then head back to the Chi."

"And you think I'm letting you travel fifteen hundred miles to stay in another room?"

"Well, I didn't want to be presumptuous. I mean, we agreed to wait as long as we could to get busy."

"I think the wait is over."

"Are you sure?"

"Yes. Unless, you don't think you can hang?"

"Shit, I don't know. You had a brother waiting so long, I'm backed up. I might also drop a few ounces."

We laughed and walked through the lobby.

"You're so nasty," I said.

"You just don't know how nasty I am."

"Any chance of me finding out?"

"Let's go find out right now."

We smiled at each other and walked to the west tower of the Circus, Circus hotel. The elevator took us to the twenty-seventh floor, room 27804.

"Nice room," he said, entering with a duffle bag on his shoulder.

"Yeah, it is."

He walked over to my window and looked out onto the street. From my room you could see the Riviera, the Hilton, and the Stardust Hotel. While he was admiring the view outside, I was admiring his firm, juicy backside. My man had a nice ass and I was imagining myself holding on to that bad boy while he was deep inside me.

I hope he will be really deep inside me, I thought.

William turned around and caught me looking at his ass. "Excuse me, miss, what are you looking at?"

"I'm looking at what's mine."

"Yours?"

"Oh, yeah, mine."

"I don't see any rings on these fingers," he said.

"I bet in twenty minutes or so, you'll be telling me that the dick is mine."

"Is that so?"

"Oh, yeah mister, that's so."

"How do you know that you won't be the one professing that the pussy is mine?"

"'Cause brothers talk that shit, but most of you all can't hang."

"I'm not most brothers."

"Prove it," I said, stepping forward.

"Can I take a shower first?"

"Yeah, you do that."

He put his bag down and opened it to retrieve a few toiletries. He then went in the bathroom and closed the door.

"Take some Ginseng, too, while you are in there! There's an old man in 27806, you want me to offer to pay him for some Viagra or something?"

I could hear laughter from inside the bathroom.

"You know, baby, you talk a lot of shit! You're going to be quiet in a minute when I'm tapping your cervix."

"My cervix? Damn! You're throwing it like that?" I said, laughing.

"Throwing it like a fastball in the World Series."

"Yeah, well make sure it ain't too fast, otherwise you may never get another shot at bat."

"Damn, baby, that's cold."

I turned down the lights in the room, cued up my laptop, and played music I had saved on my Windows Media Player. I programmed an hour of slow music just to gauge how long Mr. Man could hang. If he started at the beginning of a song and was done at the end of the same song, Thomas will get to hit this indefinitely.

I heard the shower on the inside if the bathroom. The next thing I heard was William singing. He sang "I Cry" by Anthony Hamilton. That messed me up because for a second I expected Anthony Hamilton to walk out of the bathroom. I found the exact song on my laptop and played it so William could sing along. He sang so nice that I was already beginning to get wet. My man was already fine, but he could sing too? Shit, I might have just found my husband. He was crooning too.

These tears that I shed are the trail to bring you home, Mama told me that a man's own tears can make him strong . . .

As he sang, I started peeling my clothes off. I looked through my luggage and was mad that I didn't have anything sexy to wear. I wasn't expecting to see William, so I didn't have anything ready. I wanted our first time to be special, but

I guess special would have to wait for our first time back in Chicago. The water stopped and I heard William step out of the shower. As he did, "Moments in Love" began playing on the laptop. I backed up to the bed, threw on my silk pajama top and a thong, and waited as patently as I could for William to walk out.

The door opened, the light went off in the bathroom, and William stepped into the sleeping area. He seemed shy, just as shy as many women get when they're about to sleep with a man for the first time. The first thing I noticed was the famous scar. Alicia was right. It started at his right shoulder and went completely across his body. It looked like someone tried to cut him diagonally. The scar was noticeable, but William had such a nice body that it hardly made a difference. It was obvious to me that the reason he worked out so much was to take attention away from the scar, which was long and as thick as my finger.

"About the scar . . ."

I could tell this was hard for him to talk about. I walked over to him and pressed my finger against his lips for him to hush. I then kissed him on the mouth, kissed him on his neck, licked his chest, and sucked on his nipple. I ran my hands up and down his rock hard pecks and then slowly down his ripped stomach. I then went to kiss him again and he instinctively wrapped his arms around my waist and then grabbed for my ass. I reached down for the place between his legs and was quite surprised at how well endowed he was.

He has a nice package, the question is does he know how to use it? I thought.

I began to massage his package and realized that I didn't have any condoms on me. I was on the pill, but wondered if he brought any condoms. If he had done so, I knew they had to be Magnums. Before I could ask, he knelt in front of me and worshipped my body in kisses. He peeled off my thong and kissed my stomach while lifting my pajama top. After unbuttoning it, he took my breasts in his hands and began to tweak my nipples.

"That feels good." I purred.

He gave my breasts more attention, then he stood up and swept me off my feet. He laid me on the bed and removed his towel. I was pleased with the shape, contour, and size of his manhood. He got on top of me and bathed my entire body in kisses. In between kisses, he repeated how beautiful and sexy I was. Each kiss was tempered with patience and passion. Each kiss meant something as he sent chills through my body. He snaked down my body and kissed the mound above my vagina, slowly parting my lips with his finger and exposing my all to him. He didn't go "there" right away. In fact, he kissed my labia, licked it, and then when I could no longer stand his teasing me, he licked my clit like it was a Charms pop. He sucked it like he was an infant and I was his nook. He alternated licking my clit, sucking my clit, and alternating between fast and slow speeds. He then placed two fingers in me and motioned them as if to say come here while inside me. Between his tongue and his fingers, I was beside myself with passion. He worked my clitoris until the froth between my legs must have made a milk mustache on him. I was almost ashamed at how wet I was.

My nipples darkened and became hard as he took me there. Over and over again he licked until my breathing became rapid, and the next thing I knew, I was coming. I tried hard to get away from him and the more I squealed and pulled away, the more he went after me and made me come even harder.

"So who's the man now?" he asked.

"Anybody can do that. Let's see what you're working with on the sex tip."

"In a minute, let's see if you can work with this."

He was big and I'm sure that a lot of women seeing his size might give a moment of pause. A dick like his had to be the kind that every woman dreamed about. He wasn't huge like the porn star Mandingo, but he was working with quite a bit. Either way, I worked him like a porn star. I licked his shaft while playing with his balls and bit down on him while taking in as much of him as I could without gagging. I let my throat get real wet and alternated massaging him off both hands while pleasing him at the same time. I got such a good rhythm going that I could hear his breathing become rapid like an asthmatic in a race. Not wanting to be outdone, I gave him head just as good as he gave me. Within a span of ten minutes, he was begging me to stop.

"Okay, baby, stop, okay, baby, stop, stop! Stop! Tiffany, you're going to make me come!"

Neither of us wanted that to happen, so I gave him a break. I looked up and smiled at him.

"If you were my wife, could I get head like that all the time?"

"As long as you keep giving me head like you gave me."

"Shit, that's a done deal."

It was obvious that we both had skills in the oral department. Now it was time to get to the real deal; the reason he traveled over fifteen hundred miles.

"Turn over on all fours."

I did as I was asked.

"Hike that ass in the air."

I obliged him.

"Now let's see what you're working with."

I was dripping wet and my vagina freely accepted his girth. William put a condom on and placed his manhood inside me, and at that moment, he put every man I had ever been with out of my mind. It was like clearing a history on a computer. He left such an impression on me it was like I was a virgin all over again. He filled me up, and without going all the way in, he immediately found my spot. He never went too far and the love that he gave me was just enough. He grabbed onto my waist and drove himself in slowly and methodically. Over and over again he pulled out and nerve endings began firing off. I began to experience some of the best sex I'd ever had. He stroked me and fingered my clit at the same time. He also kissed my back, the back of my neck, pulled my hair, and massaged my ass. He made me feel like a woman. He made me feel loved. He made me feel something I hadn't felt before.

Love and admiration.

He took his time. He kissed my entire backside while stroking deeply inside me. He then turned me over and had his every way with me. We did every position imaginable, and as song after song played, we treasured one another and pleasured one another. The lovemaking was so good that I cried. I reached out to kiss his face in the now dark room and my hands felt the tears on his face as well. It was like we made love on a whole new level. I didn't just feel his passion, I felt his love. I truly felt his love.

He cried, and initially, I didn't understand why, but then again I did.

"Are you okay?" I asked.

"I'm great. It's . . . it's just been a while, since . . . since I really connected with someone. It's been a while since I've felt this way about someone."

"I know what you mean. It's been that way for me too."

"You were amazing."

"No, you were."

"Perhaps, we were." We kissed and then embraced. We held each other for minutes on end afterward. We held on to each other and simply enjoyed the moment.

We'd made a connection. We touched one another on many different levels. Before we knew it, we began making love again. I felt like he was my soul mate. I knew my feeling was strange, but it was like we were making love to one another, yet telling the rest of the world to fuck off. It was like we were fucking all our sins away, fucking all the pain away, fucking all the letdowns, hurt, and disappointments away. I felt him and he felt me. It was hard to explain it, but the love we made just felt—right. In that moment, I felt as if the love we were making was magical. It was like something in a love story or fairytale. It was like this love—was meant to be. I loved making love to this man—my man, and it wasn't just the sex was good, but that we were good together. I couldn't help but share my thoughts with William, but he spoke up first.

"I can't explain it, Tiffany, but you feel so good," he said.

"So do you, baby. I know exactly how you feel."

"No, not like that, I mean . . . I feel you. I really . . . feel you. It's like . . . it's like . . ."

"Love?"

"Exactly. I can't finish. I don't know why, but I think we need to stop. I don't want to ruin it. I think this should wait until . . . until . . . *our wedding night.*"

He said it! I was thinking it, but he said it. He withdrew from inside me and held me. Before going to sleep in each other's arms, I couldn't help but think about my future with the man I now loved. When I got back home, I had to end my relationship with Thomas, but I wasn't sure how easy that would be.

THE NEXT DAY

The next day we walked the Vegas strip hand in hand. We saw all the sites from the Bellagio to Treasure Island, to the outlet mall, to the slot machines and poker at the Luxor. We ate, we went to the various clubs, and we even took a carriage ride around town. He told me about the scar and the man he used to be. I told him about all the men who'd hurt me in the past and how self-conscious I have always been about my weight.

"I don't see how two people with so many problems could find one another," I said.

"Maybe it was just meant to be. Maybe we were meant to be with one another and maybe we could love all the hurt away."

"That sounds like a fairytale. How can we love all the hurt away?"

"I wouldn't believe it myself, but there is something special about you. It's like . . ."

"Like we're Adam and Eve, or Ozzie and Ruby Dee."

"Something like that."

"Why do you think we connected the way that we did?"

"I think that when God made man and woman, he split the best of both worlds. I think that couples have a spiritual combination . . ."

"Like a safe?"

"Yes, like a safe. I think our purpose is to find one another. I think each man must seek out his Eve. That doesn't mean sex, but means that you look for a woman with those qualities you lack. I think a woman can be strong, but she should seek a man that has some of the qualities she may love, but qualities still that she lacks. In there is the combination. I think when you find someone with all the qualities you're looking for but don't possess yourself, when the two of you join . . . you become one. You learn from one another, love one another mentally, physically, and spiritually, and then you both grow while loving one another. I think finding the right combination is just like the feeling you get when you open a safe: you make what looks impossible, possible."

I leaned in and gave him a kiss. "I like the way you think."

"I know—Eve."

From that day forward, William called me Eve. That was my nickname and I loved it.

The next day, William had to catch a plane back to Chicago. I was in tears.

"Don't cry. At least now we have something to look forward to."

I smiled at him with tears in my eyes and prayed to God that he was right.

Two weeks later, I was in my new office. It was a floor above my old office and from where I sat, I could look down on Thomas's office and see him. It's funny how things like that work out. I smiled as I looked around *my office* and was given the opportunity to start interviewing for my own AA. I hung my managers training certificate on the wall and knew that one day I was going to hang my bachelor's and master's degrees there. I switched programs at NLU and went for an accelerated degree. The school had an ABS program which stood for Applied Behavioral Science. It was a program where I was given credit for my life experience as I completed a portfolio of papers showing that I knew as much about a given topic as the professor teaching the course. Being in the accelerated program, I only needed to go to class once per week, which was on Saturdays. I got in a cohort with other adults who were like-minded as me. I wasn't in my office three days before Thomas walked his happy ass in my doorway.

"Hello. May I help you?" I asked.

"Where have you been? I haven't seen you in almost two weeks and you didn't give me any type of notice?"

"Mr. Young, would you mind stepping in to my office and closing the door?"

Thomas stepped in and seemed thrown off by my professional demeanor. "You didn't tell me you were still with the bank," he said.

"It's not your business."

"Why didn't you tell me you were going to be gone these past few weeks?"

"Last time I checked, I was a grown woman without any attachments."

"Whoa, I didn't mean it like that Tiff. I was just saying that I missed you, that's all."

"Okay, so you missed me. That doesn't mean you just walk into my office unannounced."

"There is no AA outside. What do you do anyway that you have an office?"

"What does the door say?"

"It says treasury manager."

"So what does that tell you?"

"You mean you aren't just doing AA work from a new office?"

"No. This is my office."

"How did you pull that off?"

"You said that I needed to do more with my life, so I did."

"You could've told me."

"For what, so you could put me down or stifle my efforts?"

"No, I could've offered you some help or put in a good word for you in the training program. How did you get in the training program?"

"With no help from you, obviously."

"But you don't have a degree. How could you get in without a referral from a V.P.?"

"The true question is, why didn't the V.P. I was sleeping with make a referral for me to get in the program?"

"I never knew you had your eye on management."

"Otherwise, you would've helped me, right?"

"Yes, of course."

"Yeah, right. Is there something that I can help you with?"

"I just wanted to know when I can see you again."

"I don't know. I'll have to let you know."

"Let me know? What are you saying?"

"I'm saying that I'm not sure I want to do this any-more."

"What? You're kidding, right?"

"No. No, I'm not."

"Tiffany, we need to talk about this."

"No, right now you need to leave my office."

I walked away from him and to the window where I looked down at his office. I was surprised to see what looked like a heavier Meagan sitting in the chair across from his desk. A chair that he and I had made love in many times before. She had come to his job, something he said she would never do.

"Tiffany, I need to see you. I miss you. Let me make things up to you. Don't be too quick to make this decision."

I ignored him and continued to gaze at his office. "Looks like your wife has put on a few pounds."

"What did you say?"

"Your wife, the woman you're married to, the bitch that was so disrespectful to me a few months back . . . she's in your office. She looks like she's put on a few pounds also."

He thought I was playing, until he looked for himself.

"I have to go," he said, rushing out of my office.

"Yeah, you do that."

"But I'll be back."

"Please, don't."

Chapter Twenty-eight—Thomas

I walked over to the elevator and went down to my office. What was Meagan doing here? *She never comes to my job. I hope everything is okay. Chances are she either wants some money or to start a fight with me over money. In either case, I don't need any drama in the workplace. I need to address her issue quickly because I am sure Tiffany will be watching from her new office.* I couldn't believe she was a manager. I walked into my office to address my wife.

"Hey, sweetheart, what's going on?" I asked.

"Where were you?" she said with her hand on her hip.

"I was talking with a new manager in the department, what's up?"

"The credit cards are maxed out."

"Okay, and?"

"I need to know when the bill is going to be paid."

I sat at my desk and crossed my legs. "The bill will probably get paid when you pay it."

"When I pay it?"

She had a look of surprise on her face.

"You ran up the bill, didn't you?"

"Those cards are in both of our names."

"Actually, they're not. I had them put in your name last time I paid them off." I was looking at my manicured hands and speaking to her matter-of-factly.

"You did what?"

"I never use them so I had them placed in your name."

"Without consulting me?"

"Why is this such an issue? Is it because it's your credit rating being affected and not mine?"

"Don't get cynical with me."

"Fine. Was that all you wanted?"

"No." She pouted.

I let out a heavy sigh. "Okay, what else?"

"The joint account only has five hundred dollars in it."

"I know."

"There needs to be more money in the account." She had her hand on her hip and if I didn't know any better I would swear that she was about to stomp around like an upset toddler.

"I agree." I was casual, almost nonchalant.

"So what are you going to do?"

"Wait for you to contribute to the account and match it dollar for dollar. I also had it changed to a passbook account."

"Why?"

"So both signatures will be needed to withdraw money."

"And what is the purpose for that?"

"Meagan, we need to start saving some money. You're spending the shit like we have a money tree in the backyard. Now, I have to get back to work. We can talk about this when I get home. Is there anything else we need to discuss later?"

"Yes, there is. I want to go to Las Vegas next week and I want breast implants."

I liked the sound of both. I needed to get her the hell away from me for a while as I pursued Tiffany, and I loved the idea of bigger breasts.

"When do you want to go to Vegas and when do you want the implants?

"I want to go to Vegas in two months and I want the implants right after. I'm meeting with doctors now doing consults."

"Okay, we can talk about this more later."

I stood to kiss her but she walked out of my office. I was pissed but happy at the same time. If Tiffany was watching, then she knew that everything I'd been telling her about Meagan was true. I looked up at Tiffany's office, and to my surprise, her blinds were drawn—shut.

"Damn, I'm losing her. What in the hell am I going to do?"

Chapter Twenty-nine—Tiffany

Sex with William that day was incredible. What was even more incredible was the way we seem to click. After seeing Thomas with his wife, that seemed to put things more in perspective as far as my messing around with him. I wanted to tell him to just go to hell rather than being so cold to him, but I was at a point where I could take him or leave him. It had taken me a long time just to get to the point where I didn't really give a damn if he lived or died.

I see that his wife put on some weight. It looked good on her, though. I watched the two of them for a while, but then it sickened me to know how Thomas played Meagan and how I was doing the same by sleeping with her husband. What if that were me? I would feel so hurt, betrayed, and utterly disrespected if I found out that someone was sleeping with my spouse.

Speaking of spouse, I couldn't help but wonder if William might be the one. Now that the word "marriage" had come up, I'd been thinking about it again. The thing was, the last time I even thought about marriage, my heart was broken. I had to keep telling myself that although I was thinking about marriage when I was seeing Thomas, the idea never crossed his mind nor did the words ever leave his mouth. I assumed that was where we were headed and assuming things didn't get me anywhere.

When I got of work, I went home and started cleaning my apartment. William and I were going to the gym today and I thought it was time that he saw the inside of my place.

At this point, there was no more holding back anything. He needed to see the person I was and see me in my natural living space. When he met me at my apartment, I gave him the grand tour of my small, intimate place. Rather than go to the gym, afterward, William drove me to his home in Hickory Hills, Illinois. I was blown away at the six bedrooms, three baths, and three=car garage that he had. His house made Matthew's look like a chicken shack.

"This is where you live?" I asked.

"Yep."

"It's so huge."

"Yeah, it is."

"But you drive a Hyundai. It's a nice Hyundai, but it's basically a top-of-the-line economy car."

"Yeah, I know."

"Why?"

"My priorities are in order."

"What do you mean?"

"I mean, I have to live within my means. I have a nice house, but I can't have both a house and a luxury car. That's foolish. The car needs to just get me from point A to point B. Granted, you want to be comfortable riding from point A to point B, which is why I got the Sonata. It's a nice-looking, comfortable, and economical business car. My car is paid for. I know so few people in my circle of friends who can say that. The house is almost paid for. I make four double payments a year, and whenever I get taxes, a bonus, or commission, that money goes right back into my home."

"So why didn't you tell me that you were living like this?"

"Because these days, brothers who are successful need to know that the women in our lives want us for us, not what we can do for them. Matt was telling me about some idiot in his department named Thomas who married a woman because she was a beauty queen or something. From what

I hear, she can hold two crowns beauty queen and drama queen. The drama queen is the one the real brothers are trying to avoid."

Just the mention of Thomas from his lips sent chills down my spine. I had no intention of elaborating on what he'd said. "So, can I see the rest of your house?"

"You sure can, come on in."

I walked around the spacious house and saw that although it was nice on the outside, it needed some work on the inside. Not that anything was wrong with it, but you could tell that a man decorated it. His home was decked out in sports stuff. He was living like the typical bachelor. He had leather and black-colored everything in the living room, a 15 x 30 oil painting of Kobe Bryant in his living room and he had a 100-inch plasma screen TV in the living room, which is where he and his friends probably hung out. There was a pool table in the dining room, and posters of sports icons throughout the house.

"So what do you think?" He asked.

"I think it needs a woman's touch."

"I was hoping you would say that." he said smiling.

He showed me the rest of the house, which was made up in typical male style. I did what most women do when they see a man's house for the first time. I tried to see the potential that it had and tried to ignore the way he fixed it up. Surely, if allowed, I'd be adding my touch to his place very soon.

That weekend, Alicia and Matthew invited us to a party at Pazzo's in the NBC Tower, in downtown Chicago. The party was thrown by an entertainment group. These were brothers and sisters who threw some amazing parties and created an amazing atmosphere where professional black people could hang out and have a positive time. They had great DJs, who would spin some of the best mixtures of old school, new school, house, and hip-hop. People of all races were invited, but it was really a place where we all could come and kick it and fellowship and network with one another.

We went to the Capricorn Party that was held in the latter part of the month, and we drank, danced and watched all the VIPs and young black professionals party with one another. We had a great time that night, and although the party was scheduled to stop at 2:00 A.M., the lights came up at midnight.

"I'd like to make an announcement!" the DJ bellowed. "I have a young man who would like to say a really quick word in front of everyone and what he has to say takes a lot of courage. I want you all to give a round of applause to a good friend of mine, Matthew Tuskey!"

Everyone clapped not knowing what was coming next. When they saw Matt making his way to the DJ, they were somewhat dazed and confused. He came to the stage and took the microphone, looking directly at Alicia. Alicia and I looked at one another as if to say, "No, he isn't doing this here!"

"Hello, everyone, I've been blessed to have met a woman who I think is wonderful. A woman who is special and someone I feel I can spend the rest of my life with."

Matt made his way to our table and got down on one knee. I looked at my girl to see if she thought this shit was just as corny as I did, but she had tears in her eyes.

"Alicia, will do me the honor of being my wife?"

Tears streamed down her face and she was all smiles. "Yes, Matthew. Yes, I will."

The NBC Tower erupted with applause. Will and I looked at each other, and although we both tried to fight it, it was obvious that something like this was in our future as well.

Initially, I didn't know how I felt about Alicia getting married. I mean, I was happy for her, but still just a little uncomfortable that she was marrying a white man. I had always thought she'd marry a good black man and this took some time getting used to. No doubt, Matthew was a good man . . .

he treats her right, he's supportive of her career, and according to her, he's great in bed. Realistically, Matt was the bomb. I just wish she could've found the bomb with a brother.

The cool thing about her getting married was that I got to plan a wedding. Not only that, but I got to dress up and we had some serious shopping to do! It was now early March, and since Matt and Alicia decided they didn't want to wait a long time to get married, they planned their wedding for June. It was hot as hell in Chicago in June. I hoped that we'd get a break on the weather so that people weren't sweating like slaves in the tuxedos and dresses.

First we had to find a place, then we had to find dresses, invitations, limo, and a ring (for Matthew, Alicia's ring was this beautiful, princess-cut diamond that was two-and-a-half carats called "Carmen") We also had to find a DJ, minister, and live entertainment. We only had a few months to get everything together, so that meant less time for William and me. When Thomas came over on Friday nights, I generally would be doing wedding stuff. Many nights, I'd take a break, fuck him, and send him out on his way. He was still feasting on me each week like it was his last meal, and my relationship with him did eventually evolve into just looking at him as something to do.

When William and I saw one another, we had a wonderful time. I started going to his church, and every now and then, he would come to mine. We couldn't keep our little vow of celibacy. Most days after kissing and petting, we would most certainly end up in bed. I have to admit, we cheated a few times and each time was just as phenomenal as the first time we had sex.

I felt bad about sleeping with two men regularly, especially considering that I was falling in love with one of them. But I felt as long as they didn't find out, everything was cool. I wanted to tell Alicia what was going on, but I couldn't. Again, I didn't want to be judged and I didn't want to take a chance on the possibility of her telling Matt, who would in turn tell William. The only reason I kept seeing them both was because I had to be sure about William before committing. That, and I was used to being devoured once a week by Thomas. I was no longer in love with him, but I was addicted to his tongue. Right now, that was the only thing holding me to him.

Alicia stopped over so we could visit a number of halls and look at dresses at the bridal shop. We shopped all day, made wedding plans all day, and saw about 100 different dresses before Alicia found the one she thought would be best for her special day.

"So . . . are you sure about marrying Matt?"

"Why do you ask? Oh wait, I know."

"I'm just sayin' . . . there are no brothers you want to spend the rest of your life with?"

"There are plenty. The thing is, none of them want to commit, many of them have issues with the fact that I make more money than them, and if that isn't it, they have an issue with my being a police officer."

"All that aside, you still think Matt is the one?"

"I do. I love him, Tiff, and he loves me—unconditionally. What is going on with you and Will?"

I looked up at her, surprised, while I held a wedding dress up to myself and fantasized for a moment.

"What do you mean?"

"I mean, what's up with the two of you? I heard that you all got busy a while back and it must've been some powerful shit if both of you all were crying."

"How did you hear about that?"

"Matt told me, and before you ask, Will told him."

"What are they, two high school girls?"

"Girl, please. Men gossip and talk just as much if not more than we do. I'm just wondering what you did to make that man cry. What's your secret?" she said, laughing. "You have a special coochie if you got brothers weeping and shit."

"Girl, you don't need any secrets. You got a man to propose to you after a few months. Shit, I need to be asking you for tips."

We both laughed.

"So what's the deal? Is William the type of man you could see yourself marrying?"

I nodded and looked in the mirror with the wedding dress in front of me. "Yeah, he is."

"Then why were you holding back sex?"

"He told Matt that, too?"

"They're boys, they talk. But yeah, he told Matt that for a while you were waiting for your wedding day. So when is it?"

"We haven't talked about it. Hell, he hasn't asked."

"And if he did?"

"He won't."

"But if he did?"

"I don't know. I don't trust my judgment in men. I like Will a lot, but I don't trust him either. I mean, everything feels right between us, but I'm scared, you know? Plus it's still really new."

"I know. Believe me I know. I'm marrying a man I've only known for several months."

"But it feels right, right, Alicia?"

"Tiffany, it does."

"Then, hell, I say go for it. I'm happy for you."

I did think the decision was premature. I thought about today's divorce rates, the fact that you really need to know someone before you marry him, and you also need to know about a person's psychological, emotional, and financial profile. I knew that Matt was okay financially, but that doesn't mean by any stretch of the imagination that he was mentally balanced. But hey, Alicia was a big girl, and if Matt messed up, we would both be over there kicking his ass!

***

Everything was in place for Alicia and Matt's wedding. This evening Matt was throwing an engagement party for the two of them at his house. He ordered tiki lights for the backyard and around the pool; he had a number of gas grills going with his boys cooking up burgers, chicken, shrimp, and fish. He also ordered a DJ, live entertainment, a bartender, and even had a day-care provider to come out for his friends who had kids. Matt had a home theatre and there was a movie going on inside the house as well as card games and drinking games.

All of Alicia's friends and family were there except Meagan. All of Matt's friends and family were there also. Surprisingly, many of my friends were there also. Some of them were invited by Will, Matt, or Alicia. I didn't know that many of my friends knew Will. As each of them came up with a different story as to how they knew Will, I started chewing them out for not hooking him up with me years ago.

Midway through the party, Matt professed his love for Alicia in the middle of dinner. We all ate, toasted the happy couple, danced, and drank well into the night. About two hours before the party ended, Matt had a second announcement to make. I thought, *If they announce Alicia is pregnant, I'm going to go off on her for not telling me.* Matt walked up the microphone and asked everyone to come near the mini-stage that he had set up in the back.

"I know that some of you are wondering if Alicia and I are expecting a baby. Well . . . not yet! The reason that I asked you all to come up here is because on my special day, *this* special day, my boy, my friend, and my brother, Will, would like to say a few words."

We all clapped. Will knew how to make a toast. He was an eloquent speaker and he showed incredible poise in front of an audience.

"Friends, family, and honored guests, I just want to say a few words and I'll let you go back to your partying. The

Bible says that a man, who finds a wife, finds a good thing. I haven't known Alicia long, but I do know that she is good for Matt. My best friend is a lucky man." Everyone applauded again. "As many of you know, Matt is two years older than me. He has not only been a good friend, he is like a big brother to me. He mentored me when we were younger, he got me a job at the bank where we work, and although I surpassed him up the corporate ladder, he's still been an inspiration to me. I have always looked up to him and always tried to follow in his footsteps. With that being said, I would like to follow in his footsteps one last time. And if she will have me . . . I would like to ask that you all give my girlfriend, Tiffany Garner, a round of applause and then a moment of silence, as I ask her to take my hand in marriage, and become *my wife*."

I almost spit out my drink. I looked at Alicia who had tears in her eyes. I mouthed the words, "Did you know?" and she nodded. The entire backyard was full of people I knew and didn't know. They all were clapping for me, and as they did, I made my way to the stage. I was light-headed and nervous. What would I say? I couldn't just say no, could I? I didn't think that "no" was what I wanted to say anyway. This was all so . . . sudden. We could continue to get to know one another and just have a long engagement. A million ideas went through my head, and when I got on the stage, William was down on bended knee with a small box in his hand.

"Tiffany, baby, I know this is all sudden and a bit premature, but I love you and this just feels right. I know you feel what I feel. I know you know in your heart that I will do right by you. You also know there is something very special between us. I would be honored . . . no, I would be the happiest man alive if you would be my wife."

I can't remember when the tears started. All I knew was that they were streaming down my face. Will opened up a box with one of the fattest rocks I have ever seen in my life. I didn't know if it was destiny, the liquor, or the timing, but when he asked me I could only form my mouth to say, "Yes, William. Yes, I will marry you."

The backyard erupted with cheers and applause.

From the point that William proposed, I started spending more time at his place. We started having sex like teenagers and each time . . . each time, it was the best sex that I had ever had. We started acting like newlyweds as soon as he proposed; from having sex every day, to shopping, to late-night talks and walks. I was sporting the ring he gave me like it was my birthright. Together, Alicia and I were giddy as schoolgirls that our lives had just gone in totally different directions after the many disappointments with the previous men in our lives. I guess sometimes you have to put up with trifling men, so you can better appreciate the real deal when it finally comes along.

I now started to see less and less of Thomas. In fact, I spent virtually every weekend at Will's house and when I did see Thomas, it was for either a quickie or just to let him please me orally and that was it. Each time that I had sex with him, I felt like shit. It felt as if I were betraying my husband. Because of my feelings, I stopped answering his phone calls, I was never home on Fridays, and although he sent me numerous e-mails, I didn't answer one. In fact, I closed my online account. I didn't know how to break things off with Thomas. I also didn't want to do him as he did me and simply tell him that I was marrying someone else. I did the only thing that I knew to do in a situation like this, I ignored him. That is, until he came into my office and demanded some answers.

"I need to speak with you. Now!"

"What did I tell you about just walking into my office?"

"I don't give a fuck! Why aren't you answering my calls?"

I couldn't believe he was getting indignant with me. "Close the door," I ordered.

He closed my door. "First of all, don't you ever speak

to me like that again! Second of all, you're a married man and have no right to make any demands on me. Third . . . good-bye."

          "No, I'm not leaving until you give me an explanation."

          "Again, I don't owe you a damned thing! Don't forget who you're talking to."

          "Look, I'm sorry about my tone. It's just that I miss you. I need to see you. I want to just spend some time with you Tiffany, that's all."

          "My time is otherwise occupied these days."

          "What the fuck is that supposed to mean?"

          "It means that I can't see you anymore."

          "Tiffany, don't do this. Give me at least this weekend. I really need to see you this weekend."

          "What is so pressing this weekend?"

          "I can't go into all that now. Please just tell me that you'll meet with me this weekend."

          He was looking like a lost puppy. I agreed reluctantly to see him that weekend, although every fiber in me told me to tell him to go to hell. He left my office and I felt my stomach tighten as he left. I prayed to God that my future husband never did to me what Thomas *and I* were doing to Meagan.

Chapter Thirty—Thomas

I couldn't believe Tiffany wanted to leave me. I couldn't believe she was being so cold and callous. We had fun together, we had sex regularly, we laughed, we joked, and we truly enjoyed one another's company. So why was she tripping all of a sudden? I wondered if she was still seeing Justin. I wondered if she was just starting to get over me. I couldn't see how with all the fun that we had. I had to think of something to keep her. I needed to hold on to her. I don't know when it happened, but *I loved her!* I loved her with all my heart. I couldn't let her get away. At this point, maybe I needed to ask Meagan for a divorce so I could get on with my life.

Meagan had already gotten her implants. Afterward, I sent her to Vegas so she could recuperate and vacation there. She couldn't have sex with me for a few weeks, and we had to wait for the pain to subside. I was happy with the end result. Her breasts were nice before, but now, those bad boys were perfect and worth every dime of my money. I hated to admit it, but now that she was thick, that ass was fatter and her breasts were large. She was so voluptuous, that with many things, I had a hard time telling her no.

Her looks still didn't change the fact that my wife had a very fucked, up personality. Initially, I felt bad about cheating on her, but with all the money I spent on her, as well as how foul she could be at times, I convinced myself that she deserved whatever she got. Since she was under the impression that I was working late every Friday night, she started hanging out more with her sorority sisters. They would get together and shop, give one another housekeeping tips, and go to various events.

Things weren't entirely bad between Meagan and me. Somewhere along the way she softened her stance on having kids. She said that she thought it might be nice to have at least one child, only if I was willing to pay for a personal trainer and maybe get her a tummy tuck afterward. To me, we had a deal, and she jokingly told me to put the shit in writing that I would pay for whatever surgery she wanted after having our baby. I typed the shit up on my PC and signed it. That night we joked, talked about baby names, whether we would have a boy or girl, and how we would care for the child. It was three weeks after that when we started having unprotected sex and started trying for a baby.

Between the possibility of my having a child, and the fun that I had with Tiffany, I truly had the best of both worlds. I didn't realize how much I cared for Tiffany until she tried to really walk away from me. When I didn't see her for a few weeks, I felt a void in my life. I couldn't let her get away. The thing was, although my wife was a bitch, I didn't want to let go of her either. Men envied me when they saw my wife. They wished that they were the one on her arm. I also liked the prospect of having a baby with Meagan. She's beautiful, she's smart, lazy, but smart, and her parents would help me spoil the hell out of my child.

Later that day, Tiffany promised to see me so I took the rest of the day off and went to the jewelry store to get her a ring, an engagement ring. I figured I would tell her that I planned to divorce Meagan. *That should buy me some time.* I also figured if I came over with flowers, wine and a ring, that would buy me additional time. After all, we would say that we were engaged, but the engagement wouldn't really start until after I got divorced, right?

I planned to tell her that we still had to keep our relationship on the low, because I didn't want to be taken to the cleaners by Meagan. I figured doing all this would buy me at least two years of time. The thing was I really did want a divorce from Meagan. She wasn't doing anything but draining me financially. I was looking into ways to possibly divorce her, but maybe still sleep with her. In fact, for now, I thought I would stop going in her raw and trying for a baby.

I went to the jewelry store and purchased a diamond, three-stone one-and-a-half carat eternity ring. I charged it to my credit card and kept it in my car. I figured if I gave the ring to Tiffany there was no way in hell she could say no to me.

I arrived at Tiffany's house at 6:00 P.M. rather than 8:00 P.M. that Friday. I rang the bell and she buzzed me in. I had the ring in my pocket, and as soon as she opened the door, I presented her with flowers and wine. I had on a Kenneth Cole suit. It was what I call my power suit. It was black gabardine with a Geoffrey Beene shirt and red tie. This was how I dressed when I was trying to close a deal. Today I was giving Tiffany my hardest sell, and I needed to come at her with everything that I had.

"Hello, sweetheart, how are you this evening?"

"I'm fine, Thomas."

"Baby, sit down, these are for you."

She smelled the flowers and looked at me suspiciously. She cut the stems and placed the flowers in a vase full of water. She smiled a half smile at me and poured two glasses of wine. I didn't think that she was feeling me at first, but then had a look as if there was a lot on her mind. She smiled a bright smile, and all of a sudden, it was like she was feeling me.

"Thank you for the flowers. Listen, why don't I make us something to eat and in the meantime, why don't you go and jump in the shower?"

"Now?" I asked.

"Right now."

"Sure, okay."

Without thinking, I headed into her shower where I had been many times before. I took my clothes off, got under the stream of hot water, and smiled as I smelled what most certainly had to be steak cooking in the kitchen. The prospect that I still "had it" made me feel good. I washed my body with the scented soap that she kept in the bathroom, and then used her Skin So Soft by Avon and put some of that all over my body. I wrapped a towel around my waist, flexed some in the bathroom mirror, and gargled with some mouthwash in the cabinet. I winked at myself in the mirror as I headed back into the hallway.

When I opened the door, the apartment was dark with the exception of the flicker of candles in the dining area. I walked to the dining room and was surprised that there was steak and a baked potato waiting for me, as well as wine and the flowers that I brought. Tiffany was sitting at the table in a red teddy and nothing else.

"Sit down, eat," she said.

I took a seat and smiled at her. Tiffany was looking so damn good tonight. Her hair was down, she seemed to have a glow about her, and her body was just . . . tight! I ate a few pieces of steak and had a few sips of wine, but Tiffany was looking so good, I was ready to take her now. I didn't know why, but she looked happy tonight; happier than she had looked in months. I pictured myself in that instant as her husband and her lover. It pleased me that she was so happy. I hoped that she could be this happy with me. The moment felt right and I was glad that I had bought her a ring. I didn't know when I was going to present it to her, but I knew whenever I did, I imagined the time to feel just like this one. This was the woman I wanted to be with. I made up my mind that tonight I was going to quit bullshitting. Tonight I was going to propose to Tiffany and make her my wife. No more player games, no more straddling the fence. The time was now, and I was going to ask Meagan for a divorce.

"Tiffany, I think we need to talk."

"We do, but not now."

She walked over to me and sat in my lap. She kissed me on my neck and then softly on the lips. I grabbed her ass and helped her to straddle me. I slowly peeled of the straps to the teddy and took one of her breasts into my mouth. I ran circles around her areolas and nipples. I cupped her ample breasts and began to knead them, kiss them, and suck them with abandon. I ran my hand up her backside and underneath her hair to get a better grip on her to kiss her more deeply. She began to rock on top of me and ran her fingers over my head as the room filled with the sound of our kissing. I got up from my chair and sat her down in it. Then I placed both of her feet on my sides and widened her legs so I could feast on her. I separated her vaginal lips and my tongue found its familiar place between her thighs. I devoured her clit and penetrated her with my tongue. The juices were flowing and Tiffany began to moan, but it was almost as if she refused to allow herself to come. I licked her with abandon for more than twenty minutes. My back hurt, my jaw locked, and I continued on my quest. I was determined that she was going to come. It felt as if I was losing her, but I still wanted . . . needed her to come. If she couldn't come from my feasting on her orally, then my chances with her had to be almost non-existent. I needed to prove a point. I needed to make her feel good. I wanted Tiffany to feel like she was my woman again and I wanted to feel like her man. I wanted her to know that the feelings she had been getting from me once per week, she could have for the rest of her life. No matter how hard I tried to make her enjoy the moment, I could see in her eyes that she just wasn't there. Her actions hurt like hell, and my thoughts of proposing to her were slowly but surely going down the drain. Maybe, though, it was time for me to put up or shut up.

Chapter Thirty-one—Tiffany

I slept with Thomas one last time to get closure. I needed to know that I was truly over him and find out if the only thing that existed between us was sex. I was scheduled to go to Alicia's house this evening. I was surprised that Thomas got here two hours early but I was glad that he did because I didn't need to wait until 10:00 to go to Alicia's. The wedding was Sunday and she and I needed to be together to make sure everything was perfect and all the loose ends were tied.

Surprisingly, for the first time during sex with Thomas, I wasn't feeling him. I was thinking of every sexual encounter I'd had to try to get myself to come, but that didn't work. I looked down at him feasting on me with nothing but pity in my eyes. The damage between us was irreparable. After all I had been through with him from his getting married, to lying, to cheating, to breaking my heart . . . there was just so little between us left but the physical which was fading by the minute. There was nothing left—nothing. I tried to get myself to enjoy the oral sex, but I guess when it's over, it's over. I let my mind wander and I allowed my mind to drift to William. He thought I was at my brother's house. He was out with Matt getting ready for the wedding, and most likely, preparing for their bachelor party. I felt bad because here I was engaged to another man with my ex-boyfriend between my legs.

In order to come, I began to think about William. I pictured that it was him between my legs feasting on me like there was no tomorrow. I envisioned the many times that we made love and how powerful our lovemaking would be on our wedding night. As I allowed myself to go there, my breathing became rapid, my breasts heaved up and down, and the next thing I knew, I was coming.

Thomas stood up and led me to the bedroom. I didn't have the heart to tell him I was really no longer feeling him. I wanted to tell him, but I couldn't crush him like that. I simply let out a huge sigh as I headed to the bedroom for what I knew would be the last time. I made up in my mind that after sex, I would tell him this was the last time we'd ever go here.

After putting on a condom, he positioned himself on top of me and began to penetrate me. My mind was somewhere else. I thought about the wedding plans, the photographer, the time that things would start, how we would apply our makeup, and what could possibly go wrong that we could be proactive and prevent. Sleeping with Thomas was now truly just something to do. And I no longer felt the need to really do it.

I moaned at the same time that I was doing all this multitasking, and ten minutes into the sex, I faked an orgasm for the first time. I did so thinking it would be hard to get away with, but apparently I should've gotten an Academy Award for my performance. Thomas thought he was really doing something. I almost laughed as I thought, *I would like to thank the Academy . . .*

He came in the condom and collapsed on top of me. He kissed my neck and gave me a peck on the lips while still inside of me. I could feel his penis throbbing from what I guess was a hard ejaculation. With his climax he was spent. With my lack of interest I was done. I got the closure that I needed, and without warning, I got up and started getting dressed. He lay there in bed watching me. His body was glistening with sweat and he was smiling at me like he had just dropped a bomb in bed.

"Can we talk now?" he said, smiling.

"Yes."

"I want to see you more often. I want to spend time with you. Tiffany—I love you."

Without hesitation I said, "I want you to get up, get dressed, and I never want to see you again outside of a professional capacity."

"Huh?"

I dropped a bomb of my own.

"You heard me."

"But we just . . ."

"Had sex? Nothing more and definitely not much to brag about."

"Tiffany, did you hear what I said? I love you. I didn't know it until recently, but I love you. I want to be with you. I want to marry you."

"Thomas, please."

"I'm serious. I planned to ask Meagan for a divorce this evening."

"And when did you come to this revelation?"

"This week."

"When I told you I didn't want to see you anymore?"

"Yes."

"So, that's why you needed to see me so bad, because you just realized that you loved me?"

"Yeah."

"Bullshit."

"I'm serious."

"You are seriously full of shit."

I continued to get dressed and packed a bag to get ready to go to Alicia's. I would shower at her place. At this moment in time, I never felt more right about William. I told Thomas to get dressed as I grabbed everything that I needed to go to my girl's place.

"Tiffany, I need you. I want you in my life and I seriously want to make you my wife. I made the wrong choice. I can admit that now. Doesn't that mean anything to you?"

"I'm sorry, Thomas, no. I seriously never want to see you again."

"Are you sure about that?"

"I have never been more sure about anything in my life."

"You can't mean that."

"Wrong again. I mean every word I say."

"Are you kidding me? I mean, seriously, do you know how much we could accomplish together? Do you know all the things that I could provide for you? I could get you out of this raggedy apartment and move you into a huge house."

"You mean the house you share with your wife?"

"Well, yeah. But it's not like she will be there and . . ."

"Hold up, did you just call my damned apartment raggedy?"

"I didn't mean raggedy. I meant . . . average. I mean, what I'm trying to say is you can do better. Baby, you deserve better."

"You're damned right! I can do better and I do deserve better! I deserve better than you."

"Dammit, Tiffany, listen to me, you are making a mistake. Babe, I'm trying to offer you a new life. I'm trying to take you with me to the top. I want you there with me."

"A new life? I have a new life. I have a new lease on life. And in case you haven't noticed, the path that you are on right now, the career path? I'm on that same path. I may not be as far up the ladder as you are, but, baby, I'm on the ladder. Don't be surprised if I get to where you are trying to go shortly after or ahead of you."

"Okay, now you're trippin'. I'm trying to tell you and show you that I love you. Now you know where I am professionally and you know where I am in the bedroom and you have to admit that I'm not too bad on the eyes. You can't just walk away from me like all this time never meant anything."

"Why not? You did!"

"Is that what this is about? You're still pissed about the whole marriage thing? Baby, I'm trying to make that right now. I'm going to ask Meagan for a divorce. Dammit, Tiffany, I want to be with you. I could have my choice of many women, many women, and I'm trying to tell you that I want to be with you."

"Thomas, listen to me and listen to me carefully. I don't want to be with you. And as far as those other hoes that want you so bad, baby, go to them. We . . . are . . . done. Get out."

He pulled the covers back and quickly got dressed. His expression was blank and he looked at me as if we were meeting for the first time and he didn't know who I was. He paced back and forth upset, like he's done a million times before in his office when something doesn't go his way. He then started pointing his finger at me as he spoke.

"I just told you that I loved you," he explained. "What's with you, Tiff?"

"Nothing. But I just told you to get out."

I went straight to the door in the living room and opened it for him. He looked at me with shock and awe. When he leaned in to kiss me, I shied away and motioned for him to leave.

"Did what just happen mean anything to you? Did you feel anything for me?"

"Yeah . . . closure. Good-bye Thomas."

He walked out the door, and when he turned around to speak again, I closed the door in his face. Never before had I felt so liberated. Never before had I had such a weight lifted off my shoulders. I went to the phone in my bedroom and called William.

"Hello?" he said.

"Hey, baby, it's me."

"Hey, love, how are you?"

"I'm fine. I just called to say that I love you."

"Well, I just want to tell you that I love you more."

"Forever?" I asked.

"Forever times infinity," he responded.

Yeah, it was a little corny and a little high school, but that was how my man made me feel. It was like new money, new emotion, or new love. I felt bad about bedding two men at the same time. I felt bad that I did William as Thomas had done me. But the thing is, I had to be sure. I had to be sure that this was what I wanted and that William wasn't someone playing me also. I felt bad about cheating, but justified it by thinking to myself that men do this shit all the time. No, it's not right, but it's how things are. Besides, I now knew what I had in William. I finally cut my safety net loose and I was going to gamble on love again. This time, I planned to play to win.

I packed my bags and headed to Alicia's condo, which was for sale. I couldn't help but think that I was free at last, free at last . . . thank God almighty I was free of Thomas at last. Or, was I?

Chapter Thirty-two—Thomas

"What the fuck just happened? I never even got to present her with the ring. What did I do wrong? How did such a good night go wrong so fast? I couldn't lose Tiffany, not again. I had to do something. Alicia was getting married Sunday and Matt invited me and Alicia invited Meagan. Meagan said that we weren't going because she hated her cousin and had no desire to go. I could tell Meagan that I had to go because it's a work thing. *I'll ask Meagan for a divorce tomorrow and propose to Tiffany at her best friend's wedding in front of everyone.* That would be romantic, and hopefully, that would bring us back together again.

I drove home and looked down at my watch. It was 7:30 P.M. and I had just experienced what had to be the worst ninety minutes of my life. I needed to get some things off my chest and get my life in order. I needed to start with Meagan. I pulled up in the driveway and noticed a limousine parked in front of my house. The driver was waiting patiently in the car.

She must be going somewhere again, I thought. *That is some other shit that need to stop. Everywhere that she goes is on my dime. I can't wait to tell her that it's over.*

I looked at the driver as I got out of my car and he looked at me with a puzzled look on his face. I keyed in my code to the alarm and walked into the house. We just had the carpet redone, so I pulled my shoes off in the foyer and headed upstairs. My heart was beating fast in my chest because I didn't know how to even bring up the word "divorce" to Meagan. I just know that it had to be done. As I walked up the thick carpeted stairs, I rehearsed in my head what I would say to her.

The closer I got to our bedroom, the more I heard what sounded like whimpering from my bedroom. *Please don't tell me she is crying. That is going to make this shit even harder.* I walked up to the door, which was partially open, and pushed it open.

My heart almost stopped at what I saw.

On top of my wife was an older brother in his fifties. She wasn't crying, she was moaning. I stood there in awe as this brother who looked like Denzel was having his every way with my wife. The bell rang downstairs, which was obviously the driver who figured out that I was the husband.

The two of them looked up at me with fright.

"Anthony!" Meagan screamed. I looked at the man who casually got up off my wife knowing that he was in the wrong, but felt as if he was entitled to be here.

"You must be the husband," he said, reaching for his pants on the floor.

"Unfortunately, that would be me. But you need to speed it up and get the fuck out of my house."

Meagan eased out of bed with the sheet wrapped around her. I reached out and grabbed her arm. "Don't you go nowhere. I'm not finished with you yet."

For the first time in our marriage, Meagan remained silent. She sat back on the bed and encouraged her guest to hurry up.

"So how do you want to play this?" he said, looking at me while stepping into his shoes.

I laughed out loud. "However you want to handle it, player."

I could take him in a fight. *But the thing is, this might be a blessing in disguise. This might be the out that I need from my marriage. I can divorce Meagan on the grounds of infidelity, perhaps not lose any money in the ordeal via alimony and sell this ridiculously large house. I can go find a modest home that's within my budget and Tiffany and I could live there.* I could tell Tiffany, "Baby, I heard your concerns and we don't have to live in the house I shared with my first wife. We can live in this house, your house, our house." *That sounds cool. God works in mysterious ways. This might be just the thing that I need. There is no need to fight this man. I simply need to celebrate.*

"You two should leave," I said.

"So, are you fine with all this?" he said with a confused tone.

"Fine? Hell, no! But I'm not going to lose any sleep over my wife being a whore. Do you love her?"

"I could grow to love her."

"You want her?"

"I do."

"Then take her with you. She's not doing me any good here."

Meagan was shocked that the two of us were talking about her as if she were chattel.

"Wait just one goddamned minute!" Meagan said.

The bell rang again, "That's probably my driver," the older brother said. "I need—"

"You need to decide if you're taking my wife with you. I'm leaving, and by the time I get back, I hope the two of you will be up and out of here."

Before I left, I turned and gave Meagan and her new man another hard look. "You look familiar to me. What's your name?"

"Ja . . . James Grafton."

"The attorney?"

"Yes."

"You just made my damn day. Now, she can have your money and your services."

"So, your divorce to Meagan . . ."

"Won't be contested."

Meagan was pissed that I was calm and didn't allow her to get underneath my skin.

"Do you even care that I'm cheating on you?" she asked.

"Only if you care that I've been cheating on you."

"I'm no fool, Anthony."

"I never said you were."

"Do you have any idea how many times I've been to your office on Friday nights?"

"No, not a clue."

"Well, several times."

James crept by me as I stood at the door. "Looks like you two have quite a bit to talk about. I think I'll leave."

He was ignored as I turned my attention back to Meagan. I thought about fucking his old ass up, but then it dawned on me, why bother?

"You've been cheating on me for a while now," she said.

"You're right. I haven't been happy with you for a long time, and I wasn't even happy before we got married."

"Then why did you marry me?"

"For a long time I was infatuated with you, Meagan, but I never loved you."

"I never loved you either."

"Then why marry me?"

"I used to think it was your earning potential. Now that I think about it though, I think I did it to piss off my father. You could never keep me in the life I am accustomed to."

"So this was just . . ."

"Simply put . . . one huge mistake."

"Then you don't mind granting me a divorce?"

"Mind? Oh yeah, I mind. I'll give you your divorce, but a part of me hates you for seeing another woman behind my back. I know who you've been seeing. I checked your emails, phone bills, and I even hired a detective and used your money to pay for it making you the dumbest MF in the history of cheaters. You paid for your own investigation into your own infidelity, which I intend to hold against you in court."

"Why get ugly when you have one of the richest brothers in the city now?"

"Because I can't believe you cheated on me with that fat girl. I can't believe that you had her at my wedding. I can't believe you were screwing my cousin's friend."

"I didn't know she was Alicia's friend."   .

"No, but you knew you were marrying me. We were supposed to be in a relationship."

"And with all that being said, we both just sat here and agreed that our relationship was built on lies! We just admitted that neither of us really loved one another!"

"That still doesn't make what you did right."

"What about your shit, Meagan? What about the fact that you damn near put me in the poorhouse?"

"One thing has nothing to do with the other."

"Are you serious?"

"Our relationship might not have been much, but at the time it was real enough. You need to pay for what you've done!"

"And this isn't payment enough?"

"No. Cheating on me is one thing, but cheating on me with someone like the fat girl is a step beneath me."

"That's something else that I've always hated about you. What the fuck makes you think that you're better than everyone else? Your father really didn't do you any favors by spoiling your ass!"

"And your parents did you a disservice by not ever getting you out of the hood."

"You know what? I'm out of here. Do your worst,

Meagan. I'm going to ask the fat girl to marry me. She's more woman than you'll ever be!"

"She can't help but to be more woman than me, she's big as hell!"

"Was big. If you've seen her lately, you'd know how slim and beautiful she really is. You're the one who seems to be blowing up. I used to think you were so pretty, but the truth is, on the inside, you're one of the ugliest people I know. Good-bye, Meagan."

Meagan stood with her mouth wide open. I shook my head and was kind of relieved that she was cheating on me. That made my decision so much easier. I raced down the stairs and headed back to Tiffany's house.

This was great! Tiffany and I could be together. We could get married and I'd be able to give my all to her. We could have a future without my having to worry about finances or living beyond my means. I drove as fast as I could back to her apartment. I noticed that her car wasn't there and hoped that she was still at home. We just had sex not more than an hour ago and I figured she was probably asleep. Since her car wasn't there, I assumed she just ran to the store or something. It was only 9:00, so I rang the bell and there was no answer. I walked around back and knocked on her bedroom window and still nothing. I sat in my car and waited for her to return. Nothing. I called her cell phone and it just rang and rang. I left a number of messages stating that I was divorcing Meagan and I really wanted to be with her. I left message after message and waited there in the parking lot of her complex for a response. Nothing.

"Where the fuck is she at?" I asked myself.

I stayed in the parking lot until almost 2:00 A.M., but she never returned. I started to get a feeling as if it was too late for us and Tiffany had moved on.

***

I headed back home at 5:00 in the morning. When I got there, Meagan was gone, as was her lover. She found a wealthier man, and even though I could have kicked myself for being so stupid, I was glad she was moving on. I could never give a woman like that everything she wanted. Perhaps he could, which would be a financial relief for me. I went to sleep that night and tried to dream about a future between Tiffany and me. When I woke the next morning, I tried desperately to think of ways to make this dream a reality.

Chapter Thirty-three—Thomas

I woke up the next morning with a mission on my mind. I knew that Tiffany would of course be at Alicia's wedding tomorrow, so I went to the Men's Warehouse and bought myself a really nice suit. I bought new shoes, socks, underwear, and went to the barbershop and got my hair cut by Big Meechie at Imperial Kutz in Calumet City. From there I went to Marshall Fields and bought a bottle of Chrome Cologne. I made sure that my shit was on point. I tried calling Tiffany all day Saturday and once again my calls went unanswered.

She is starting to piss me off with this not answering me bullshit, I thought.

Meagan never returned to the house and I never inquired where she was. I figured she was either with her new man or was at her parents' house. I called my broker and moved some money around in my portfolio. I also called a realtor so that I could put the house on the market. I liked my house but the way I saw it, Tiffany and I wouldn't need all that space. I just hoped in my heart and mind that it was not too late for Tiffany and me. I rehearsed in the mirror what I would say to her and how I would propose. I figured that Meagan would serve me with divorce papers within the next few weeks. That being the case, I figured that Tiffany and I could get married in December and possibly get married on Christmas day in Las Vegas.

I got up bright and early Sunday morning. I had breakfast, and the first thing that I did before sitting down to eat was phone Tiffany both at home and on her cell phone. To my surprise, both had been disconnected.

"She couldn't be that damned mad at me, could she?" I said aloud.

I tried the numbers again and sure enough, they were disconnected. The wedding was at 3:00 P.M. so I ate, went back home, and tried to figure out my next move. When I got home, I sent Tiffany an e-mail. It bounced back and the screen said "undeliverable." I shook my head in disbelief as the thought that Tiffany might be serious about no longer seeing me entered my mind.

At 2:00 P.M. I was on the road to the wedding which was held at The House of Lynwood. It was practically down the street from my house so I got there fairly early. I signed the registry and shook hands with people I saw from work. I was wondering if Meagan would show up. After all, the invitation was actually sent to her although I think that was just Alicia being courteous to her cousin. I sat down on one of the benches toward the front of the hall and was astonished at how many people were here in attendance. I had about 160 people at my wedding. This wedding looked as if it was an event for almost 300 people. I had no idea this couple was that popular.

It was 2:45 when the groom walked out and I scanned the room frantically for Tiffany. She had to be the maid of honor. After all, she planned this wing-ding. I thought that she would've been out at the very least to check on the hall, greet guests, and make sure that everything was perfect on Alicia's special day. I figured that she might not want to see me here today, but the ring was in my pocket, and at this point, all I wanted to do was find the right time to pop the question. I figured the best time would be after Alicia was married and during the reception. I was nervous about proposing because I didn't know what Alicia's response would be. She would know that in order to marry her best friend, I would have to divorce her cousin. Alicia had a hot-ass temper, too, so I really needed to be cautious in my approach.

Matthew walked in as well as one of his groomsmen. The guy with him was a nice-looking brother who looked like he should be modeling or some shit. I knew that Matt hung out with brothers, but I didn't know that they were as tight with him as I was with my boys. The two men took positions on either side of the minister who was in the middle which I thought was odd. A few minutes later, "When Two Are In Love" by Prince began to play. As the music started, in walked two more gentlemen who stood on either side of Matthew and the other brother. The two groomsmen who walked in were in white tuxedo jackets and black tuxedo pants. The tuxedos were by Pierre Cardin. What struck me odd was that Matthew and the first brother were in black-on-black tuxedos. I figured that the first brother had to be Matthew's best man, whereas the guys in white were the other groomsmen.

As Prince continued to play overhead, in walked two bridesmaids dressed in lilac dresses, that were off the shoulder. I recognized the dresses from a catalog that I saw when Meagan and I were doing our wedding plans. The bridesmaid's dresses were from a very expensive collection. The two women walked in and took their place on either side of the two groomsmen who had preceded them. As the second bridesmaid took her place beside the groomsman, the music overhead stopped.

Thirty seconds passed and "So High" by John Legend began to play overhead. Everyone stood up and in walked Alicia, who looked simply stunning in her off-white wedding dress. The dress was strapless with a corseted bodice that was beaded with little pearls. It had a form-fitted, formal-length, beaded pencil skirt that flared at the bottom to form the train.

The dress accentuated her curvaceous body. She wore a cathedral-length veil that was attached to a diamond tiara. Her hair was swept up off her face and held in place by pearl pins.

She walked into the hall and down the aisle to stand by Matthew. In her hands were a dozen long-stemmed red roses. As she took her place beside Matthew, she handed the bouquet to her bridesmaid. Turned to face Matthew and they joined hands as they gazed longingly into each other's eyes and smiled. Matthew whispered, "You look breathtaking," with a single tear in his ice-blue eyes.

Where the fuck is Tiffany? I wondered as the music stopped. I couldn't have scared her off. I just knew that she would be here. The only thing that I could think of was that she might not be here for fear of seeing me with Meagan. I thought she would be in the wedding considering that this was her best friend getting married. I couldn't believe that she wasn't here. She should have been standing beside her best friend on her special day. As I was in deep thought, I noticed that everyone around me was still standing. Just then, the music began again, only this time, "Never Felt This Way" by Brian McKnight began to play.

What the . . .

I looked at the double doors, which opened a second time as the music played overhead and my heart almost jumped out of my chest. As I caught my breath, I became weak at the sight of the *second bride* walking down the aisle. I became light-headed and couldn't breathe as I was in a state of shock and awe. I tried to focus beyond the tears that were now forming in my eyes. Were my eyes deceiving me? Was this some sort of cruel dream? Was it karma gone mad? I tried to pinch myself to make sure this was real and not a dream. I saw the bride dressed in an off-white halter-top wedding dress with a low cut back. The dress was lace with a tulip bottom, and it hugged *Tiffany's* hips and curvaceous figure. Her hair was down and around her shoulders in soft curls. Around her neck was a diamond pendant and in her hands was also a bouquet of long-stemmed red roses. She walked in slowly and gracefully, also fighting back tears as she made her way to the man I had thought was the best man. I imagined in more than one way, he must have been the best man. It was becoming more evident that he was the better man.

What do I do? What can I say? What can I do to awaken from this dream—this nightmare. This can't be happening. Wake up Ant, wake up! She can't do this. She can't do this to me. She can't do this to us. God, no, I know what it is that I want now! I want Tiffany. I have to have her, I need her. I'm incomplete without her. I searched the room for the exit. I looked around at the faces of the people around me. I suddenly felt alone and ashamed. I was hurting on many different levels. Everyone looked so happy, most of all her. How could she do this? Just forty-eight hours earlier, she was in my arms. She was in my life. I was in her bed. When did she meet him? Who was this guy? Didn't she know that I loved her? I told her I was sorry. I told her that I would change. Didn't she know that given a second chance I would give her the world? I imagined this must be karma. Either that or God is a woman with an ironic sense of humor.

My stomach was in knots and I felt acid in my throat. The room was suddenly warm and too small. The walls began to fade and to change to a yellowish and orange tinge as if I were on some sort of psychedelic trip. I felt the heartache and the slow burn of the cancer inside me. The cancer that was God giving me what most certainly had to be my just due. I was hurt by the deception and crushed by the irony. I had to do something but was at a loss as to what that something was. I glanced down at the invitation which read, that Meagan and I were cordially invited to a *double wedding*. We were officially invited as the guests of Matthew and Alicia.

I looked at the woman next to me and noticed that she had *two invitations*. I asked her if I could I see them, and in her hand was an invitation like mine and another that stated that she was cordially invited to the double wedding of Tiffany Garner and William Alexander.

Two invitations? I thought.

It stood to reason that she wouldn't have invited me. It stood to reason that this was where all of her down time was spent. She had been trying to break things off with me for months just as I had wanted to do with her the closer that my wedding came. As I looked up from the invitation, Tiffany was just about to pass me. She looked in my direction and I gave her a look of hurt and confusion. I expected her to look at me with fright, shock, or fear, just as I had when I saw her at my wedding. Instead, she gave a smile and looked at me almost as if she looked *through* me. She looked at me as if I were nothing—as if I didn't exist. She didn't miss a beat and gave no hint of emotion or remorse. She continued on her trek down the aisle and took her place beside the man who, in just a matter of minutes, would become her husband. As she stood beside him the music overhead stopped and the minister motioned for everyone to be seated. I sat down and my heart raced at 110 MPH.

"Dearly beloved, we are gathered here this day in this place to join four souls in the lawful and wedded bliss of matrimony. They say that he who finds a wife finds a good thing. Today, brothers and sisters, it warms my heart that these two men have found happiness with the beautiful women who stand beside them. It gives me great pleasure to see them joined as they pledge their love for one another among family, friends, and the Almighty. Before the ceremony begins, I would like to ask that if there is anyone here with a lawful and just reason that these couples should not be joined in marriage, that they speak now, or forever hold their peace."

I took in a deep sigh and moved forward in my seat as I got ready to stand and stop this thing before it got any farther. As I moved in my seat, I felt a heavy hand on my shoulder.

"You're Thomas, right?"

I looked over my shoulder where a nicely built brother who stood about six foot three inches and was about 250 pounds of muscle glanced at me with fire in his eyes.

"Yes, I'm Thomas. Who are you?" I whispered.

"We've never been formally introduced, but I'm Kyle Garner, Tiffany's younger brother. You were just moving in your seat because you needed to shift your weight, right, brother?"

His hand was *so heavy* that I knew standing wouldn't be a wise decision on my part.

"Yeah, I was just . . . uncomfortable, that's all."

"I thought so."

He sat back and I didn't move. I watched the ceremony and not once did Tiffany look my way to see if I was going to interrupt her wedding. Not once.

The ceremony went on and as it progressed, I bit my bottom lip and let the tears flow. I let a damn good woman get away from me; a woman who just might have been my soul mate. Initially, I couldn't see past her weight or her lack of further education. As she took another man's hand in marriage, the weight of the wrong decision as well as my indecision came crashing down on me like a hangover. I thought about the times that Tiffany and I had shared. I thought about the walks, the talks, the dinners, and the sex. I thought about not only everything that we had done, but the potential that we had. I thought about what could've been, as well as the reality of what will never be. I didn't even hear the minister's final words.

"Ladies and gentlemen, I would like to present Mr. and Mrs. Tuskey and Mr. and Mrs. Alexander!"

The hall erupted with applause as everyone stood up and clapped. Once again, I felt that heavy hand on my shoulder as I was ushered to stand and applaud.

I did. With tears in my eyes and a broken heart, I did.

The couples retreated from the hall, and as they left, Tiffany walked down the aisle hand in hand with her new husband. As they both passed me, she didn't look in my direction not once. Not once.

I had to see her one last time. I stood in the receiving line and Kyle, her brother ushered me to leave. I assured him that I wasn't there to start any trouble. He assured me that if I did, the remainder of my life would be spent in intensive care. I stood in line looking at Tiffany, trying to read her. I wondered was she as scared as I was, in our meeting one final time. She looked unfazed. Alicia saw me and looked around as if she were seeing things. She then started looking around almost as if she were looking for her gun or something to hit me with. I mustered up the courage to make my way to Tiffany. First, I shook her husband's hand who simply gave me a smile not knowing who I was. I assumed that he figured I was a guest of Matthew and Alicia. I then reached out and hugged Tiffany who gave me a light and meaningless hug. I whispered in her ear.

"Congratulations . . . it should've been me."

She whispered back, "No . . . it should've never been you."

I walked away and out of her life.

I placed the ring that was in the box among the wedding gifts on the table in the hall.

Chapter Thirty-four—Tiffany

I took the semester off from school to redecorate our home. *Our home . . . wow, that has such a nice ring to it.* I bought a few new items here and there. Nothing major, but our house definitely needed a woman's touch. William told me to do whatever it was that I needed to do to make our house a home. I did just that. I have a garden in the back, a swing set on the porch and I turned one of the guest rooms into a nursery. We were not expecting yet, but I want a bunch of babies with this man. Being with William is like living in a dream. We are in love, we make love all the time, and most importantly, we're friends.

My man works and he works damned hard, but on the weekends, he plays hard also. We go to the entire city's latest plays, we hit all the museums, and every weekend for us is an adventure. We hold hands like teenagers, cuddle like teenagers, and smile just thinking about one another. Some weekends are lavish. Others are just quiet times spent alone at home watching movies. I am truly having the time of my life.

I still work out and I am still going to continue going to school. I work now because I want to, not because I have to. William has tried to get me to quit quite a few times now. I told him I will take a leave of absence when we decide to start our family, but as far as not working, I can never let myself be that dependent on a man. Not even a man as nice as my William.

I have to keep it moving. I have to keep striving at work to be the best I can be and do the same in school. I need to keep doing my thing in the gym and stay in church and let

God guide me on this journey. I thought when I became a married woman that meant I was living the happily-ever-after part of my journey. I've come to realize that this is just the beginning and my life is still a work in progress.

As I sat on my couch reading in the day room, I took a few moments to look at how much I have been blessed. I have a man who loves me, a beautiful home, and my life has new direction. I sat there in silence thinking and reflecting on my life and running my hands through my hair as I pondered many of the decisions I had made.

I still regret sleeping with Thomas. I still regret cheating on my then boyfriend now husband. I regret all the times that I let some man disrespect me, or sex me, or take advantage of me as Thomas had. I regret being so hard on myself and all those days that I sat and wallowed in self pity. Days that I beat myself up about my weight and my mistakes, which were many. Come to think of it, perhaps they weren't mistakes. Perhaps they were simply the decisions that I made at the time.

They say that which doesn't kill you makes you stronger. Well, I think I'm a pretty strong woman now. I should be mad at Thomas Anthony Young, but he made me strong. His deception prepared me to be the best woman I can be for my husband. His betrayal . . . the hurt he inflicted on me . . . well, it makes me appreciate what I do have even more.

Over a year ago there was no way that someone could tell me that I would fall in love with a handsome man with rugged looks and then lose that man to another woman who ended up being his wife. You couldn't tell me a year ago that I would accidentally get invited to my boyfriend's wedding and bounce back like I did after the depths of betrayal that I endured. When my relationship with Thomas ended, for a time, I thought my life ended. I thought being with him was the best that I could do. I was wrong . . . man, I was wrong. Sometimes we as women have to go through heartache and trials and tribulations so that God can prepare us for the real deal when it comes along. I used to pray sometimes that God give me the man of my dreams. I thought that man was Thomas. I used to pray that God change Thomas's heart when I first began dating him. What I should have been praying for was that God help me to make the changes in my life that needed to be made.

I was so upset with Thomas. I was so taken with him. I took so much crap from him and I let him walk all over me. I was in denial for a long time. I wanted so much for him to change, not realizing until now that I was the one that needed changing. When I started taking care of me was when I discovered the real me and who I have the potential to be. It's been an incredible journey so far. I can't wait to see how things go the rest of the way.

Chapter Thirty-five—Thomas

I had just settled into my new place and was sitting at the dining room table of my apartment where I was working on my new budget. I now owed Meagan a considerable amount of alimony and I was trying to figure out how I was going to fight a paternity suit that she served me with just a few days ago.

So far, I'd been compelled to sell the house, pay alimony, and also pay for the amniocenteses to determine whether or not I was the father of the child she was carrying. I knew in my heart I should've never married that bitch. I married her for her looks and it took me way too long to realize exactly what a mistake that was. It was my night to host the card game with my fraternity brothers. I didn't want to be bothered, but the guys insisted. I knew they were going to give me shit the second they saw the place. Still, sometimes when you are friends, you have to take shit from your boys when you mess up. The doorbell rang and in walked Don, CC, Fred, and Chuck.

"Nice digs," Chuck said sarcastically.

"Oh, how the mighty have fallen," Don said.

"Back in the hood, huh, bruh?" Fred chimed in.

"It's not that bad," CC said. "Y'all lay off the brother, you know his ego is killing him right now."

We sat down and played cards. Sean didn't show up and I wondered where he was.

"Hey, where is Sean?"

"Oh, Sean is on punishment," Don said.

"What do you mean?"

"He's got a new woman now and she's friends with Tiffany and she told him that she didn't think you were the type of person he should be around."

"You're kidding, right?"

"Nope."

"And he listened to her?"

"Yep."

"What kind of grown-ass man lets a woman make his decisions for him?"

"Uh, the same type of man who lets a woman go through all his money, spend way too much on a wedding, and looks down on his boys because they work blue-collar jobs."

Ouch, that hurt a bit. Don was never one for holding his tongue.

"Hey, guys, about that . . ."

"It's okay man," CC said.

"So what's this broad look like?" I asked.

"Oh, she's fine as a MF! Believe that!" Don said.

"So you mean to tell me that this brother put off his boys for a woman just because of her looks?"

Silence fell over the table.

"Okay, bad choice of words, but clearly he's whipped."

Again silence. Then laughter.

"Okay, okay, maybe I was a little whipped."

"A little!" they all shouted.

"Okay, a lot. Whatever, but you all have to admit, you were all envious of the fact that I married a woman that fine."

Again laughter from all of them. I had a confused look on my face.

"What?" I asked.

Don said, "Man, no one envied your relationship with that bitch. I'm sorry, dawg, but we have been talking about your ass since day one. Stevie Wonder could see that bitch was playing you from the get up."

"Man, get the hell out of here. If you all knew, why didn't you say anything?"

"Shit, we all did. Hell, at the bachelor party each of us toasted you and said, 'Yo', Ant, don't marry that bitch!'"

They were right. They had. But I didn't see it. I thought marrying Meagan gave me society status. I thought making six figures and having a wife with supermodel looks meant that I made it. I thought it made me somebody.

"A'ight, whatever, let's play cards."

We began playing and I could see that something was on Chuck's mind. He kept looking at me as if he felt sorry for me or something. We would each look at our hands and Chuck just kept looking at me as if he were trying to gauge my pain or something.

"Chuck, man, what? What's wrong, dawg?"

"You okay Ant?"

"Yeah, yeah, man, I'm good."

I wasn't good. Tiffany had been on my mind day and night and I have to admit, I wasn't taking care of myself like I should, but this is not the type of thing that guys talk about. Not unless we're dogging women out, and I had no right to say anything negative about Tiffany.

"Why do you ask?" I asked Chuck.

"You just don't seem like your normal self, and it looks like you are picking up a little weight there, bruh."

Don was getting upset with the line of conversation. He threw his cards down.

"Aw shit, okay, that's enough. Are you two niggas going to play cards or are we turning this into a *Lifetime* special?" Don said angrily. "The nigga picked up a few pounds, so what? Chuck, you've picked up a few pounds too, we all have, now can we get back to the game? It's your play. Ant fucked up, now everyone get over it."

" He didn't mess up" Fred said. "I think he did good not getting with the heavy set sister."

"Shiit . . . she ain't heavy no more," Chuck said. "I

saw her a few weeks ago in the grocery store and man, she looks better than a MF! That ass is like BLAM and her thighs are strong as hell. She had on this form-fitting skirt and this top where her titties were sitting up like this and . . ." Chuck was going on and on until he realized he was the only one speaking and speaking out of turn at that.

"Uh, . . . Ooops. . . my bad. All I'm saying is the bitch looks good as hell now. Don's right. You fucked up."

Don started laughing. "Yeah, he did, we established that. Now, for the last time, can we play cards? Why don't you two grab a few beers and let's act like men rather than the Sisterhood of the Traveling Pants or some shit."

We played a few more hands, but Tiffany was still on my mind and I just couldn't shake what happened. My boys were here to cheer me up; to help me forget about her. *But I don't think I need to forget about her right now. I think what I need to do is think about the mistakes that I made and learn from them. As it is I'm not only depressed, I'm wondering if I will ever find a woman as good as Tiffany again.* I was playing cards with my boys, but I would be lying if I said I was playing to win. I felt as if I had just lost everything. When I couldn't keep the charade up any longer, I asked my boys to leave.

"Fellas, tonight isn't a real good night for cards. I'm sorry. Can we take a raincheck?"

"Aw, shit man, come on!" Don was really upset now. "Nigga, do you need a hug? Is that what this is about?"

"Naw, man. Right now I just need some space. Fellas, I'm sorry."

One by one the guys got up to leave. There were a few grunts and moans but they all understood. Each one gave me a fist pound as they left. Don was the last one. He was the player of the pack and the most insensitive, but even he gave me dap.

"You're getting soft, Ant," he said while pointing at me and walking away.

"Naw, I think I'm growing up."

"Well, finish growing up before our next card game. Leave ya personal shit at home. For now, you go ahead and wallow in self-pity, listen to some Sade or Keith Sweat or something. Hurry up and get this shit outta your system. Holla at me if you need me. Maybe next week before the next card game we can go out looking for some broads or something. I think if we get you some new pussy you will be a'ight. You just need a new distraction, that's all."

"I don't know about all that, but I'll call if I need you."

"Peace."

"Take it easy."

He left and I sat in my small apartment in silence. I fucked up with Tiffany. I really fucked up.

Just as I was thinking about my problems, a UPS truck pulled up in front of my house. I assumed it was the remainder of my things that I ordered to furnish my new apartment, but instead, it was a small box. I signed for the package and opened it up. Inside was the ring that I left at Tiffany's wedding and a note.

Thomas,

Here is your ring back. I'm sorry that I did you the same way that you did me. I thought it would make me feel better, but it didn't. I used you. I used you as you used me and for that . . . I'm sorry. I'm grateful to you. Without your cheating, I would've never found my soul mate. I guess God does work in mysterious ways. I don't hate you. I never did. In fact, on behalf of my husband and me, thank you. I hear that you're a new father, and all I wanted to say was . . . CONGRATULATIONS!

—Mrs. Tiffany Alexander